PALE MOON WALKING

paula altenburg

Paula Altenburg

This book is a work of fiction. Names, characters, places, and incidents are the product of the author's imagination or are used fictitiously. Any resemblance to actual events, locales, or persons, living or dead, is coincidental.

Copyright © 2015 by Paula Altenburg. All rights reserved, including the right to reproduce, distribute, or transmit in any form or by any means. For information regarding subsidiary rights, please contact the Publisher.

Entangled Publishing, LLC
2614 South Timberline Road
Suite 109
Fort Collins, CO 80525
Visit our website at www.entangledpublishing.com.

Select Otherworld is an imprint of Entangled Publishing, LLC.

Edited by Vanessa Mitchell
Cover design by Syd Gill
Cover art from Shutterstock

Manufactured in the United States of America

First Edition October 2015

Chapter One

The year was 1877

United States Federal Marshal Sam Kyote of the Special Division entered the Red Room of the White House—the same room where Rutherford Hayes had been sworn into office only a few months before.

Sam switched a hidden lever beneath the mantel above the fireplace. The fireplace swung aside to reveal what was known to the Special Division—which occupied three full levels beneath the White House—as the Seventh Door. He ducked through the narrow opening. Steep steps spiraled downward, the tunnel walls illuminated by gas lighting. At the very bottom and third level, an underground research bunker had been carved from the earth. He cracked open the heavy steel door and peered inside.

The bunker's thick gray walls had been wired so that the lights worked off an electrical current running through special filaments rather than gas, which was far too volatile for the experiments conducted here, Louis AuCoin, the government's lead scientist, swore the filaments were an invention that would someday revolutionize the world.

Sam wasn't naive. He knew the United States government was involved in some serious top secret technological research, and that a lot of the technology Louis tested hadn't necessarily been acquired by honest means. And he'd joined the Special Division with a full understanding he'd be investigating things with no clear explanation.

But he hadn't expected any of those things to be him.

A little over a week ago he'd been called in to the bunker for a physical—standard practice for all Special Division marshals—although this would be his second in less than a year. The last thing he remembered after opening the door was a bright flash of light that knocked him flat on his ass, then a heavy pressure as if someone were standing on his chest. An explosion, he'd been told. He'd awoken on an examination table in one of the bunker's back rooms, shaking with fever, chills, and an incredible pain throughout his aching body, and been sick to his stomach for hours.

The more disturbing repercussions, however, had begun several nights later, after Louis released him. He'd been at home and alone, staring in horror at a spider as it crawled up the wall of his bedroom.

His pitch black and windowless bedroom.

A newfound ability to create illusions was another unexpected side effect. It had manifested itself two days after the extraordinary night vision. This was what had brought him to the bunker this morning. He had nowhere else to turn.

Louis AuCoin was a short man, slight of build, and around forty years of age. Wiry black hair, untouched by gray, was currently shoved to the top of his head by a pair of safety glasses so that it stuck out in all directions. He wore a white coat and held a blazing blow lamp in one hand.

"I need to speak with you," Sam said.

Louis straightened, his attention divided between a lump of gray metal on the worktable in front of him and the bunker door where Sam stood. While whatever the scientist was working on this morning appeared to be harmless enough, Sam stayed by the door just in case. One accident was enough.

Louis extinguished the blow lamp and set it on the table. "Sam. You're supposed to be on sick leave. What is wrong? Has your fever returned?"

"I have something to show you. Can you turn off the lights?"

Within moments, the bunker was plunged into a thick darkness so profound it penetrated pores. Yet to Sam's enhanced vision, Louis appeared as a sharp silhouette— a white cutout against a black backdrop. He watched his friend move around the bunker by memory alone, feeling his way in what, to him, must be complete blindness.

"Any time now, *mon ami*," Louis said with impatience, a hint of curiosity tempering his tone. "But whatever you're doing, don't touch my experiment. The metal is quite caustic."

Sam had no plans to stray from the bunker door. His palms were sweating. In his head he formed an image of the bunker, turning it bright as the sunny day outdoors, and added the same cloud-speckled blue sky. He then projected the illusion he'd carefully constructed into the bunker—an image, overlapping reality. He watched Louis's face go slack as he gazed at the ceiling-turned-sky with amazement, tilting his face toward a sun that was shining underground.

But Sam had an even better trick to show him. He'd had almost a week since the accident to perfect it.

The sunlight-drenched contents of the research bunker disappeared. So did the sky. Carefully, using images pulled from his memory, he reconstructed the Red Room, three levels above them. The result was perfect to the very last detail, even though if he'd been asked, other than an impression of their colors, Sam could not have explained what the paintings on the walls really looked like. He'd never been interested in art. But it was as if his brain had captured a tintype that he'd then been able to recreate and step inside.

Louis's face went pale in the bright, artificial light Sam had manufactured from nothing. He reached for one of the chairs as if about to sit down, but it was an illusion. His hand connected with air and he tumbled to the floor, cracking his head on the side of the very real worktable he could no longer see. He swore under his breath in his native language as he picked himself up.

The more detailed an illusion Sam projected, however, the more difficult it was for him to hold it for any length of time. He allowed the one of the Red Room and the blue sky to drop, plunging the bunker back into inky darkness. This wasn't even the best part of his newfound abilities—or the worst, depending on one's perspective. The few times he'd ventured out in public over the past three days he'd accidentally projected the unguarded daydreams of two complete strangers who'd been staring off into space, lost to the real world. The first time it happened, the illusion he'd unwittingly projected had been of a woman's face. The second, a page from a book—as if the owner were mentally reviewing some particular subject he'd been studying. It might have been law. Each time, Sam had been able to drop the illusion before bystanders took more than a passing notice of what he'd been doing. But they'd noticed something about their surroundings was...

Off.

These illusions weren't as complete or detailed as the ones he'd constructed in his own head, however. Not everyone thought in pictures—at least, not as vividly as some. He expected Louis to excel at it, though. The scientist noticed many small things other people missed. He dried his palms on the tail of his sack coat before adjusting his bowtie, using movement to disguise his nervousness.

"I want you to think of something," he said to Louis. "Some image you can picture in your head, with as much detail as possible. An object or place I couldn't possibly know about."

Louis concentrated. Sam stared hard into his eyes. A dark-haired woman appeared, clad in gartered stockings and a black corset and nothing else. On her inner right thigh was a small, diamond-shaped birthmark. The scientist sucked in a sharp breath. He again reached blindly for something with which to steady himself. He was about to place his hand on the lump of metal he'd warned Sam not to touch.

"Be careful. Your experiment!"

The Frenchman snatched his hand to his chest. "What did you do to me?" Louis demanded, his voice hoarse.

"That," Sam said, "is the question I came to ask you."

Twelve hours and almost a hundred tests later, Sam and Louis sat over dinner in an eatery several streets away from the White House. It was very late at night and the room nearly empty.

Louis was frowning as he chased a meatball around his plate with a fork. "You have heard the stories about Sky People," he said. "Creatures from another world who crash-landed on ours. They're the reason the Special Division was created."

"Those are stories made up by the seasoned marshals to torment the new recruits."

"Those are truth," the Frenchman corrected him. "Sky People claim they have nanoparticles in their bloodstream — miniscule pieces of technology — that allow them to survive in an atmosphere hostile to them by altering their anatomy to suit their surroundings. They can take on human form. Pass for one of us. I was given the task of proving whether or not those nanoparticles exist and if they can be of use to us. You were part of that assignment. I transmitted that nanotechnology to you."

Cold anger flowed through Sam, undiminished by assurances he was in good health. A fierce headache disputed that claim. "You had no right to experiment on me without my permission."

"I had every right. You are Special Division. One of the elite. It's your sworn duty — and mine — to help protect the country from dangers most men cannot even begin to imagine."

The headache worsened with his level of anger. "Protecting my country shouldn't mean sacrificing my right to make my own choices."

"You knew when you signed up it involved taking risks. You and I, *mon ami*, have been chosen for a very top secret assignment. A situation that requires absolute secrecy. I couldn't tell you about it until I knew if the experiment would be a success."

"Then should we be discussing it here?"

Sarcasm was lost on the Frenchman. "Better here than back at the White House. The staff here is…discreet."

Meaning someone paid them to be.

Politics was a dangerous game. Sam had been in Washington long enough to witness the intrigues and machinations taking place on a daily basis. He'd wanted no part of them. He resented being forced to do so.

And yet a part of him was curious.

Louis was right. He had known there'd be risks involved when he'd signed up for the Special Division two years ago, although this was the first time he'd experienced anything up close and personal. He reached for his glass of wine.

Louis grabbed his wrist. "Careful. Alcohol could affect your new abilities. Even an establishment as discreet as this one is perhaps not the best place to find out."

Sam set the glass down again. Cold sweat formed between his shoulder blades. "How long before the effects of having Sky People blood in my body disappears?"

"The blood itself isn't causing the effects. The blood transfusion was merely a vehicle. Unless the nanotechnology fails, the effects should be permanent."

Sam rubbed his temples. "I can't change form."

"The technology definitely seems to have a different effect on you. My hypothesis is that you're already adapted to this world so there's no need for you to change. And you have a different physiology from theirs. But it *is* having an effect. That's what is important."

"Why?"

"In order to fight our enemy, we have to think like them. Do what they can. We need a weapon to use against them. You, Sam, will be that weapon. Now we need to learn how to use what you've got."

"I have excellent night vision and I can create illusions that the entire world can see. Sometimes, if a person is a visual thinker, I can project what they're daydreaming about. I can't walk on water."

"Those are better skills than ordinary men possess. You're also a trained marshal," Louis said. "You know how to hunt fugitives."

"I haven't agreed to anything."

"You did when you signed up," Louis reminded him.

"I could quit."

"I'm afraid it's too late for that."

That remained to be seen. But if Sam did decide he wanted out, it was best not to say so. He'd have to disappear. Change his identity. And he wasn't ready for that. Not yet anyway. The Special Division's outreach was vast. To evade them effectively, he'd have to take precautions, make preparations. He schooled his features, protecting his thoughts.

"What happens next?" he asked. His headache had begun to abate. So far, that was the only positive event of the day.

Louis jabbed the meatball and stuck it in his mouth. He chewed for a few long moments as he stared at the flame on the candle between them, lost in deep thought. Then he tossed back most of the contents of his own glass of wine.

"I write a report," he said, shrugging his shoulders. "You came to me for a physical. How are you feeling? I mean," he amended, "do you *feel* like your normal self?"

"Other than the headaches, I feel the same as always."

"Your eyes have changed color."

"What?" Sam tried to look at them in the shining silver blade of his knife, but the light was too dim. He repositioned the utensil on the crisp white tablecloth, next to his untouched plate. "They were still green when I shaved this morning."

"They now have little flecks of yellow in them. In the candlelight, it's more pronounced. They look like gold."

Sam didn't want to admit how much that scared him. "If you're flirting with me," he said, "I think you should know that my taste runs more toward long-legged women than short Frenchmen."

Louis didn't share in the joke. "I'm a scientist, *mon ami*. I am trained to be observant. You should hope no one else notices such an unusual change in you." He played with the fork, turning it over in his fingers. "I don't think Washington is the best place for you right now, at least until you have learned the full extent of your abilities, how to control them, and how best to use them. We need to find out if the headaches get better or worse over time. Until then, this must remain secret."

Again, Sam was lost. "Why would I want to hide them if the Division plans to use them?"

"I told you. This is top secret. The Division's director knows nothing about this and he cannot find out. He's an ambitious man. He will have only one use for your abilities. For *you*. You wish to become one of my research experiments while I study you on behalf of your government?" Louis lanced another meatball. He tapped it on the side of his plate. Somewhere at the back of the eatery, dishes clattered and laughter erupted, jangling Sam's nerves. "You are too trusting. You think the government is working for the good of the country, when in reality, the government is run by men who are working only for themselves. Those are the men who must be stopped." He pointed the meatball at Sam. "That is where you and I come in. The report I write on these follow-up tests will indicate to the director that you are a very sick man, and I think you should be placed on indeterminate sick leave. You need to recover. To learn what you can do, but learn it in secret. You should go West."

"*West*?" Sam stared at his friend. "Why would I want to do that?"

"Think of the benefits. The people are few and far between. They don't ask too many questions. You'll be able to practice your new abilities without any undue influence or attention. And if you go West, I can help you," Louis added, an air of triumph in his manner. "It just so happens I know of a ranch outside a little place in Nevada Territory called Coyote Bluff that recently came up for sale. I believe the previous owner's heir can be persuaded to sell it to you for a reasonable price."

None of this was what Sam wanted to hear. "I don't want to go West. I don't want to own a ranch in some little hellhole miles from civilization." His anger resurfaced, fed by a helpless frustration foreign to him. He didn't like not being in control of his own life. He hated being backed into a corner. And yet he couldn't deny he'd been made aware of the risks. He simply hadn't *known* them. "You did this to me. If I'm too trusting, why should I trust you?"

"You shouldn't. Trust no one. You should be thanking

me, though. This is the beginning of an exciting future for you. May it be a long and prosperous one." Louis reached for Sam's untouched glass of wine, lifted it in the air as if making a toast, then took a hearty sip. "The government isn't your friend, Sam Kyote. Luckily for you, I am."

Louis plunged his hands deep into his overcoat pockets as he walked the dark streets of Washington, heading for home. Sam was a good man, and he didn't feel right about what he'd done to him, but of all the marshals Sam was the best and the best had been ordered.

Still.

"You should pay more attention to your surroundings," a familiar voice scolded Louis from the shadows, making him jump and grab for the derringer in his right pocket. "The night is full of cutthroats and thieves."

Louis's fingers uncurled from his weapon. "*Mon dieu, mon ami,*" he complained, conscious the night also had ears. His heart rate spiked, steadied, then inched toward normal. "Must you scare me to death? A gun or knife would be more merciful."

His friend was correct, however. Street lighting this far from the Capitol was almost nonexistent, the crime rate very high, and Louis had a scientist's tendency to become too lost in his own thoughts.

His friend fell into step beside him, keeping his face well hidden beneath a broad-brimmed hat despite the cover of the night. Neither of them wished to be seen in the other's company. They both had reputations to protect. "What did you discover?"

"The blood transfusion I gave him was a partial success," Louis said.

"What do you mean…partial?"

When his friend came to Louis with a blood sample from the Sky People for him to examine, he'd been over the moon. Unfortunately, he hadn't been able to see the actual nanoparticles beneath his microscope. The magnification simply wasn't enough.

Since he hadn't been able to identify these nanoparticles under the microscope, and therefore assess their functionality, it had been his friend's idea to test it on one of the division's best marshals by injecting the sample into his bloodstream.

Louis had insisted on caution. Blood transfusions sometimes proved fatal even under the best of circumstances. He would have preferred to use federal prisoners for this sort of experimentation. Unfortunately, that would have raised too many questions.

After the first hour, however, when Sam had shown no serious side effects from the first injection, Louis had given him a larger amount. Sam's body had argued, but not openly rebelled. Now, health-wise, he seemed fine.

And the results were intriguing. They also had scientific proof that Sky People blood contained a substance of value to humans.

"Sky People physiology is much different from ours," he explained. "Combined with the nanoparticles their blood is said to contain, and the fact blood transfusions aren't always reliable under the best of conditions, we simply can't expect the results to be the same. Sam can't change form the way the Sky People can. What he can do, however, is create visual illusions that are quite detailed and very impressive. He manufactures them from his own imagination, as well as intercepts them from the thoughts of receptive individuals. Early tests suggest they're visual thinkers. He's also had significant changes in his eyesight. His night vision is extraordinary. His eyes have altered appearance, too, although only slightly." Louis trembled with an excitement he hadn't felt since the day he'd been hired away from the Canadian government in the province of Quebec and asked to work on top secret projects for the Americans. "It's likely that's how he's intercepting other people's mental images—by looking into their eyes. I never considered the possibility."

"How long before we know if the nanoparticles in Marshal Kyote's blood will remain stable?" his friend asked.

"I can't be sure. I plan to place him on sick leave until we find out." Louis took a deep breath. "It's best if he spends as little time around the Special Division as possible. It will keep Carson Whitley from finding out about the transfusion or that it has had positive results. And Sam needs to be protected. I told him you'd sell Billie Hernandez's spread in Coyote Bluff to him. I trust you'll give him a fair price."

He sensed his friend's displeasure. A precarious thing.

"You shouldn't have done that. I never meant for a federal marshal to take up residence in Coyote Bluff. Having one living there could create...complications. Besides, that ranch is next door to Libby."

Libby Mayden was the daughter of notorious outlaw Lord Maxwell Mayden. Even though Mayden was dead now, Max's men remained loyal to him—and therefore, to her. They kept each other safe. But Sam Kyote had just taken on a role he hadn't applied for. He deserved a level of protection, too. And compensation."

"Things are beginning to unravel for Whitley, *mon ami*. We both know he has connections to Sky People. What we don't have is proof. And think of how safe that marshal will be with Libby next door."

Almost six years ago a ship carrying deported prisoners from another world had blazed across the sky and crash-landed in New Mexico Territory's desert near an area the Mayden gang called home. Twenty-three Sky People had survived the crash, claiming all they wanted was to live out their lives in peace. At the time, Mayden had said to let them alone. He wasn't a man who'd deny anyone a second chance. That was what the Wild West was built on.

But for Max Mayden, second chances were all anyone got. And some of those Sky People were proving less peaceful in their intentions than others. Allowing them to take up with ambitious men such as Carson Whitley could bring no good to the world. The world needed a way to fight back.

Sam Kyote was it.

They were almost to Louis's street corner now and would soon have to part ways.

"Only the Sky People and a few men know where that ship crashed. If anything you think might have come off it shows up in your bunker, or anything unusual at all, you're to tell me at once," his friend finally said. "I want to know where—and how—Whitley acquired it." He stopped near the intersection in an area where the shadows were deepest. "Can this marshal be trusted? Is he up to a challenge like this?"

"Sam is a man of integrity," Louis replied. "He's angry right now. Justifiably so. But he's also curious. And he wants to serve his country. He's one of the best. Guaranteed."

Chapter Two

Sheriff Libby Mayden listened hard as she stared into the gloom of a half-mooned night. The homestead below her consisted of a house, barn, small corral, and one tiny outbuilding. She counted three shadowy figures moving in from three different angles.

The math was easy. Since she was alone, that made the odds three to one.

She'd heard the sharp crack of gunfire from a mile away, where she'd been sitting in a rocker on her front porch, admiring the wedge of pale moon and the wide, starry desert sky. Duty and neighborliness drove her to investigate. Billie Hernandez, the last man who'd owned this property, had been dead for a week before anyone found him. Heart attack, the local doctor had said.

At least he'd died peacefully. That was looking like less of an option for her mysterious new neighbor.

A rock dug into her hip, and Libby shifted long, lean

legs on the cactus-strewn knoll in an effort to get more comfortable. All was now silent in the night. Too silent. Sam Kyote had to be either dead or deaf, because she saw no outward indication he knew he was under attack.

The well-worn walnut grip of her pistol fit smooth and familiar in her hand. It had been a while since she'd last shot a man, and while she wouldn't hesitate to do so if necessary, she didn't much care to be starting up the practice again. Coyote Bluff had been the ideal place to hang up her holster because of its peaceful reputation. Normally nothing stirred out here but the tumbleweeds.

Something about the movements of the man approaching the back of the house caught her attention. Then a spark flared, a bright orange beacon in the shadows, and Libby's gaze zeroed in on that. If Kyote was alive, it appeared to her as if the intruders meant to burn him out of hiding.

She set the pistol on the ground and eased the wide, buckskin strap of her repeating rifle from her shoulder. While not her weapon of choice, the rifle was more accurate and its range was better, and there was no way she could allow that house to be set on fire. In this dry environment it would go up like well-seasoned kindling, and no doubt take the other buildings with it. If it caught the weeds, desert scrub, and manzanita surrounding the homestead, there was an even greater danger of igniting a wildfire that could spread for miles.

She sighted down the long barrel, opting for the easier body shot than the head shot, aware she might only get this one chance. She wanted him incapacitated yet hopefully able to answer questions, but as soon as the other two men realized they were no longer alone out here, they'd be after her, too.

The orange spark became a yellow ball of dancing flame. The intruder had lit a torch. She couldn't wait any longer. The rifle bucked against her shoulder when she thumbed back the hammer and squeezed the trigger, leaving her ears ringing.

Her bullet slammed into her target, and the way he spun halfway around from the force of it, then went to his knees, told her she'd hit something vital. The torch he carried dropped to the ground as he fired an instinctive but wild return shot in her direction.

Libby rolled away from where she'd been lying and sprang to her feet, scooping up her weapons, then ran in a low crouch down the exposed slope toward the shelter of the small outbuilding. Her long, thick braid of hair thumped between her shoulders. She'd lost track of the other two men, but counted on still being out of range of their pistols for a few more crucial minutes.

Excitement pounded hard in her chest. She'd almost forgotten how much she loved a good gunfight. The uneven odds served to increase her pleasure, not diminish it, but that didn't make her stupid. She'd need to be careful with her ammunition. Both her gun and rifle repeated, but once their chambers were empty she'd have a difficult time reloading them, especially in the dark.

But so would her opponents.

She heard the report of a gun, then the whine of the bullet as it kicked up dirt a few feet in front of her. She darted for the safety of the black shadows behind the outbuilding.

And collided with someone already in hiding.

The grunt of pain as her forehead connected with a

solid chin told her she'd bowled into a man. Although she managed to retain her grip on her pistol, the rifle spun from her hand and clattered against the clapboarded side of the outbuilding. Her arms wrapped around him, her forward momentum and weight taking them both to the ground in a tangle of limbs.

He swore as they landed, Libby on top, and tried to push her off him. Libby brought the barrel of her pistol up to rest against his temple and cocked the hammer. There was an audible click as the bullet slid into its chamber.

"Who are you?" she demanded. It could be her neighbor, but she wanted to be sure. She hadn't survived to twenty-five years of age in the West by making careless assumptions.

He went still beneath her. "You're a woman."

"Sheriff Mayden," she corrected him, her voice crisp with authority, and she burrowed the barrel deeper into his flesh to compensate for any weakness he might have perceived. "Don't make me ask you again."

"The name's Sam Kyote," he replied. "I bought this place three weeks ago. And in case you haven't already figured it out, Sheriff Mayden," he added with a drawn out, faintly mocking emphasis on the word *sheriff*, "my home is under attack."

The heat in his voice curled around her. She uncocked her pistol, lifting it away from his head, and slid her weight off his stomach so he could breathe. She couldn't see his face because of the clouds and the deep shadows cast by the outbuilding, but with her knees pressed into the dirt on either side of his hips and her backside now sitting on top of his groin, there were other things she noticed. One in particular, which made her think that the West could definitely use more women.

She scrambled to her feet as if her trousers had caught fire, glad for the blanket of darkness because her cheeks were now burning. She had no illusions about her feminine charms. She was as tall as a man, in fact taller than most, and slender as a twelve-year-old boy. Her blue eyes were too large for her face and her hair could best be described as a light, brindled brown. She was better with a pistol than a butter churn, and the kindest thing the locals could find to say about her was that if she gained a few pounds, she'd make some lucky farmer a sturdy wife. She'd had seven proposals of marriage thus far, and none of them came from a man under fifty. All offers were withdrawn as soon as the whispers regarding her reputation reached their ears.

Libby Mayden, outlaw. Pardoned for killing five men in as many shootouts.

Those same whispers suggested the pardons came about courtesy of the lack of jails for women in the Territories. In reality, each shooting had been tried and judged self-defense. All of the dead men had wanted to see if she was as good as her father, famed outlaw Maxwell Mayden, always claimed her to be. They'd found out she was better.

Her new neighbor, too, got to his feet, although without as much spring, and dusted off the seat and back thighs of his trousers. Libby strained to hear any movement from their assailants, but even the one she'd shot remained mute. He had to be dead.

Uneasiness rippled over her skin. That shouldn't have been a killing shot.

Not on an ordinary man.

"Well, Mister Kyote," she said. He was taller than she'd

anticipated, surprising her, and she tipped her chin up to stare at his face even though she couldn't quite see his eyes in the dark. "It appears to me you could use some help from the law. I—"

"Look out!"

Life was fragile in the West and people learned to react fast to danger. Libby dropped to the ground, needing no second warning from him.

He fired a shot over her head.

Two shadows slithered through the inky black night. Conscious of the danger, and her dwindling number of bullets, Libby took instant advantage of the thick slice of moon as it peeked through the clouds. She planted her elbows in the dirt, steadied the pistol with both hands, and fired a shot, too.

The shadow she'd aimed for faltered. For a crazy second, the shape of it shifted and lengthened. A gasp of shock rushed past her lips before she could stop it. She hadn't seen anything like that in nearly five years.

She blinked and the image was gone. It had likely been nothing more than her unsettled imagination, pulling her back to her last real gunfight—the one that had caused her to hang up her holster and turn herself in.

But it could explain why her first was a killing shot.

And why this second one wasn't. Another shot from Sam finished it off.

Darkness settled around them again, silent and still, blinding her for precious seconds and leaving her vulnerable and exposed. Her skin prickled all over, anticipating danger.

"My apologies. Are you hurt?" Sam Kyote slid his fingers beneath her arm and helped get her boots under her.

"I'm fine."

Her response came out a little too terse. She wasn't used to receiving gentlemanly courtesy and therefore had no idea how to react to it. Or to a gentleman's touch, for that matter. It sparked quite the internal reaction.

"I don't mean to be rude, Sheriff Mayden, and I thank you for your timely intervention, but I believe the trouble has passed. They won't be back tonight. Do you need me to escort you home?"

The offer threw Libby off even more. No one had ever questioned her ability to take care of herself. Not when she was armed. And a sheriff didn't require an escort.

"What I'd like is to take a look at the body of the man I killed," she said. "I have a number of outstanding warrants in my office. My files are full of WANTED posters, and he might be one of them."

Sam Kyote caught her wrist, holding her back when she would have walked away to find out. His thumb, perhaps innocently enough, rubbed against the soft under pad of her flesh. The contact—so innocuous, and yet so…disturbing—burned as if she'd been branded.

She eased her hand free of his grasp. He took a step back as if to give her more personal space, but she noticed in doing so, he'd blocked her path.

"Best let me handle this," he said. "You don't know for certain he's dead."

She couldn't make out her new neighbor's expression. If she were to guess at his age by the sound of his voice and the confident authority in his stance, she'd hazard somewhere between her age and thirty. The way he dragged out the letter *a* suggested he hailed from the East.

Maybe he was simply trying to be a gentleman, protecting her delicate feminine sensibilities. But she didn't think so. His insistence on taking charge of the situation was not about him being a gentleman toward her. Her instincts had never let her down before and she trusted them now. Underlying the polite manners, Libby caught the distinct, watchful air of a predator. He was hiding something.

Maybe it was Sam's face she'd recognize from one of those WANTED posters in the files on her desk. Maybe that was why he'd avoided town even though he'd been here three weeks.

"It won't be the first time I've had to confirm a man dead." Or the first time she'd been wrong. She had a few old bullet wounds of her own, and she'd learned to approach a man who might possibly be playing possum with caution.

With a shrug, Sam stepped aside.

Staying tight to the shadows, she walked around the perimeter of the yard until she came to the spot where she was certain the first man she'd shot, the one from the top of the knoll, had fallen.

She found nothing. No body, no sign anyone had ever been here at all, and yet the telltale smell of something dead lingered. A skitter of cloud slithered over the moon. She waited until it passed and the thin wash of light it provided returned, but it wasn't going to be enough.

"Do you have a lantern?" she finally asked Sam, who had followed her.

"There's no need for one. There's nothing to see. If you did hit someone, you only winged him."

Libby frowned. Something about this wasn't right. She was certain she'd killed at least one of them. She never missed.

Her past again reared its ugly head. It scared her, and that made her mad. She rounded on Sam, her pistol tight in her palm, wishing even more that she could see him better so she could read his face for the truth.

"Who are you, Sam Kyote?" she demanded. "I mean, who are you really?"

Louis's experiment on him had backfired. It was no great success. An ability to create illusions was entertaining, occasionally useful, but hardly a great secret weapon. After three weeks this was still the best he could do.

And the illusion of shadow he'd projected to hide the remains of whatever these were from the beautiful, if somewhat trigger happy, sheriff wasn't going to hold up forever. It took too much concentration and made his head hurt.

He had to get rid of her.

"I'm a US Federal marshal," he said, in answer to her question. He thrust out his hand, ignoring the gun she had trained on him. "Pleased to make your acquaintance."

"A US marshal, huh?" She didn't relax, or accept his hand.

He let it drop to his side. It seemed Sheriff Mayden was the suspicious type. To make matters worse, marshals weren't highly regarded in the Territories—where frontier justice tended to be swift and ruthless, and federal laws too often contradicted the local ones.

"Why were those men after you?" she asked.

He'd been wondering the same thing himself. Louis's

experiment on him, and all his talk of top secret projects and ambitious men in the government who couldn't be trusted, had left him a tad suspicious of pretty much everyone. "I'm not taking it personal. They were most likely trying to rob the place. Or maybe just testing my mettle, seeing as how I'm new here and all."

He could sense her examining his every word, looking for lies, and she was having none of his explanation. "What brings a US marshal to a peaceful place like Coyote Bluff?"

"You just answered your own question," he said. "When we aren't working, marshals like peace and quiet as much as the next man. Maybe more. I could ask you the same question," he added. "What brought *you* here?" He didn't believe for a moment it was a burning desire to be sheriff.

She deliberately misunderstood him. "I heard the gunfire from my place, a mile this side of the gorge. I thought I should check it out."

So the sheriff had her secrets, too. It came as no real surprise. Women had to be as tough as the men in these parts. A lot of the lawmen in the Territories were reformed outlaws and gunfighters, and she handled her pistol with well-above-average skill. He'd ask a few questions about her in town. A man being curious about a woman sheriff—in particular, one as beautiful as this—wouldn't draw undue attention.

And he was very curious. A diverting image of her had been branded into his brain. He didn't need to be recreating that particular fantasy. Not right here and now. She'd shoot him for sure.

"I'll see you home," he said. Since he was a marshal, his insisting on it should rile her enough to speed her on her way. Already, the raw smell of the recently dead was slipping through his illusion. He couldn't hide that.

After a few more long, drawn out moments, she holstered her pistol. Night sounds returned. From what he could discern, most were benign.

"My horse is hobbled on the other side of the knoll. It knows its way home." She turned her face away, peering into the shadows, and sniffed. "Where's that smell coming from?"

"Could be my pigs. The pen's over there."

"It doesn't smell like pigs to me."

She began pacing off a widening circle. The toe of her boot missed one of the bodies he'd hidden from her by the breadth of a hair.

It was time to be blunt. His head was pounding.

"I don't know about you, Sheriff, but I've got to make an early start in the morning. Everything's under control here. If you want to talk more, or look around, why not come back when it's daylight?"

She finally nodded, although it was plain to see she was far from satisfied.

He accompanied her as she headed into the night, tense and alert and not really welcoming his company. Sheriff Mayden wasn't a woman who needed to fill long stretches of silence. That piqued his interest even more.

Once they were out of his yard he let the illusion behind him fade. The cover of darkness gave him an opportunity to examine her with more leisure than could be considered polite. She was feminine without being fragile, and obviously independent. He liked that in a woman. Most days, it was hard enough looking out for himself.

And she was well beyond passable pretty. Damn near poetic, if he was being honest. He hadn't minded at all having her curvy backside pressed tight against his crotch after she'd tackled him.

They reached the spot where her horse waited amongst the sagebrush and creosote. Now that he was no longer trying to hold an illusion in place and the headache had eased, he wasn't as eager for her to depart. He helped her into the saddle over her awkward and charming protests that she didn't require any assistance. "My mama raised me right, Sheriff. She taught me to be a gentleman."

The distrust in her cool gaze told him she thought he was making fun of her. Sherriff Mayden had no true idea of her appeal to a man.

Curious.

He took in those long legs of hers, hugging her horse. His tongue went dry at the thought of them wrapped around his hips instead. Coyote Bluff gained more appeal by the second.

He still had his hand on her mare's bridle.

"Good night, Marshal Kyote," she said, all pointed politeness, and waited for him to remove it.

He did so, but with great regret. "Good night, Sheriff Mayden."

He watched as she rode away. The pretty sheriff might be good with a gun, but anything could be lurking in ambush. He considered following her to make sure she got home safe, then reluctantly discarded the notion. She'd shoot first and ask questions later if she felt at all threatened—and a threat well might include being trailed by a man she wasn't sure she could trust.

He returned to his yard and the remains he had yet to examine.

When he was done, he had more questions than answers.

He rocked back on his heels, puzzling things through. For his part, his aim was a source of Division amusement. It was a few rungs above awful. He could hold his own, but he'd never be crowned Sharpshooter of the Year. Sheriff Mayden's shots, on the other hand, had been clean and accurate. He could tell she'd meant to incapacitate the two men she'd targeted, not kill them, by the location of the bullet wounds. She'd nailed the same spot on both of them, from two different angles, with a precision that spoke of long hours of practice and a solid knowledge of basic human anatomy.

These weren't human. That meant they could only be Sky People. Why would they be here, in this out-of-the-way little town? And on his property, no less?

No one but the Division knew where he was.

Sam scratched his head. He had no one to ask. No one to trust.

Except for Louis.

And he had no real reason to trust him either. He'd come West to Coyote Bluff as suggested because if it turned out Louis was telling the truth about a special assignment, then he was right where he should be. If not, it was easier to disappear here than in Washington.

But he wasn't ready to run. He had the proof at his feet that Louis was being at least partly honest with him.

He made a decision. He'd settle for doing quick sketches of the internal organs, then send the sketches to Louis. Louis could do with the information as he pleased. What happened after that would decide a few more things for Sam.

In the meantime he'd try not to think about how he'd had the blood from one of these things pumped into his body. The only purpose that served was to make him angry.

He was well beyond that.

"Your task was straightforward," Carson Whitley said. "Watch Sam Kyote. Find out what the Frenchman did to him. Apply a little pressure if necessary. I don't believe I mentioned anything about starting a range war."

The tall, beanpole-thin man Carson addressed removed his hat and wiped his brow with his sleeve. Heat shimmered in waves off the narrow mountain valley's stark granite walls. Scraggly larch and spindly pine grew from its crevices, offering little by way of shade. The pulsing heat of the sun bordered on brutal. After nine years in the western desert region around the silver mines of Utah Territory, Carson had grown used to it.

Jace Birch hadn't been here as long or adjusted quite as well. Five years ago, he and a dozen of his companions had stumbled into one of Carson's mining operations. They were dirty, starving, and looking for work. It hadn't taken long to figure out there was something…unusual about them. For one thing, they were mechanical geniuses. Their innovations for shoring up tunnels meant he'd been able to dig deeper and farther than current modern mining techniques allowed. He'd made a second fortune off selling the patents for the designs.

"Someone interfered," Birch replied.

Carson dusted imaginary dirt off the knee of his gray wool britches in an attempt to mask a mounting impatience. "Someone…who?"

"I don't rightly know."

Carson rested his forearms on the saddle horn, lacing the reins through the fingers of his gloved hands, and asked himself if Birch was being honest about that. Sam Kyote's sudden decision to take sick leave on a ranch near an outpost next door to hell raised a number of red flags. The little Frenchman's report on Kyote's poor health was also rife with ambiguity. There was a distinct possibility that one of them—or both—were working against him.

Carson knew firsthand how easily friendships and loyalties could be bought. The money from his highly profitable silver mining ventures and an investment in the national railroad had earned him a seat in the senate as the lone representative for the Territories. That seat had gained him access to almost every government secret imaginable. Secrets worth more than silver or gold.

Once he'd established his government connections it had been so easy to set up the Special Division and have himself instated as its director, a position he'd held for the past two years. Its primary mandate was to investigate sightings of Sky People, which he supposed was as good a name for them as any. Carson's personal mandate was to draw as little attention to them as possible. Someday he meant to be president. Having Sky People behind him gave him an advantage most people couldn't dream of.

But right now they also gave him a headache. Three Sky People were dead. Another had vanished. A US marshal from the Special Division, one whom he had personally signed off on sick leave, had seen proof of their existence. In a tiny town called Coyote Bluff, where a change in the drift of the tumbleweeds was cause for celebration.

He would have to wait and see if Kyote raised an alarm. If he did, Carson would find a way to deal with it. If he didn't, however...

Well. That would have to be dealt with as well.

"Get your men back out there and find me information on Kyote's accomplice so we know what we're up against. Remind them to be more careful this time." He nudged his blue roan into motion, turning it back down the steep, narrow trail leading to his silver mine operation. "I want to know every move Sam Kyote makes."

Chapter Three

The better part of the week had gotten away from Libby, leaving her little time to check into her new neighbor's past—or the motives of whoever had been behind the attack on his homestead.

She frowned over the latest message in front of her. She'd sent off a few telegrams, and gotten confirmation that Sam was indeed a US federal marshal, but she'd found nothing else. It was as if the man hadn't existed before 1875. He hadn't done much since, either—a fact not uncommon. Plenty of people came to the Territories to escape from their pasts. Coyote Bluff harbored more than its fair share of them.

The reason her week had been ruined ran a tin cup back and forth along the bars of her cell, creating a racket fit to wake the dead.

Libby sighed and looked up from her desk toward the other side of the small room. She had two cells in the jail—

one for the men, and one for the women. She'd only ever had Mary Lou Bennett in that second cell, and every time she did, it meant Libby had to sleep at the jailhouse. Propriety, and the local pastor, dictated Libby couldn't leave a male deputy alone with a female prisoner overnight.

Libby's deputy used that as a convenient excuse to never be alone with this particular prisoner at all. Mary Lou might be a tiny little thing, with a face as sweet as pie, but she was meaner than a bear with a rotten tooth. Her husband, easy-going of manner and weighing three hundred pounds at the very least, brought her up on charges of assault every two or three months so he could shut both eyes for a few nights and get some uninterrupted sleep.

This time, however, he'd needed stitches to close the gap above one bushy eyebrow from where Mary Lou had cracked his head open with a cast iron griddle. Libby often wondered why William Bennett didn't up and abandon her, and for that matter, why he'd married her in the first place. The fact she was dainty, blond, and China doll pretty probably had a lot to do with it. Maybe Mister Bennett had finally given up on her though, because this was day seven and he hadn't yet made an appearance to post bail. Mary Lou was getting meaner with each passing hour and Libby seriously feared for his life if he did.

The racket with the tin cup grew louder. "Sheriff!"

Libby prayed for patience. "What is it now, Mary Lou?"

"I need to use the outhouse."

Libby reached for a pair of handcuffs and the key to the cell. The key hung from a heavy iron ring on a hook on the wall behind her desk. She tossed Mary Lou the handcuffs and waited until she put them on before unlocking the cell door.

The outhouse was behind the jail. When they reached the end of the narrow dirt lane that led to it, Libby removed the handcuffs.

Finicky as a fine lady, with her nose in the air, Mary Lou lifted her skirts and stepped into the outhouse. Libby stood in front of the door so she couldn't slip out again and make a run for it, a lesson learned the hard way about three arrests back.

Someone shouted her name.

"Libby!" Deputy Pete Gaster peered around the corner of the jailhouse. "That new neighbor of yours you was asking about is over at the general store."

Libby winced, but tried to keep it on the inside. The general store was across the street from the jail, and if Sam Kyote was in it, he'd just heard every word.

"Thank you, Pete. I—"

The door of the outhouse burst open behind her, slamming her in the back and knocking her to her knees, and Libby cursed her weak leg. She glimpsed a flurry of gingham as Mary Lou sprinted away, her skirts hiked to her knees, no longer presenting a lady-like appearance at all.

She dashed past Pete, who stood aside and let her go.

"Stop her!" Libby cried, furious.

Pete held up his hands, his eyes wide with alarm. "I ain't havin' nothin' to do with that."

Libby gave chase, glad her pistol and holster were hanging over the back of her office chair, because otherwise, she didn't think she could have stopped herself from shooting Mary Lou in the back.

By the time Libby reached the street her escaped

prisoner was in the process of liberating a horse from the hitching post in front of the general store. A crowd had started to gather.

Mary Lou spotted Libby bearing down on her, dropped the animal's reins, seized a spittoon off the boardwalk, and sent it hurtling at her with surprising strength for such a small woman. Libby dodged the spittoon and made a dive for Mary Lou, hooking an arm around her waist and carrying her to the ground. Puffs of dried-out horse manure, ground to a fine powder by traffic and time, rose in a dusty cloud around them. It shot up Libby's nose and tortured her nostrils. She sneezed and Mary Lou tried to wriggle free. It was like tickling a fish to try and hang onto her, but by this time, Libby was taking the matter personal.

One of Mary Lou's pointy-knuckled fists caught her in the eye. Pain exploded.

Libby'd had enough. Resisting arrest could be added to Mary Lou's long list of legal transgressions. She drew back a fist of her own. Before she could take a swing, however, a large hand closed over her shoulder and hauled Libby upright.

She found herself staring into an amused pair of the oddest eyes she'd ever seen on any man. They were green in color, but with distinct flecks of gold surrounding the pupils that caused them to sparkle almost yellow in the sunshine. He had tawny hair that was blonder than brown, and a firm, smiling mouth bracketed by laugh lines. The size of him actually made Libby feel dainty.

So this was how Sam Kyote looked in the light of day.

He was aptly named. Despite the hint of good humor, the predatory air to him hadn't diminished. If anything, it was much more pronounced. He had a grip on Mary Lou's arm as well, but he wasn't looking at her, he was watching Libby with an ill-concealed interest that left her as tongue-tied as the gangly, awkward, thirteen-year-old girl she'd once been.

And acutely aware that half the town was watching the show.

"Careful," Libby warned him, but it was too late. Mary Lou sank her teeth into the hand restraining her. Sam yelped in pain, releasing both women.

Mary Lou made another break for it, with Libby again in pursuit. The crowd parted, well aware of Mary Lou's reputation. Besides, Libby thought, resigned to looking like a fool, she could hardly blame them. This was better entertainment than the tired Sunday sermons.

She heard footsteps pounding behind her.

Sam brushed Libby aside and caught up to Mary Lou in several more easy strides. He grabbed the back of her dress and lifted her so that she dangled above the ground, her feet and fists whirling. Mary Lou kicked at him, angry but harmless.

"Pass me the handcuffs," Sam ordered Libby, careful this time not to take his attention off the smaller woman. "That was my horse she was trying to steal, Sheriff Mayden, and I'd like to press charges."

Mary Lou's cheeks paled, then reddened in outrage. Horse theft was a hanging offense. No one in town would have dared bring such a charge against her, but Libby could see she wasn't as certain of this tall and intimidating stranger. Since Mary Lou hadn't actually stolen the horse the charges would never amount to anything, but she couldn't know that. A few days of worry would serve the little tyrant right.

Sam was waiting for the handcuffs, but Libby didn't like having someone else do her job, especially when that someone was a US federal marshal. It called into question her professional integrity. She hesitated, but decided not to create a bigger scene for the spectators than she already had. She passed the cuffs to him without a word, then trailed behind him as he escorted Mary Lou back to the jail.

To Libby's deep annoyance but not surprise, Pete Gaster had vanished. She'd learned a long time ago that any place there was trouble, the deputy was anywhere but.

Once the prisoner was again behind bars, Libby turned to Sam, who was looking well pleased with himself. She counted to ten in her head. Then she said, "May I have a word with you in private, Marshal Kyote?"

"Of course, Sheriff."

They stepped to the boardwalk in front of the jail. All eyes were on them, but thankfully, the townspeople remained out of earshot. They'd make up their own stories as to what was about to transpire, Libby did not doubt.

"There's no need to thank me," Sam said.

His straight blond hair was cut short in back and longer in front, and it fell forward over his brow despite an absentminded effort to push it back. He smiled at her with those unusual eyes, and Libby tried to recall why she was angry.

Mary Lou shouted curses at her from inside the jail.

Oh, yes. That.

"Tell me something, Marshal." Libby kept her voice low and pleasant, although inside she was fuming. "Would you thank me if I did your job for you, and in front of your employers?"

The smile in Sam's eyes slowly died. "No one else was helping you."

"They were letting me do my job," she lied. She knew full well no one cared she was sheriff. Nothing ever happened in Coyote Bluff and they'd been looking for entertainment. Helping her would have denied them of that. "I'd already caught Mary Lou." That part was true.

A slow minute passed as he mulled over her words.

"You're right, Sheriff Mayden. I crossed a line." His smile returned, this time spreading to his mouth. A slight dimple deepened the cleft in his chin. A faint scruff of beard, very fair, shadowed his lean jaw. "How about I make you supper tomorrow night as my way of apologizing? I swear to you, I'm a good cook."

Libby blinked. She wore men's trousers and boots, now covered in a powdery dust of questionable origins. She stank of weeks-old dried horse droppings, and her tangled hair needed a good brushing and re-braiding. Yet her handsome new neighbor had just invited her, sturdy Libby Mayden, to dinner?

She wondered what he was up to. Perhaps it had something to do with the events that had transpired at his homestead. She couldn't ignore her suspicions that his visitors might have had some connection to certain events from her past. If she accepted the invitation, it would give her a chance to find out more.

The way he looked at her while he waited for her answer filled her with a pleasant and gratifying warmth. He might have ulterior motives for cozying up to her, but she couldn't deny she felt flattered by the attention. She tried to recall if she had a dress to wear. Or for that matter, the last time she'd worn one.

"It all depends on whether or not Mary Lou's husband intends to bail her out before then," she said. "And there are those horse theft charges to attend to."

"We both know I can't make good on those charges so there's no point in laying them," Sam said. "But I'd appreciate it if you not tell her that for a few more hours so she can think on it." He drew back his sleeve and showed Libby his forearm, which had a perfect, half-moon bite mark on it. "She drew blood."

Most of the crowd in the street had dispersed, no doubt disappointed that the fun was over since Libby and Sam didn't appear to be arguing or about to exchange anything other than pleasantries.

"You might want to have the doctor clean that bite for you. Mary Lou Bennett is meaner than a rabid dog," Libby said. "And I'd be happy to come for supper, Marshal Kyote," she added. She tried a cautious smile. "Thank you for the invitation." If William Bennett didn't come for his wife before then, the heck with the pastor's decree. Pete would have to take over the jail for a few hours until Libby's return. It would serve him right.

Sam tipped his hat to her and sauntered across the dusty street to the general store. Libby sneaked a quick peek at his backside and allowed herself one wistful thought. It would be nice if Sam Kyote had invited her to dinner because he found her equally as attractive as she found him. Even old maids could dream.

But there were two types of men she knew to steer clear of, because lawmen and outlaws were two sides of the same tarnished coin. She had too many secrets, and she'd had her fill of worrying whether or not loved ones would come home. She'd go to dinner, but she'd keep it professional.

Assuming, of course, she'd be given a choice.

"Libby?"

She jumped, startled. Pete had reappeared behind her with a broad grin splitting his skinny, gray-stubbled cheeks, as if he could tell what was on her mind.

"What is it?" she asked.

"You know what they say about Coyote Trickster around these parts."

"No," Libby said, "I don't." Her stomach twisted because she knew she was about to find out. Pete loved local Indian lore, but his translation of the language was often convenient. He had an odd sense of humor.

"Local legend has it that when a pale moon walks in the night sky, Coyote Trickster wins the maiden he's been pursuing." He spat into the dirt in front of the boardwalk. "That there Marshal Kyote is after you, Libby Mayden. Get it? Kyote? Mayden? And ain't it interesting that tomorrow night's a full moon?"

Yes, she got it. She didn't find the joke as amusing as he seemed to, either.

Because a tiny part of her—the more feminine side—wouldn't mind overly much if she were pursued by Sam Kyote.

Watching Libby wrestle another woman to the ground had to rank as one of Sam's all-time top favorite events. Where he came from, entertainment like this couldn't be bought. Her gentle chastisement of him for interfering in her work, and those gorgeous, over-serious, cornflower-blue eyes, had been a close second.

He'd finished his business at the general store. While he waited for his purchases to be packaged, he moved on to the telegraph office to see if they had any telegrams for him. Seven days had passed since the shootout. The crude autopsies he'd performed had revealed little useful information, at least to his untrained eye, although he'd sketched the perplexing layout of the internal organs so he'd have a better idea of their vulnerable spots if he ever needed to know them again. He'd posted those sketches to Louis in Washington, along with a carefully worded note.

The telegraph office had no messages for him. He could do nothing more until he got a response and waiting was driving him crazy. Patience wasn't one of his virtues. Libby with the gorgeous blue eyes offered precisely the distraction he needed.

He left the telegraph office and returned to the general store. As he walked through the swinging door, the shelves behind the cash register caught his eye. They were neatly stacked with rows of porcelain dishware and serving plates. If he had Libby coming for dinner, he should offer it to her on something other than the battered tinware he used on the trail.

"I have a few more things I'd like to add to my bill," he said to Mae Miller, the store owner's portly wife.

Mae might once have been an attractive woman. In middle age her peppered hair had thinned. Her face sagged into drooping jowls. When she smiled, she revealed speckled gums and three brown, crooked teeth. The first two fingers of her right hand were stained an unhealthy yellow, suggesting a fondness for tobacco.

"What things might those be, Marshal Kyote?"

He nodded at the shelves. "I'd like a service for four, if you don't mind."

Missus Miller's smile disappeared, replaced by an expression of disappointment and genuine concern. "I'm sure your intentions are good, but speaking as a woman, I believe Missus Kyote will want to choose her own dishes."

The two elderly gentlemen playing checkers on the cold stove in the center of the room pretended not to listen. Sam didn't see how this could pose a problem for him since first, he wasn't married, and second, the store's selection was limited to one choice of pattern. Plain white.

"Thank you for your concern, but there is no Missus Kyote."

Her eyes lit up and Sam realized he'd walked straight into a trap.

"Then you'll need help outfitting your kitchen," she said. "My Bess will be happy to oblige. She's a great little cook, too."

"She's got to be a great cook," one of the checker players muttered under his breath to the other. "Claiming she's little is what's a stretch."

The other man kicked him, and Missus Miller cast a surly look in their direction.

"Thank you," Sam said again. Without thinking, he glanced out the window at the jail across the street. "I don't need help with my kitchen, but if the requirement arises, I've already got someone whose opinion I can ask."

"Surely you can't mean the sheriff."

The checker players both lifted their heads at that, scenting gossip, the game forgotten.

Sam hadn't been speaking of Libby, only making an excuse, but their reactions surprised him. "Why not?" he asked. "She's a beautiful woman."

"She's a little…" Missus Miller paused as if struggling to find the right description. Frowning, she traced a knothole in the worn pine counter with one finger. "Independent."

The checker players nodded their agreement.

Independent was polite speak for *experienced*, which was more polite speak for a woman of loose morals, but Sam figured something must have gotten lost in the translation somewhere because Libby didn't give that impression at all. Missus Miller had to mean the word in its original context.

Westerners were as nosy as the next person about most things, but in a land where an inordinate number of people came to make a fresh start, they believed a man's past was best left alone. He was judged by who he was, not what he'd been. He guessed the same rule applied to the women.

Since she'd brought up the subject, however, he felt safe in asking a few questions. "Nothing wrong with a woman who can take care of herself," he said easily. "I hear Sheriff Mayden is good with a gun."

"Killed five men in five shootouts," one of the checker players chimed in, sounding as proud as if the accomplishment were his own. "She's Lord Maxwell's daughter, y'know. Rode with the Mayden gang her whole life."

"Really?" Sam wondered why he hadn't made the connection when Libby had first given him her name. Everyone in the country had heard of Maxwell Mayden, the exiled British aristocrat turned outlaw who'd been killed by

Pinkerton detectives during a stagecoach robbery. Him having a daughter appeared to be the lesser told tale.

"Shut yer mouth, Saul," Missus Miller said. "Sheriff Mayden ain't no outlaw."

Saul's voice quivered with indignation. "Never said she was. I said she rode with them, which she did. That don't make her no outlaw."

Sam wasn't planning to quibble over the finer points of the law. Libby wore a badge, so whatever she'd once been, the West no longer recognized it. But he guessed now he knew what Missus Miller meant when she called Libby independent, although in his mind, the correct word to use would be *unorthodox*.

"You know," the other man interrupted, speaking with slow and thoughtful deliberation, "if anyone is going to be offering the marshal kitchen advice mebbe it should be the sheriff. Pretty girl like that ain't gettin' younger."

Missus Miller and Saul forgot their blossoming argument. Everyone looked at each other and nodded their heads.

Missus Miller reached for the dishes. "Give me a few minutes to wrap these up proper," she said over her shoulder to Sam. "If you're going to be entertaining, you'll want a tea service, too."

When Sam left the store a half hour later, his head was still spinning. He strapped his purchases carefully to the back of his horse. He had no logical explanation for what had just transpired or the conclusions that had been drawn. He suspected, however, that soft-spoken Sheriff Mayden was going to be unhappy about it when she found out.

And she would.

He contemplated the past week's events as he followed

the dusty road out of town, whistling with contentment, and came to some conclusions of his own.

Between the late night visits from Sky People, and Coyote Bluff's colorful residents, his temporary exile from Washington wasn't going to be the dull hardship he'd thought it would be.

Beautiful outlaw-turned-sheriff Libby Mayden was the frosting on the cake.

Chapter Four

The next day was a Tuesday. More precisely, it was the second Tuesday of the month, which was when Judge Roy Rowe held court in Coyote Bluff's Evening Lily saloon.

Judge Roy, as Libby called him, was an impressive man. There was nothing noticeable about him physically. He was in his fifties, had graying brown hair, and was of average height and build, although remained fit from all his hours in the saddle. His face was weathered and tan for the same reason.

It was his eyes that set him apart. They could be cold and expressionless or hot and overwhelming, depending on his mood. Either way, they made people cautious. He'd told Libby more than once to always look a man in the eye, because it was the best way to get a handle on him. If she saw nothing, she should either shoot him or walk away.

Libby had only ignored his advice once. She'd never do so again.

The Evening Lily was owned by a man named Eldon Caudel. He was calm, quiet, and kept a sawed off shotgun loaded with buckshot under the bar. Consequently, Libby rarely had occasion to visit his establishment in her official capacity.

Since nothing of significance ever happened anywhere else in Coyote Bluff either, she spent court days keeping Judge Roy company while he drank on the town's tab. She was particularly glad of today's excuse to get away from Mary Lou. Although she held onto her faith that William would collect his wife, he still hadn't done so.

"I could order her hanged," Judge Roy suggested, spinning his empty shot glass. "William's always been a decent fellow. I'd be doing him a favor. Coyote Bluff, too."

"You can't hang her," Libby said. "The town would have nothing left to talk about."

Judge Roy didn't appear convinced. "She's unadulterated evil. I'm fairly certain the devil spawned her."

Libby's lips twitched. "I've heard that rumor."

"Speaking of rumors." He lifted his glass and gestured for Eldon to bring him another. "I hear you have a new neighbor."

"A marshal, yes. Sam Kyote. He bought Billie Hernandez's place."

"A marshal, huh?" His gaze narrowed. "What's he like?"

She shrugged, noncommittal. "Seems nice enough."

A rare smile slipped into his eyes. "I hear he's planning to ask for your kitchen advice. If so, that boy's going to starve."

She tensed up. "I have no idea where you'd hear such a thing."

Eldon, delivering Judge Roy's next shot, insinuated himself into the conversation. "At the mercantile. The marshal was buying new dishes."

Judge Roy thanked Eldon for the drink. The bar owner nodded and retreated back to the bar. He and Judge Roy had been friends a long time, but he knew better than to hang around once he'd been dismissed.

"Missus Miller is always on the lookout for a husband for her daughter," Libby said when they were alone once again. "The marshal was no doubt using the only excuse he could think of to divert her interest."

"If you say so." Judge Roy leaned back in his chair and moved on to the next topic. Despite three double shots of whiskey, he remained sober. "I came through Buckwheat a few days ago. Seems people have been asking questions there about a certain lady sheriff rumored to be in the area, and speculating as to whether or not the stories about her family connections are true."

She fidgeted on her hard wooden chair. Whatever else Maxwell Mayden might have been, he was particular about who he trusted around his daughter. The Mayden Men, as they were known behind their backs, might have been killers and thieves, but they had their own code of ethics. They were loyal to him, and therefore, to her. They'd all watched out for her as if she were their own daughter or sister. They continued to do so.

And, while Maxwell Mayden might no longer exist, Judge Roy Rowe always made sure no one who mattered got too close to where she was.

Until now, it seemed.

Cold crawled up her poker-straight spine. "I hardly need

to remind you my past is a poorly kept secret."

He eyed her with concern. "Max had a lot of good friends. I figured you keeping his name would protect you. Unfortunately, you have your own reputation to live down, not just his."

Talk of her abilities had died down over the past few years. She'd kept her head low. People had been content enough to let her past be the past. Most had no idea where she'd gotten to. Even here in Coyote Bluff, while the locals liked to brag about her abilities, it was the legend they liked. Only a few truly knew her to be as good as was claimed.

"It's been five years since my last gunfight."

He threw back the fourth shot and plunked the empty glass on the table. "They asked specifically about your days in New Mexico Territory, and if you ever took work on your father's behalf."

If she didn't know Eldon would take exception to serving a woman—sheriff or not—she'd order one of those shots for herself. It required control of every muscle she possessed to repress a full body shudder. Her eccentric and infamous father had sometimes taken honest work from dishonest people by having him or his men act as desert guides and armed protection. Yes, she'd accepted work on his behalf. Work he'd turned down.

But only once.

And once was enough.

"My father would never have allowed me to ride into the desert with strangers," she hedged, mindful there were ears everywhere, even here. She kept her face blank, careful to stick close to the truth. Judge Roy had his secrets, too, and he could smell a liar faster than a rat hunting cheese.

"But you were in New Mexico Territory with your papa, right up until he died."

Under the table, she spread her palms on the thighs of her trousers and flexed her fingers. There was no way anyone could know what had happened on that trip into the Chihuahuan Desert. She'd told no one. The only witness was dead.

But she couldn't help wondering if maybe Sam's late night visitors had found themselves on the wrong ranch. If that were the case, then sooner or later they'd find hers. She intended to be ready for them when they did.

"You know I was."

"They were also talking loud in a public place about how you're supposed to be the fastest gun in the country." His blue eyes sparkled with concern against the sun-ripened brown of his skin. "Are you still the fastest?"

"I can't speak for the talents of other people. But I'm as fast as I ever was. Maybe faster."

"Now's the time to tell me if anyone has a reason to be gunning for you. Should I be worried?"

If she trusted anyone, it was Judge Roy. In his own way he loved her. She knew that. In this regard, however, he wouldn't be sympathetic.

Seasoned gunfighters followed their instincts and she went with hers. "Not at all."

He tapped the rim of his glass with his fingertip and frowned at the table. For a few seconds, she thought he might call her for lying. Then, he looked up.

She pressed her palms harder into her thighs and prayed nothing would show on her face.

"Make sure you look any newcomers straight in the eye,"

he finally said. "And it might not hurt to get a bit friendly with the new marshal. Just in case. I hear he's a man who can take care of himself."

Sam eased a beef pie from the bowels of the wood stove's temperamental oven. The rich smells of meat and pastry filling the airy kitchen advised him of his culinary success.

He'd opened all the windows and doors, but the room was still hot as all get out. As he placed the pie carefully on the counter he decided he'd entertain the town's lovely sheriff out on the front stoop where the air was cooler.

And Libby was lovely, there was no arguing that. Pretty Sheriff Mayden had a past that defied all conventions, which made her all the more interesting to him. He hoped to get to know her better. And he had a few tricks up his sleeve to make it happen. He hoped to convince her to spend the night. His property was isolated, as was hers, so no one would know, although propriety wasn't likely to be a serious obstacle with an independent woman who'd been raised around men.

He sat on the steps to watch for her arrival. With the pie cooling, the new dishes set out, and the table and chairs outside and ready for supper, he had nothing to do now but wait. His thoughts drifted to Washington and the lack of response. He hated not knowing what was going on. Other than that one brief run-in with Sky People, this so-called special assignment was duller than dirt. He'd practiced illusions to the point of boredom. He was anxious for action. Any would do.

A cloud of dust kicked up from the direction of Libby's

ranch.

When she rode into the yard he helped her dismount from the saddle. As his hands closed around her waist, her cheeks bloomed a bright, rose-petal pink. He found that charming. The more awkwardly she received gentlemanly attention, the more of it he wanted to shower on her.

He set her on her feet, although he didn't remove his hands right away. Her light brown hair fell in a heavy braid to the small of her back and smelled of lilac soap and fresh air. She hadn't changed to a dress as he'd half expected she might. He didn't know what message it was meant to convey to him, but for his part, he was glad she wore trousers. They suited her best, gripping her hips and thighs in a way that was hardly decent for any respectable woman. The open-collared white shirt she'd tucked into the waistband stretched across a pair of full breasts to reveal more than a hint of creamy-fleshed cleavage. He had it on good authority her papa was dead, which was just as well, because right now the poor man must be spinning in his grave.

Those lovely, wide blue eyes, tipped at an exotic angle, lifted to his as she eased away from his touch, placing a few discreet feet of distance between them.

"Good evening, Marshal," she said. "Sorry about my manly attire, but I was delayed at the jail. I had a prisoner to release and my deputy was late for his shift."

He didn't know whether to laugh or cry. She believed she looked like a man, when nothing could be further from the truth. He had no doubt her jail was full most Friday nights. If not, the male residents of Coyote Bluff were either exceedingly well-mannered or dead from the neck down.

"Don't apologize. You look beautiful," he said. Her eyes

dropped from his. "Supper's ready. First, let me take care of your horse for you."

He didn't give her a chance to argue, but took the mare's bridle and led the animal to the barn. When he rejoined her she was sitting on the front steps, her knees drawn almost to her chin, watching the last rays of sun settling over the desert.

He couldn't resist. He had talents no normal man should possess and he wasn't above using them to impress a beautiful woman. The headache they gave him would be well worth it. The sunset she admired so intently suddenly exploded with light. Streaks of red and gold shot high into the deepening sky.

"Oh!" she exclaimed, her eyes going wide. She stared, entranced, until the fireworks subsided. While she watched the lights, he gazed at her. "I've never seen anything so pretty before."

Neither had he. And the headache he'd anticipated turned out to be nothing at all. He was getting better at the illusions every day, particularly simple ones such as this.

"Local legends claim that when a woman sees the sky flashing red and yellow, she'll find the man she's been waiting for her whole life," he lied.

She laughed, a genuine, feminine sound that made her even more attractive. "What makes all these local legends so certain a woman will wait her whole life for one man?"

"Doesn't every woman want to find the right one?"

Her expression turned serious. "No, Marshal Kyote, they do not. Freedom is a wonderful thing. Some women are content with the worry-free lives they create for themselves." She dusted off her trousers and stood. On the first step she was at eye level with him.

She changed the subject. "If you don't mind, I'd like to discuss what happened here the other night when those men attacked you. Is it possible they were after you because of your work as a marshal? Can you think of anything they might hold a grudge against you for?"

Was this the only reason she'd come here tonight? To get information?

Rather than being disappointed by the possibility, he was intrigued. He'd turned on the charm. Now he'd have to pull out all the stops.

"No," he said. "Nothing."

She didn't need to say the words outright. The look she leveled at him was enough to accuse him of lying. "You're a US federal marshal in a relatively lawless land, Marshal Kyote. You honestly believe you have no enemies?"

"Sam."

Her blue eyes widened. "I beg your pardon?"

"My name is Sam."

Twin lines formed a vee that narrowed over her brow. Uncertainty mingled with her suspicion. "Are you *flirting* with me?"

He decided to lay his cards on the table and gauge her reaction. "I invited you out here alone and offered to cook supper for you," he said. "I'd say that flirting is one of my objectives, yes. You're a very beautiful woman, Sheriff Mayden," he added, taking a step closer, but careful not to touch her. He didn't want her to feel threatened, simply aware of him as a man who found her appealing. She did, after all, carry a gun—and she knew how to use it. "Any other objectives that happen to get satisfied this evening are all up to you."

Her reaction was not the one he'd anticipated and hoped for. She stiffened, drawing back as if he'd slapped her, and folded her arms across her chest. "Despite what you may have heard, I'm not an adventuress."

It was his turn to be flustered. He'd been confused by the term *independent* when used in relation to her because of its various interpretations, but a*dventuress* was a polite term for *whore*. No mistaking that one. He couldn't deny he'd invited her out here with less than proper intentions, so he guessed he could understand the confusion. He'd rushed his agenda because of her mature age and unconventional background, and made assumptions based on her lack of regard for proprieties. Just because she wasn't a conventional woman, that didn't make her a loose one. He should be thankful she hadn't already gone for her gun.

"I'm profoundly sorry. I've heard nothing of the sort. The townspeople hold you in high regard. My apologies for offering you such an insult, no matter that it wasn't intended."

She didn't believe him. He could see it in the depths of her lovely eyes. But he also read curiosity. And interest. As if she were testing him and he was in danger of failing.

Right then, his plans for the evening took a distinct turn. He still wanted her. In truth, now more than ever. But the approach he'd planned wasn't going to work with her and now he had no clear idea of what would.

"I'm widely regarded by the townspeople as sturdy." Humor, as sudden as it was unexpected, touched her tone. "I've never milked a cow in my life, Marshal Kyote. Rest assured I don't intend to start now."

A single coyote barked off in the distant desert, followed

by a series of answering yips from its pack. Somewhere, the animals hunted.

Well, Sam was hunting too, and he was about to change tactics. "Is it so hard to believe," he said, slowly and with great deliberation, "that I find you a beautiful woman?"

"I'm too tall, too old, and with too much reputation behind me to appear attractive to respectable men. That leaves us with brood mare or work horse. And neither one of those options is attractive to *me*."

He didn't dare speak for fear of saying the wrong thing. Her height was nothing to him. He liked a woman he didn't have to bow down to in order to kiss. She couldn't be more than twenty-five, which made her mature but hardly over the hill. And as for having too much reputation…

Her independence had been part of the reason he'd rushed her. He liked an independent woman. And he liked her to be all woman. Libby Mayden fit those requirements. He knew what he wanted. The trick was to find out what she wanted, too.

He set his hands on her hips and tightened his fingers so that she couldn't pull away too easily, but at the same time, wouldn't feel trapped. He gave her a few seconds to figure out what was coming. He saw the flare of interest in her eyes. The way her pupils dilated.

When she showed no signs of undue alarm, he leaned forward and placed his lips over hers.

Libby had been kissed before. Aside from one or two, most had been pleasant.

None, however, had produced quite this reaction. She quivered from the tips of her polished leather riding boots to the roots of her freshly washed hair at the smooth glide of his lips on hers.

Without any thought for propriety or the impression she might give, she lifted her hands to Sam's shoulders and clung to him, afraid she might fall, because her knees had become unreliable. She blamed it on the old bullet wound that sometimes caused her to limp, but somehow, with a few words of flattery and a simple kiss, he'd unbalanced and unsettled her.

That was a first.

The kiss ended. She opened her eyes and stared at his chin, unable to meet his gaze. His hands remained on her hips. Hers, she discovered with a start, continued to clutch at his shoulders. Her shaky legs had not yet recovered. She felt awkward and unsure of herself, which was ridiculous. She could outdraw most men—had killed five of them as proof—and yet she lost her head over a simple, uncomplicated, undemanding kiss.

Sam gave her one of those wide, humor-filled smiles that seemed to come so easily to him. "I'm fond enough of horses," he said, "but I confess, I don't often think of them in relation to women. If I ever need a brood mare I'll buy one with four legs."

Libby's face flushed with heat. She'd been indelicate and spoken without thought, another failing of hers. On occasion, her years of riding with her father's old gang of outlaws came back to haunt her. Lord Maxwell Mayden had been a gentleman in the old country, and tried to raise her to be a lady, but the lessons never stuck. If she'd learned anything from watching her delicate, genteel mother wither away, it was that real ladies didn't survive for long in the West. And Libby was nothing if not a survivor.

Her legs regained their reliability. She withdrew her hands from Sam's shoulders. The smooth, tightly woven fabric of the shirt he wore felt expensive to her. A US marshal appeared to be well compensated for his work.

"I apologize if I insulted you," she said.

"Not at all." The setting sun caught the gold flecks in his unusual eyes. He held out his arm for her to take. "Supper's getting cold."

It smelled wonderful, and she said so as Sam escorted her to a table he'd set outside on the stoop, near the kitchen door. A bright linen tablecloth and china plates adorned it, along with crystal stemware and an unlit hurricane lantern. He'd gone to a lot of trouble for her and she'd shown up in men's trousers. It was no wonder civilized men found her so lacking in feminine charms.

He pulled out her chair and held it for her. As he did, his hand brushed her arm. She went as limp at the casual contact as she had from his kiss. The heat in his eyes when she glanced up—the way they dipped to the open neck of her shirt—said he'd meant for it to cause that reaction.

He *was* flirting with her—as if he really did find her beautiful.

Sam, she discovered, had a good sense of humor when it came to his work. The stories he told her, while outrageous and far from believable, made her laugh.

They also made her forget why she'd come here, and instead of finding out more about him, she talked far too much about herself. He was good at gathering intelligence, she had to admit. Very good. Because she had never been much of a talker.

The evening passed far too quickly.

"We should do this more often," Sam said. "It gets lonely in the desert at night."

The smooth inflection in his tone—the way his eyes lingered again on the open neck of her shirt—suggested this might well be a subtle invitation for her to stay over. The problem with living under Max Mayden's—and then Roy Rowe's—thumbs for so long, however, was that any man who dared turn an eye in her direction was most likely offering attentions she didn't want. Since Sam's attentions were hardly unwanted, she had to assume he either didn't know or didn't care. If he didn't know, she should feel guilty. She should walk away before things got out of hand. If he didn't care, then he was foolish.

The light of the lantern flickered, sending shadows dancing across the yard and into the night. Unlike the last time she'd been here, when it was too dark to see, a pale, full moon now rose in the sky and she could see for miles. Her deputy's words slipped into her thoughts. *Local legend has it that when a pale moon walks in the night sky, Coyote Trickster wins the maiden he's been pursuing.*

The moon wasn't walking, and Pete's words were nothing more than foolishness he'd made up for amusement. Coyote Bluff, while it had its fair share of secrets, was hardly exciting.

"It's getting late," she said. "I should be going." Mary Lou's husband had finally retrieved his wife, so she didn't have to rush straight back to the jail, but she had chores to do at home before her next shift in the morning.

She started to gather the dirty plates to help clear the table, but Sam caught her wrist. As the pad of his thumb ran across the soft flesh underneath, heat scorched through her. Flirting, she suspected, was part of his nature, harmless and fun, because really, she'd be crazy to think a man as handsome and fun as Sam was, a man who could have any woman he wanted, would dally with someone like her.

"Leave the dishes," he said. "I'll get them later, after I take you home." He cut off her protests that she didn't need an escort, sending her another one of those careless, disarming smiles. "Tonight, you're my guest. Since I invited you here, I prefer to see you to your door at the end of the evening."

She couldn't help being flattered by that.

She walked with him to the barn and helped saddle the horses.

So far, she'd uncovered no good reason why anyone would want to kill Sam—other than that he was a US marshal. From what he'd said though, and she'd read in the reports, he'd done very little work here in the West. It wasn't his territory.

His being here didn't make sense. Those missing men she'd shot made even less.

And Libby liked for things to make sense.

Chapter Five

They were almost halfway to her place, talking softly because sound carried over such long distances in the desert, when Libby realized the world wasn't right.

The coyotes, raucous and playful all evening, had fallen disturbingly silent. No night birds twittered or flew overhead. No small animals rustled in the desert scrub. Even the wind had gone dumb.

Sam picked up on the change, too. He reined in his horse, grasping for the bridle on hers to draw the animals closer together. Libby's leg brushed against his, and out of long habit she groped for the rifle in her saddle boot.

"Wait here," he said.

All hints of a smile were gone from his tone. Now, Libby could well imagine him as a federal marshal with an impressive capture record. But she wasn't used to overt male protectiveness, nor did she believe she needed it. She was the sheriff around here. When he spurred his horse into motion, heading for a narrow arroyo that cut a thin line through the desert and created one of her four property lines, she stayed right behind him.

Beyond the line stretched government land, too arid for cattle ranching but holding enough promise of silver and gold that miners continued to flock to it. Only one other homestead existed out here and its buildings were dark, the residents no doubt asleep. The Rosenbergs had a young family.

"I don't see anything," Sam said, but he still spoke in his marshal tone. That meant he thought things weren't right either, no matter how they might seem on the surface.

"Maybe it's—" she began, only to be cut off by a terse command.

"Get down!"

He rolled from his saddle and she was quick to follow his lead. He slapped the horses on their rumps and sent them running.

A rifle shot rang out. A bullet struck a boulder close by, blasting the rock to bits. Swearing, Sam threw himself over her to protect her from flying shards of broken basalt and clumps of dirt. She waited, holding her breath.

How on earth had he known that shot was coming?

After long seconds of silence, she lifted her head. She could see the desert, drenched in pale moonlight, past the black shroud around them—but Sam's face was hidden from her, even though he had her pinned on her back to the ground and they were pressed so close together she could feel the beat of his heart against hers.

"Why can't I see you?" she whispered to him.

"Magic trick." His breath brushed her cheek as he spoke into her ear. "An illusion. Picked it up from a year spent with a traveling road show. Have you still got your rifle?"

"Yes."

She had it clenched tight in her left hand. It was a wonder it hadn't gone off and killed one of them when he landed on her. The ridiculous story of an illusion, she'd call him on later. She knew better than to take a man at face value. Sam Kyote was more than he seemed. Whether that was good or bad remained to be seen.

"Good." He pressed a fast kiss to her forehead. "For luck. We're going to crawl to the edge of that arroyo. It's my guess that whoever they are, they're hiding in there. When we reach it you're going to start picking them off, quick as you can. But you keep your head down," he ordered. "They'll know what direction the shots are coming from."

She didn't ask any questions or even think beyond what needed to be done. With a little luck there'd be time for talk later.

They crawled side by side, their progression to the edge of the arroyo slow. When they reached it, she peered over the lip into what was little more than a dry creek bed at this time of year. She had to wait for her eyes to adjust to the deeper shadows at the bottom, no more than fifteen feet below her. When they did, she made out two figures. They both carried rifles.

She lifted hers, taking careful aim, her finger slowly tightening on the trigger. She had no qualms about shooting at men who'd shot at her first. But she wasn't convinced these were men and there was only one way to find out.

She pulled the trigger.

Sam had no weapon on him. He hadn't anticipated a need for one over dinner with a beautiful woman.

It didn't matter, however. Libby had matters well in hand on her own. She fired off two shots in rapid succession—striking each man where the right kidney would have been on a human. Both men went down. Neither moved.

Sam and Libby stayed perfectly still, not speaking, waiting to see if there'd be any return fire. When there wasn't, and Sam felt confident there wasn't going to be, he took a slow, careful look around.

The danger appeared to have passed. He'd have to take care of the two bodies in the morning. Right now he had to get Libby home. She was a little too quiet for his peace of mind.

"On your feet, Sheriff Mayden," he said. "This is no time to go delicate on me. We have a bit of a walk ahead of us. The horses are gone."

Delicateness, however, was hardly one of her failings. She hadn't screamed, fainted, cried, or fired accusations at him, or done any of the things he'd expect of a woman who'd been shot at, even one who was a sheriff—because this was Coyote Bluff, after all. She knew how to kill Sky People, too. That wasn't something she'd picked up by accident.

She groped for his arm. "I can't *find* my feet."

He'd forgotten the blanket of darkness he'd wrapped around them. As he disassembled it, peeling it off like multiple layers of old paint, he reconciled himself to the inevitable. She'd have questions for him. Fair enough. He had a few of his own. He wondered if either of them would respond with the truth, and supposed that would all depend on the question. He'd let her go first so he could make up his mind.

They walked for fifteen minutes before she finally found

her tongue.

"You're quite the illusionist, Marshal Kyote. I've been rolling it around and round in my head, and no matter which way I look at it, I can't for the life of me figure out how you tricked everyone into seeing nothing."

"If you could figure it out, then it wouldn't be much of a trick. For my part, I confess I'm puzzled as to why your first question wasn't about us being attacked by men with no apparent reason for hostility."

"You mean that wasn't part of your illusion?"

He had to smile at the tartness of her response. "No," he said. "It wasn't."

"Why do *you* think we were attacked by them, then?"

"I have no idea. But I'm sure you'd agree," he added as they trudged through the moonlit desert night toward her house, "that this is turning out to be a different type of courtship than any you're most likely used to."

He was as surprised as she seemed to be by his choice of words. She said nothing for a long minute that threatened to cause him considerable embarrassment and discomfort.

"Is that what this is? A courtship?" she finally asked.

The question, from any other woman, might have come across as coy. From Libby, he discovered it created a warm spot near his heart. He took her hand in his and laced their fingers together. Women like this one weren't easy to find.

"Libby," he said gently, trying her given name out loud for the first time, "after all that's transpired since you rode into my yard this evening, we're both still alive and on amicable terms. What else could this possibly be but a courtship?"

He pretended he couldn't see her cheeks reddening, or the cautious, sidelong glances she slid his way as she mulled over his words.

"I've never been courted before, so I can't speak with any authority," she said.

He stopped, forcing her to stop, too, since he had a firm grip on her hand. The moonlight shone on her hair and in her eyes in a way that he found made it difficult for him to speak. He reached for her free hand as well.

They stood toe to toe, their joined fists pressed between their touching bodies, and a soft laugh caught in the back of his throat at the ludicrousness of the situation. How romantic had this entire evening proven to be?

"It's not just any girl I'd take to a gunfight," he said.

Then, he kissed her.

She'd been cautious with their first one back at his place, as if not knowing what was expected of her. This time she returned his kiss with more ambition, her tongue tasting his, and the soft sounds of pleasure she made said she liked what she found. That she didn't try to hide her reaction told him beyond any doubt that some decision on her part had also been reached, and it was one in his favor.

Desire exploded, deep in his gut, and he freed his hands to wander the curve of her back and swell of her hips. She pressed against him, her breasts to his chest, and his manhood instantly stiffened. A true gentleman might take into account that she'd come to an amorous decision after the euphoric rush brought on by surviving a gunfight, but it didn't matter to him. Lovemaking was the best thing he could think of for working off stress. After, they'd both sleep better for it.

But he had to slow things down or their first moment of intimacy was going to take place out here in a patch of sage brush, not a bed, and he planned to do at least part of courting her right.

When he lifted his head from their kiss, however, the sight of her almost changed his mind about waiting. She looked all doe-eyed soft and a little confused. Satisfaction sang through him that he could unsettle her when nothing else tonight had.

"I forget what we were talking about," she confessed, so shyly and with such wistful charm that Sam could have kissed her again.

He would, but not here. When they reached her place, where they weren't out in the open and exposed to the world, they could pick up where they left off. Right now it was best to change the subject. He planned to be honest with her about what he did for a living. He hoped she'd be honest with him in return. Mutual trust would do wonders for their fledgling relationship. Besides, he had a suspicion that her secrets were more interesting than his.

He reclaimed her hand, and again, they began walking.

"Let's talk about something else for a bit," he said. "Have you ever seen Sky People before?"

She caught the toe of her boot on a rock and might have stumbled, but Sam saw it coming and steadied her. He'd already noticed she sometimes favored one leg and he wondered about it.

She recovered nicely. "You mean the Acoma?"

He played along. "Who?"

"People who live in pueblos. A sky city. I met a few in New Mexico."

"These Sky People come from a city a little higher than that. They come from the stars. Or so I've been told."

"Talking about something like that would sound crazy to most people, wouldn't you think? But I suppose," she added, peering at him from under those long eyelashes, "it'd be no crazier than someone who can make people see what he wants them to see."

The way she dodged the question and turned it around amused him.

"So this is how it's going to be," he mused. "Tit for tat. Information for information."

"We both work for the law, S-Sam."

She stumbled a bit over his name, which made him smile because he intended to hear it on her lips again tonight, but with a much different inflection next time.

"I know about your past, Libby," he said. "Your father was Lord Maxwell Mayden, killed by Pinkerton detectives during a stagecoach robbery. You were pardoned for killing five men in self-defense after they called you out. I hear your daddy bragged about your skills with a gun maybe more than he should have." Especially when he was drinking, but Sam didn't see the need to completely disparage her father. "And I know you've been inquiring into my past, too."

"Yours isn't quite so well documented." She sounded put out by that.

"No. And for good reason." Sam studied the desert night. A rattlesnake slithered through rocks and dirt fifty yards to their right, following an unsuspecting pocket mouse about to become dinner. He saw a lot more things going on around them than Libby did. His instincts were as good, if not better, than those of most people, too, and if he didn't show trust in her, she'd never have any in him. "I'm a US federal marshal, but I work for a special division. We hunt anything out of the ordinary. Rumors of strange things, like people who come from the sky. Although," he confessed, "until I came to Coyote Bluff, my job's been a mite dull." He jerked a thumb at the arroyo behind them. "Now those Sky People appear to be more than rumor. And I can't help but think that these aren't the first ones you've run across."

He'd already learned that she never said much without careful consideration, so he let her take her time, willing to wait—even though it meant he'd have to think harder about her response when she gave it.

"How do I know you aren't one of them?" she finally asked. "Maybe that's how you know about them. Maybe that's why you can make me see things that aren't right. Maybe you aren't a marshal at all."

"If I was one of them, then why are they trying to kill me?"

"Are they trying to kill you? Or are they trying to make it look like they are? Because it occurs to me that they're terrible shots."

"That's a lot of trouble to go to in order to trick you. And it ended up with them dead. I'm not one of the Sky People, Libby. You're just going to have to trust me on that. Or shoot me, too. Take your pick."

Seconds stretched to minutes. He took that as a good sign. If she'd decided to shoot him, she'd have done it straight away. Just to be safe though, he kept hold of her hand.

She tightened her fingers, squeezing his in return. "Just before my father was killed we had a stranger ride into camp looking for an armed escort across the desert. Papa accepted, even though he didn't like the man's looks. Once we got close to our destination, it was obvious something wasn't quite right. He didn't try to look as much like a man anymore. And I started to think that the reason he didn't care was because he wasn't planning to give anyone an opportunity to talk about him."

"So your father killed him," Sam said.

"No. I did. It took me three bullets."

Yet Libby was an excellent markswoman. That explained how she'd discovered where best to shoot them. Sam debated pushing for more details, but decided not to, just yet. He'd let her think on it some more, and tell him the whole story when she was ready.

"Could they be back for revenge because you killed one of them?" he asked. They'd attacked his ranch, not hers, so he didn't think it was likely, but still, he had to ask.

She dug the toe of her boot into the dirt. "My father accepted the job. How would they know it was me who killed him?"

He'd swear she was lying about something, but let it go. Libby had relived enough of the past for one night, and it was a lot more than most people could take. The pieces of her story, however, didn't all fit together.

By now, they'd reached her property. The house was a neat and tidy one-level cabin. He could hear a few animals rustling about in one of her barns. A soft nicker and snort told him what had become of his horse. It had followed Libby's mare home.

He saw to Libby's safety first. A quick glance inside the cabin showed it to be undisturbed.

"Mind if I check on the horses?" he asked, gesturing toward the barns.

Libby shook her head.

He found his gelding chewing on hay in one of the

outbuildings. He unsaddled both horses and bedded them down for the night, then took a quick look in the other buildings just to be sure. She owned the usual assortment— a milk goat, a pig, and some chickens. A fat, lazy-looking cat lounged on a beam in the rafters overhead. Her beef cattle would be out on the range somewhere, most likely mingled in with the herd he'd bought with his ranch. Branding made them easy enough to separate come roundup time, still a few months away.

He returned to the house, climbed the low steps, and walked through her front door, passing a quaint wicker rocker on the verandah. Inside, Libby had lit a lamp. It rested on the pine slab kitchen table where she sat waiting for him. Now that she was home safe and sound, and the excitement had passed, uncertainty regarding his intentions colored her expressive eyes.

Sam found it endearing. Promising, too.

"Thank you for seeing me home," she said, all prim and proper, as if she didn't want to presume. "And thank you for a lovely evening."

That made him grin. He kicked the door shut behind him with his heel. He checked to make sure her guns were holstered.

And he went with his instincts. If he walked away, and let her think on things for too long, he might not get another opportunity like this for a very long time. He gathered her into his arms so he could kiss her again.

"It's not over yet," he said, once she was breathless and clinging to him. "Not unless you want it to be."

Chapter Six

Libby fought to collect her scattered thoughts, a hard thing to do when she was being held in Sam's arms.

He claimed they were courting, but he'd seen for himself she was no ordinary woman. He needn't fear she'd take him too serious. She knew better than to get too deeply involved with any man working either side of the law. They liked women well enough, but in the end, they had only one true love—and that was adventure. She understood. She liked it, too.

And if men could be adventurous, why couldn't she?

Her greatest concern was that if he spent the night, someone might report back to Judge Roy. Or that some of the locals might take exception to her keeping company with a marshal.

She liked Coyote Bluff. She liked being its sheriff. She liked Sam Kyote, too. Especially alive. Surely a federal marshal who chased Sky People for a living would know how to keep his mouth shut about private affairs, especially when it was in his own best interest to do so.

She toyed with the hank of straight blond hair that wouldn't stay back from his forehead, twisting a lock of it around her index finger. His eyes, golden and green in the light of the lamp, smiled into hers.

She gave a gentle tug on the lock of hair, then spun on her heel and out of his arms. "The bedroom's this way, Marshal."

He grabbed the lamp off the table.

"I like for a woman to be able to see what I'm doing," he explained when she lifted her eyebrows in question. The smile in his eyes spread to the corners of his lips. "And I like to know if what I'm doing does what I mean for it to."

That sounded promising. Her stomach bumped upward in anticipation as she led him through the front parlor to the bedroom at the back of the cabin.

Her home was tidy but spare. She'd indulged in a double bed. After years of sleeping in bedrolls, often under the stars, when she'd finally settled down and bought property with the small legacy left by her father, she'd opted for comfort at night. Other than that she had no sense of style, or any idea how to turn a house into a home.

Sam didn't seem to mind. His eyes were on her, not the sparse décor of the room. He set the lamp on the nightstand beside the bed. Then he hooked one finger into the waistband of her trousers and tugged her toward him. He unfastened the top button of her shirt, lifting her shirttail free. Libby worried her bottom lip as he worked at the second button, then the third and fourth. She wasn't self-conscious of her body exactly, but she had a few scars that might require some explaining.

"I can't recall ever stripping men's clothing off a woman before," Sam said. He kissed the side of her throat, making her catch her breath, before upending her onto the bed so that her long legs dangled over the side. The bedframe creaked. "But I'd say it's best to start with the boots." He yanked off one, then the other. With another smooth motion, Libby was trouser-less, and down to her pantalets and unbuttoned shirt.

She felt indecent. Wicked.

And very, very curious.

"So how is it so far?" she asked. He looked blank. "Stripping men's clothing off a woman?" she prompted.

Mischief brightened his lean face. He dropped to the bed beside her. "Better than one might expect." He dragged a fingertip along the line of her jaw, staring into her eyes. "Although I suspect that's got more to do with the woman than her clothing."

He surely was a sweet talker. Libby couldn't help but smile at him in return.

"I should probably start with your boots, too," she said, "but being as how you're this close to me…"

She unfastened his shirt slowly, exposing a broad chest and rippled muscles on a torso that made her tongue go dry. She trailed her fingers across his abdomen, curious how he'd react to her touch. It didn't take long to find out.

He gave a low growl, shrugged the shirt off his shoulders, then tossed it aside. He wore preacher boots, wider in the toe and easier to remove than hers, and he kicked them off without help. They hit the plank floor with two solid thuds.

Her shirt followed his. Libby lay beside him in her corset

and pantalets. The sensation of wickedness grew, even as her curiosity spiked. She reached for his trousers. He lifted his hips to help her ease them off. In seconds he was stretched fully naked on her bed, and unashamed of the fact.

She'd been raised around men so she saw nothing that surprised her, but she'd also been sheltered in many respects. She'd had no idea a man's...weather vane...could be quite so large, not based on the artwork she'd seen in her mother's old books, and admitted to fascination.

Sam was a breathtakingly beautiful male—golden-haired, golden-eyed and golden-skinned. While she thought she could stare at him all night and consider it no hardship, other than that, she hadn't a clue how to proceed.

She decided to wing it. If he had no trouble with nudity, then neither did she. The corset she wore was a simple affair, meant more to support her breasts than to narrow her waist, and she shed it easily despite him watching her movements the whole time. As she let it fall to the floor, he touched her bare shoulder.

"How did you get this?" he asked.

She'd forgotten about the old bullet wound. It wasn't even the worst one she owned, which made her stop and wonder if she wanted to show him the rest.

"Really?" she demanded, resting her hands on her hips and masking awkwardness with bravado. "I'm sitting here three quarters undressed and you notice a bullet hole first?"

Sam grabbed her wrist before she could reach for her shirt to cover herself.

"I don't care how the scar looks," he said, going straight for her real source of concern. "I've got a few of my own and they aren't pretty, either. I'm not counting coups with you,

Libby. I was just curious how you got it."

Libby'd patched up so many bullet holes in her father and his men over the years that she failed to notice them anymore. Sam was right, though. His were no prettier. He had one above his elbow, and a ridge of scar tissue along his hip where another bullet had grazed him. What looked like a stab wound marred the fleshy underside of one forearm. She didn't have any of those to compare. A bicep had a fading bite mark on it, courtesy of Mary Lou Bennett. That one served him right.

He ran his hand up her arm to her shoulder, then eased it over to cup one of her breasts. He flicked a thumb across the nipple, at which point Libby forgot how to breathe.

The gold flecks in his eyes gleamed. "For the record, I noticed a lot more about you than a bullet hole. But I wasn't sure you'd appreciate me praising it."

"While granted I can only speak for myself," Libby replied, "also for the record, I suspect most women would rather hear compliments about their bodies than have to justify imperfections."

Sam touched her scar with a fingertip. "Nice try, but most women don't have these kinds of imperfections. So how did you get yours?"

Libby straddled his hips and placed her palms flat on his bare chest. He reached to untie the front laces of her pantalets. "I was in six gunfights," she reminded him. "Just because I won them doesn't mean no one else got off any shots."

All the humor left his face at her words, as if she'd utterly stunned him.

He quickly recovered. "I can only speak for myself too, but I doubt very much if most men like the idea of their women being shot. Although a few compliments are, indeed, a good idea." His smile returned, but it didn't seem as bright to Libby as before. "You have very beautiful breasts."

He cupped her buttocks to ease her forward so he could kiss each of those breasts. Then he flipped Libby to her back so that he was kneeling above her, and slowly slid the pantalets down to her thighs, his thumbs browsing lazily over her flesh as he did. His eyes paused in their inspection of her at the long, ugly scar on her thigh—the one that left her with an occasional limp. Other than that pause, and a tightening of his lips, he made no mention of it.

Instead, he said, "You have the softest, smoothest skin. And I love long legs on a woman. I've been thinking about yours since we met." He pressed a soft kiss to her lips. She watched his eyes darken from gold-flecked to a deep, forest green. "You're an exceedingly beautiful woman, Libby Mayden. I figure right now, I've got to be the luckiest man alive."

She could feel her cheeks burn with heat. She'd never been told she was beautiful before. Not in that tone of voice, nor with that particular look in a man's eyes that said he meant every word.

She set her hands on his knees, resting at either side of her hips. "I'm not real sure what we do next," she admitted.

He didn't seem bothered by her confession. "It's all about doing what feels good," he assured her. "There's no right or wrong thing. No particular steps. What comes to mind first?"

Libby gave it some thought. At her advanced age she might not get too many more opportunities to be an adventuress, not with a man she found so attractive, and she intended to make the most of this one. "Can I touch you anywhere I want?"

A muscle twitched in his jaw. "I'd be pleased if you did." His voice came out raspy and hoarse. His erection, thick and already hard, bobbed against her flat stomach as if in mutual agreement. "But remember, that means I get to touch you, too."

That seemed fair enough. Cautiously, she caressed the round tip of his manhood. A tiny drop of fluid moistened her fingertips, and when he didn't complain, she stroked along the full length of him.

Sam let out a low growl of pleasure that shot a bullet of heat through her belly. He rested his forehead against hers.

"It won't break," he said. "You can be more assertive." He reached between them to show her what he meant.

His breathing quickened with each of her strokes. A bead of sweat ran along his hairline to his jaw, and he closed his eyes. After a moment, he gently took her hand away and kissed her palm.

His eyes met hers, rueful and filled with heat. "On second thought, maybe it had better be my turn to touch for a while."

The night would end far too soon if Sam didn't take charge of things now.

He intended to make certain this night was memorable for her because it would set the tone for the next ones to come. He sank his fingers into her hair and kissed her mouth, parting her lips with his tongue. Then he ran his tongue along the curve of her neck, enjoying the little pants and gasps as she tried to breathe out. He toyed with her nipples, taking first one in his mouth, then the other.

Libby clutched at his shoulders, arching her back.

Lord, she was lovely. It was fortunate for him she had no idea of the way other men watched her, and that her reputation with her guns was so good, or he might never have gotten this chance with her. Some other lucky bastard would have captured her first.

He slid a hand between their bodies, and stroked one finger along the cleft between her thighs. He dipped the finger inside her, making her gasp again, and started a gentle rhythm—in and out, in and out—careful against her delicate flesh. She was hot and moist, and he had to take shallow breaths to keep from exploding, himself.

Seconds later Libby let out a sharp cry of pleasure, one laced with a faint and enticing surprise. Her nails dug into his shoulders, and he knew she was close. Quickly, trying not to break the rhythm they'd established, he eased his erection into position.

Thrusting into her, deep and hard, he gritted his teeth when she cried out in pain.

Well. That was unexpected.

"I'm sorry," he said, over and over, kissing her cheeks, then her eyelids. "I promise this is the only time it will hurt. Give it a few minutes and you won't mind at all. Or I can stop altogether, if you'd like."

A spark of determination entered her eyes.

"Don't think you can use this as an excuse not to finish what you've started," she warned him. "I've survived gunshots. I can endure one night with you."

"I'm glad to hear it," Sam said dryly. Still hard inside her, his erection ached painfully with prolonged and unspent lust. "But I'm confident I can make this better than something you have to endure."

She glided her hands down his back to his buttocks and lifted her hips so that her pelvis rocked against his. A jolt of heat knifed up his spine. His arms shook with the effort it took to remain unmoving as he gazed down at her face, flushed with a passion that made it almost impossible for him to think.

"I'm hearing a lot of bluff, Marshal," she said. "Maybe it's time to show me your cards."

"Are you calling, Sheriff?" he asked, amused, and she nodded as she took her bottom lip between her teeth.

Sam was past ready to oblige. He thrust again, slowly at first, then faster and harder. Libby's eyes darkened, her lids drooping, as she moved along with him.

He felt her inner muscles as they clenched, gripping him tight, and Libby cried out his name as she came. Her fingers dug into his buttocks, and with one last shudder and jerk Sam erupted too, a groan of intense satisfaction passing his lips. He collapsed, rolling to one side so that Libby had one knee draped across his thighs and he remained deep inside her.

When she'd said she didn't know what to do next, he'd assumed she was talking about in this particular instance and with him in particular. It hadn't occurred to him she meant overall.

God, he was stupid.

He raked the damp hair off her face with his fingers. He had hoped they'd be spending the rest of the night making love, but Libby, a loner who didn't readily welcome the attentions of men, was far less experienced than he'd anticipated.

He hadn't counted on complete innocence. Once was all he could ask of her and still consider himself a gentleman—which was already questionable under the circumstances. He'd taken a lot for granted tonight.

And a true gentleman, he thought, uneasiness niggling at his conscience as he felt her breathing return to normal against the side of his neck, *would have withdrawn rather than releasing inside her*.

Her innocence meant the only honorable thing for him to do was marry her. He tried to decide how he felt about that. He'd never considered marriage, before. He'd been too caught up in his career.

But honor had little to do with this sudden desire to make Libby his. Long-legged and naked and glorious beneath him, all rosebud pinkness and creamy-skinned wonder, she'd make any man happy for long nights on end. She'd be no hardship to come home to at the end of the day.

A marriage to him would suit her, too. She'd never have to worry again about getting called out by gunfighters when she had a federal marshal, former or not, for a husband.

He'd have to marry her fast, though. While more than one child had been born long before the first nine months of marriage had passed, he didn't care to subject Libby to that sort of gossip. She had enough reputation attached to her because of her name.

First, however, he had the Sky People to contend with. Sam remained a member of the Special Division. He had a duty to uphold. It appeared as if Louis had taken no action with those sketches he'd sent. That meant he had some thinking to do, too.

He eased out of Libby, reluctant to do so because he

could feel himself already stiffening again, and she murmured in protest as he did.

Another time, he thought. She'd be tender enough in the morning already, and wouldn't thank him for it. He wanted her grateful and begging for more. He trailed his fingers along the naked line of her back, and she nestled closer against him, her eyes drifting closed. Before long, she fell asleep.

He snuffed out the lamp, the flame dying away as he turned the wick down, plunging the windowless room into darkness. The bedroom door remained open, and moonlight from the front of the cabin streamed across the wood floor. All was silent and peaceful.

Sam yawned, even more relaxed now than he'd thought he would be, and fairly confident Libby was, too, the aftereffects of the gunfight behind them. He drew her close, draping an arm over her shoulder and tucking her head under his chin.

They would talk in the morning.

Birch showed up on Carson's doorstep a few hours before dawn.

Carson jerked the sash of his dressing gown tight over the sprawling girth of his belly. The lantern he'd brought downstairs and set on a side table cast a warm yellow glow across the marble floor of the wide foyer.

He moved out of the doorway so Birch could step inside. He had no family to speak of and no staff around at this hour of the night to be troubled, and yet he was annoyed by the intrusion.

Birch held his broad-brimmed hat in his hand. "Two more of my men are dead."

Carson frowned. "I thought I told you to be careful."

Birch shrugged. "You also told us to watch him and put a little pressure on him. I can't say what went wrong. Their bodies were found this morning when they never checked in. I do know that Kyote's new friend is the local sheriff."

To find out Sam Kyote's new accomplice was the local sheriff came as an unwelcome surprise. Men became sheriffs in remote locations based on how good they were with a gun. They rarely became good by abiding the law. So Carson had plenty of questions as to why Kyote would strike up a friendship with a sheriff who no doubt had a colorful past.

"Do you know anything about this sheriff?"

"Turns out she's a woman named Libby Mayden. Her pa was a famous outlaw down around New Mexico Territory, killed a few years back. We knew him and his men."

Carson pieced it together. The Sky People's ship had crashed deep in the Chihuahuan Desert, an area the Maxwell Mayden gang used to call home. Now Maxwell Mayden's daughter was a sheriff in a remote location far from New Mexico Territory—and had apparently struck up some sort of alliance with one of the Special Division's marshals.

A marshal placed on sick leave by a Special Division scientist who'd once worked in the West.

Carson wasn't a big believer in coincidence. Something was up. Someone else had gotten to Kyote. He intended to find out what and whom.

"Change of plans," he said.

Chapter Seven

Libby awoke to find she was naked, with a man's thumb caressing her breast.

She peeled one eye open. Sunshine puddled on the floor in the open doorway and she bolted upright, the sheet falling to her hips, suddenly panicked. What was the time?

"It's still early," Sam said from beside her, on the bed.

His eyes slid up, from her waist to her eyes, then lowered again, and Libby, remembering her state of undress, grabbed for the sheet to cover herself. Heat started at the tips of her breasts, spreading upward until the roots of her hair felt on fire. All things considered she'd slept better than she'd expected to, deep and dreamless, and she had him to thank for it. Becoming an adventuress had obvious advantages she didn't regret, but she hadn't accounted for the awkwardness of the morning after.

This, she could do without.

She wondered how to get him out of her bed, and her

house, without appearing ungrateful or rude, because she wasn't against repeating last night and didn't want to spoil her chances. Next time, however, she'd sleep alone afterward.

"Thank you," she said, hoping he'd take a hint.

He smiled up at her with those lazy, gold-flecked eyes. "I'm supposed to be thanking you."

"I meant for waking me."

Stretched out in her bed like he owned it, with his hands linked behind his mussed head and his bare chest on display, Sam made no move to go. He looked relaxed and content as he contemplated a thin crack in the whitewashed ceiling, while she felt the exact opposite.

She had a lot to learn about being a fallen woman.

The silence lengthened. Libby realized with a start that he was deep in thought and not paying the least attention to her. Caution caught seed in her chest. She hadn't forgotten their confrontation with the Sky People or that she hadn't told him everything. Nor did she plan on it. Some things were best left alone.

Sam rolled to his side to study her, propping his head on one hand, forcing her to play tug of war with the sheet. A night's growth of blond stubble grazed his chin and jaw. Lord, that was attractive. She tingled all over.

"We can be married wherever and whenever you like. Lady's choice," he said.

He wasn't making any sense, at least none that she could determine. "How did we go from dinner, to courting, to marriage?"

"Call me old-fashioned, but this," he gestured between them, "is several steps beyond courtship."

"Just because we were intimate is no reason for us to

get married." She was embarrassed—and a little annoyed—that she had to explain it to him. "The circumstances were… extenuating. Last night was about letting off steam."

His lean face froze, the humor it had displayed only seconds before wiped away as if he couldn't quite believe what he heard. He sounded calm enough when he spoke, however. Dangerously so.

"I'm not sure which one of us should be more insulted right now."

Libby tried again. She crumpled the sheet in white-knuckled fists. "This is only the fourth time we've spoken. We don't know anything about each other. I've been an outlaw. You're a federal marshal."

"People marry after a lot less acquaintance than we've just had. I know enough about you to be satisfied I can live with you. And I think you'll find I'm fairly easygoing."

Libby didn't want marriage. Not to Sam or any other man. So far, as an entire institution, she wasn't impressed by what she'd seen. Her parents had married as strangers and it had proved to be a disaster. She assumed William Bennett hadn't known Mary Lou very well either when he'd proposed, because that had to be a decision he now regretted.

Aside from all that, Libby had a graver concern. Sam didn't know nearly as much about her as he might like to think.

"I like my life the way it is," she said.

"Would you like it quite as much if you were an unmarried mother?"

She grasped the sheet tighter, trying to follow the shifting threads in the conversation and getting woefully tangled. "What are you talking about?"

Sam rubbed above the bridge of his nose with his thumb as if massaging a headache. "Where do you think babies come from?"

She felt foolish and ignorant, and out of her depth. And to be honest, a little afraid. She knew where they came from. But the thought of a baby hadn't occurred to her. Annoyance took over. If he knew so much, why was he bringing this up now instead of last night?

"How in tarnation does a woman become an adventuress without having babies?" she demanded. "Is there some sort of handbook I should be reading?"

Sam shot upright beside her, looking a little the way William Bennett had after Mary Lou hit him on the back of the head with the cast iron frying pan. "An *adventuress*? You think that's a more attractive option than marriage to me?"

He swung both feet out of bed, and ignoring the fact he was naked, scrabbled through the discarded clothing on the floor for his trousers. He yanked them over his hips, his movements jerky with anger. He turned to where she now knelt on the bed, the sheet clutched to her chest, watching him with wide-eyed fascination. She'd never seen a grown man throw a girlish fit before.

He shook his finger at her. "You are not an adventuress now, and you won't be one in the future. If you even suspect you might be pregnant, we're getting married straight away. If not, you can have more time to get used to the idea. But make no mistake. My intentions are honorable toward you and I expect the same courtesy extended to me."

He finished dressing, then took her chin in his hand. He kissed her with a fierceness that left her dizzy and aching with a rekindled want that shot all the way to her toes. His eyes glittered like gold, as if he could read her reaction and it satisfied him.

He let her go, and reached for his hat on the floor near the foot of the bed.

He paused at the door, one hand on the frame. "Mark my words. Sooner or later, Libby Mayden, you're going to have to make an honest man out of me."

Angry, but unsure with whom, Sam saddled his horse and headed for home. He had one stop to make along the way.

The morning was bright, the sky was blue, and all things considered, his mood should have been better. He'd spent the night with a beautiful woman who wasn't deep into making commitments. He'd never really been keen on the idea of marriage. It tied a man down. He'd made the offer for her benefit, not his.

There were other options available to them than marriage. In many areas of the West pastors were rare. As long as a man and woman who set up housekeeping together without the benefit of the clergy behaved married their neighbors tended to look the other way.

Their children, however, were still labeled bastards. No respectable woman, not even an independent one like Libby, would want that. Sam sure as hell didn't, and he could guarantee his mother, a proper Southern lady, wouldn't care for it, either. Besides, Coyote Bluff had a pastor. And Libby was its sheriff. The townspeople would no doubt frown on any casual housekeeping arrangements she made.

Western women were an entirely different breed from the ones he was used to, and calm, beautiful, independent Libby, more so than most. She was the sort of woman who did what needed to be done. She'd make the perfect wife for a marshal. So there was a benefit to him, after all. Several, in fact.

Her unwillingness to commit also meant some other man could as easily step in and win her over, however. He wasn't about to let that happen. Maybe he should give more thought to courting her properly. Trouble was, aside from the gunfight, last night had been pretty much his best effort.

Still no closer to a solution, he reached the scene of the ambush. Instead of following along the crumbling top of the shallow arroyo, Sam rode his horse into its dry bed. Bright pink, desert sand verbena littered his path. Between the chunks of gray rock poking from the sand, Indian paintbrush bloomed. The desert was a pretty place, he'd been discovering.

That was all he discovered this morning. The bodies were gone.

He scanned the ground, then the ridge. His eye caught on a flash of bright metal. Directly above where the bodies should have been, on a rock overlooking the desert, a long cylinder, about fifteen inches in diameter and at least six feet in length, had been mounted. It rested on a tripod, and from where he stood, appeared to be made of brass.

Sam climbed up the short embankment for a closer look at the contraption. It swiveled on the tripod. He peered in one end. It was a high-powered telescope, the likes of which he'd never before seen. And it was trained on his homestead. Sky People had been spying on him.

The sun crawled higher in the sky, scorching the back of his shirt. He scratched his head where the band of his hat itched his forehead as he contemplated his next move. He couldn't leave it out here where anyone might stumble across it. After a bit of grunting and swearing, he got it tied to the back of his horse so he could drag it home.

He wasn't far from his ranch when he saw he had company. He unfastened the flap on his holster so he'd have easier access to his gun if need be.

It turned out he had nothing to fear. The young boy sitting on his stoop came from the Coyote Bluff telegraph office.

"Mornin' Marshal. You're out bright and early," the boy said, his eyes alive with curiosity as he stared at the dusty contraption Sam hauled behind his horse.

"Doing a little surveying," Sam replied, dismounting. He left it at that.

The boy passed him a folded piece of paper. He waited until the boy mounted his mule and was on his way back to town before he opened the telegram.

TO MARSHAL SAM KYOTE OF COYOTE BLUFF STOP RETURN TO WASHINGTON IMMEDIATELY STOP LEAVE TERMINATED STOP CARSON WHITLEY

Well, wasn't that curious.

He folded the paper and tucked it into a pocket. He wondered if Louis was behind this. Or if Whitley had finally found out about this so-called special assignment. Louis's warning about the director hadn't been forgotten, and right now, Sam trusted no one. The presence of Sky People said something was, indeed, going on.

Either way, this telegram contained a direct order. But it would take him eight days to get to Washington and another eight to return. He had no desire to leave Libby—what with her being the only law in the area—to fend off Sky People alone. Not for that length of time. He didn't care how good she was with a gun.

He considered refusing the order. He could simply send a reply, tendering his resignation. But that wasn't going to be enough. He'd have to disappear and he wasn't ready to do that. He had parents to think of. Libby would never go with him, either. Not yet.

He also wanted to know the reason behind the telegram. Why had his leave been terminated? What was happening in Washington that he didn't know about?

Honesty compelled him to admit that Sheriff Libby Mayden could handle herself. She could plug a tossed nickel at fifty paces. She knew how to kill them. Besides, they hadn't been gunning for her. Both times, they'd come after him.

So that left him his answer. He'd go to Washington. He'd talk to Louis and insist on answers as to what this special assignment really was. He'd find out why Carson Whitley wanted him. And he'd return to Coyote Bluff as fast as he could. Then—only then—if he had to, he'd disappear.

Because no matter what happened, he wasn't disappearing without Libby.

Libby sat at her desk in the empty jailhouse, staring off into space, and tried to figure out how she'd ended up on the wrong end of a shotgun marriage.

She could come to only one conclusion. Sam would have to rethink his position. For her part, she wasn't going to think on it at all. Even if she were interested in marriage, which she wasn't, Maxwell Mayden's gunfighter daughter, retired or not, was no proper match for a marshal. She knew where her loyalties lay. It was a pity, though. The mere thought of Sam's smile—those unusual eyes—lit a fire that curled through her insides.

Pete Gaster strode into the jail. He hitched his trousers and hooked his thumbs in his suspenders, sizing her up with one squinty eye.

"Your neighbor just grabbed the stagecoach, and he was traveling with a big ole' trunk. Why d'ya think he'd be skipping town in such a hurry?"

She had to drop an elbow to her desktop to steady herself. If he regretted that marriage proposal, all he had to do was say so. For him to flee without saying goodbye was downright insulting.

She left Pete in charge of the jail as she walked to the post office to collect any mail that came in on the stagecoach, more deflated by the news that Sam had left town than she had a right to be.

The day was a hot one, even by local standards. She walked the length of the dusty boardwalk and entered the combined post and telegraph office, a single room attached to the stagecoach station next door to Coyote Bluff's single hotel.

At the most, the post office interior was one degree cooler than the street outside.

"G'day, Sheriff Mayden," the postmaster greeted her. A thin sheen of sweat covered his shiny, bald scalp, and his white linen shirt was no longer crisp. His grin widened, showing a gold-capped incisor. "The marshal got an urgent early morning telegram requesting he head back to Washington at his earliest convenience. The boy I sent out to deliver it said he met the marshal riding home from the direction of your ranch."

The explanation for his speedy departure came as far too great a relief. She shot the postmaster her haughtiest look, complete with an uplifted brow. "There's a lot of land between my spread and the marshal's, Mister Townzen. You're an intelligent man. Don't waste your energy on foolish speculation."

She thanked him for the mail and left, the weather no longer entirely to blame for the heat she now suffered. As she neared the jail, she heard someone call out her name.

A heavily pregnant woman was weaving between the dried out piles of horse droppings in the street and hurrying toward her. A baby slept in her arms while two small children toddled behind, dragging on her peplum skirts.

Greta Rosenberg. She was a plain-faced woman, weathered and wrinkled by a life spent crossing the prairies with first her parents, then her husband. Although a few years younger than Libby she looked a good ten years older.

Libby liked her a lot.

"Greta," Libby scolded her. She lifted the sleeping baby from the tired woman's arms and tried not to think about Sam's comments on pregnancy. Right now, her friend made it look downright frightening. "It's too hot for you and the children to be out in this sun. Where is Ira?"

"He's getting the wagon wheel fixed. We'll be on our way as soon as it's done. It won't be so hot once we're moving."

Greta's blue eyes were anxious beneath her wide-brimmed bonnet. She kept an eye on the two small children hiding in the folds of her skirt. "I heard gunshots coming from the arroyo last night."

Libby gently rocked the sleeping baby in her arms. She knew why Greta was worried. A few of the men in Coyote Bluff—Ira Rosenberg included—had a bounty on their heads, and even though Judge Roy did what he could to protect them, there was always someone who wanted to make a name for himself. Men like Ira, who'd once ridden with the Mayden gang, would begin shooting strangers on sight if they were worried enough. She couldn't let that happen. There had to be some semblance of law. If not, the whole town would fall apart and all Judge Roy's hard work undone.

Neither could she come right out and say that Greta had nothing to worry about. While Sam figured those men had been after him, and it certainly looked to be true, they didn't know that for a fact.

She'd have to do something about the bodies in that arroyo before someone went poking around. She'd forgotten about them.

"I'll look into it as quick as I can," she promised Greta. "It's probably nothing. In the meantime, you and Ira stay away from that area and let the law handle it."

Sam would have gone to say his goodbyes to Libby in person if he wasn't still so annoyed with her. Instead, he'd crawled through her window, the one with the broken latch, and left a note on her pillow.

He made his way down the dusty street to the stagecoach station without even a passing glance at the jail.

The stagecoach arrived right on schedule. With the help of the driver, and a lot of grunting and groaning, the heavy trunk was soon lashed in place to the roof. He climbed up beside the driver to ride shotgun. The day was too hot to sit closed in with the other three male passengers. He cradled the butt of the Winchester repeating rifle the driver handed to him, resting its long barrel across his knees, and rocked in the swaying seat as the stagecoach drove out of Coyote Bluff. He'd be catching the train in River's Bend to start the eight-day journey to Washington.

As he watched the miles of desert roll by he allowed himself a few warm fantasies regarding Libby and the night he'd return. He became so lost in them that he wasn't paying as much attention to the potential dangers of riding the stagecoach through isolated stretches of desert as a federal marshal should.

The first bullet, accompanied by the sharp crack of a rifle, whined past his left ear, too close for comfort. Sam brought the Winchester up, and without thinking twice, fired off a few shots as the driver wrestled the horses under control and whipped them into a run.

The stagecoach careened back and forth, threatening to topple. Sam braced his feet in the boot and grabbed onto the sway handle. He held the rifle in his free hand, watching for signs of pursuit. A well-executed robbery involved killing the driver and spooking the horses. If the coach overturned, so much the better. The bandits then had less worry that the passengers might be armed, which no doubt they would be, and able to fight back.

"What's your cargo?" Sam demanded of the driver, whose complete attention remained focused on keeping the frantic horses under control. The value of the cargo determined how hard they'd have to fight for their lives.

"The joke's on them fellers," the driver replied, his voice grim. "Other than the mail, we don't pick up no cargo until we reach Buckwheat."

After a few minutes, with no indication anyone was in pursuit, the driver slowed the horses to a steadier trot.

Sam leaned over the side of the box to call into the coach. "Everyone all right in there?"

A trio of shaky yeses came back in response.

That, Sam thought, settling back in his seat, was one of the most poorly planned and executed robbery attempts he'd ever bore witness to. It was almost as if the bandits were scared to get too close. As if they didn't want to be identified.

The stagecoach might not have any cargo, but it had four passengers. One of them was a federal marshal who'd been ambushed by Sky People. At least twice.

And it led Sam to wonder how many people might have known he'd be leaving town in a hurry today.

When Libby went to look in the gorge that afternoon, as she'd promised Greta Rosenberg she would, the bodies were gone. Either Sam had gotten to them first, or they'd had companions who'd returned.

The gorge meandered for several miles, cutting a long, deep scar through the desert that filled quickly with water during the heavy spring rains. Right now it was bone dry.

She could see traces in the dirt from where the men had camped, and tumbled earth along the gorge walls from where they'd climbed to the top. What they'd been doing here, she couldn't say.

But she didn't like it.

Her next stop was the Rosenbergs' homestead, where she was able to report to Greta with a clear conscience that she'd found nothing of interest.

Greta hadn't been reassured.

"Let me know if you see anything more," was all Libby could think of to say in response to her friend's concerns.

She left the Rosenbergs' and headed for home, skirting the mouth of the gorge, more troubled than ever. If there was one lesson she'd learned in her life, it was to never dwell on the past. Hers, however, had caught up with her present, and her thoughts wouldn't seem to let it go.

At home, she went about her chores and her usual routine. She hung out the last bit of laundry. Then, still in her work shirt and cotton trousers, she stood in the open door and watched the black sky come to life. She'd spent more time in wide open spaces than she had in a house, and she slept best out under the stars. Without Sam here to distract her, the thought of crawling under the blankets alone was too much.

He'd left her a note, confirming he hadn't rushed off to be rid of her, which came as more of a relief than she'd anticipated, although she didn't doubt his leaving without saying a proper goodbye was his way of making a point. He was a man who liked to get his own way.

But Libby was happy enough with things as they currently stood. She'd watched her father's men go all foolish over women they'd only just met any number of times. They fell out of infatuation equally fast. Sam would eventually see reason.

She got out her bedroll, saddled her horse, and headed into the night. Even though she'd told Greta there was nothing for her to worry about, when those chubby, little Rosenberg faces crowded into Libby's thoughts, she decided she'd spend her night watching over their property.

She chose a spot on a hill where she could best see their house. It was a long, low, single-story stone cabin, too small for the growing young family, because Ira Rosenberg continued to debate whether or not they'd be staying in Coyote Bluff. A lot depended on how much silver remained in his mining claim and the price of cattle that fall.

The site had the added advantage of a view of the gorge. She'd be able to see if anything came or went in the night. She unrolled her bedding between the fragrant brittlebush and sweet-scented lupine, snuggled in, boots and all, and gazed up at the sparkling umbrella of stars.

A chill wind had sprung up and Libby wrapped herself tighter inside her blankets. The strong tea smell of the brittlebush tickled her nose. The soft glow of lamplight from the Rosenbergs' cabin window winked out, and all around her, the day dwellers settled in for the night. Her horse grazed nearby, untroubled.

Tired as she was from the previous night, and feeling safe and secure, sleep nevertheless continued to dodge her. A tiny worm of fear had burrowed its way into her head and it wouldn't let go. For months after she'd killed the Blue man, as she'd called him, she'd awoken from nightmares, dripping in sweat. She rarely had them anymore, at least, not so severe. Time had faded them. But every once in a long while Libby still clawed awake from a troubled sleep, gasping in panic, her night clothes soaked through.

Eventually, after much tossing and turning, she dozed off.

At first, little pieces of the past surfaced, to drift into her semi-consciousness. An image of her father's face. A few whispers of sound. A man's fingers on a horse's reins, shifting from normal to long, flat-tipped, somewhat hooked, and colored in a pale blue hue. Through the range of emotions the memories evoked—from caution, to suspicion, to fear— Libby had one overriding goal.

She had to get away from the Blue man.

With that crystal-clear thought, the images settled into focus. She was riding through the worst of the desert heat, already feeling dry, anxious to conserve energy and body moisture. The Blue man's eyes bored through her back and she didn't dare turn around to see why. She kept one hand close to her hip and her gun, the reins loosely clasped and carefully arranged so that she could drop them in an instant if need be. Her free hand, she rested on her thigh. She debated whether or not she should kill him, but a part of her hesitated. Life was cheap in the West. She didn't need to cheapen it further.

The next moment, the desert and the Blue man were gone, and Libby was sitting beside a campfire late at night with a tin mug of coffee warming her hands. Her father sat next to her, his face shadowed because of the flickering flames, the darkness, and the wide brim of the hat he'd tipped low. He always did that when he was thinking things over. He didn't like people reading his expression. In public, he cultivated the impression he was a hard drinker and a loose talker. It made people think he was careless, when nothing could be further from the truth. Max, as she used to call him, did little without careful consideration.

They'd just come from a meeting in a nearby town with a potential client, one who wanted an escort into the desert during the worst heat of the summer.

"We're not taking this job," Max said to her. A log popped in the fire, sending sparks spraying like miniature fireworks. "He's after something that will bring no good to the world."

"We need the money," Libby replied. While it might not be honest work, it was no more than a step or so removed. "I could do it."

"You aren't going into the desert with him." She heard the steel in her father's voice, but only because she knew him so well. "None of us are. I'll get us money another way. Pay attention when you look at a man, Libby Mayden. This one had nothing in his eyes."

The scene shifted again, and even though she was all alone in the world now except for a few of the men who'd survived the Pinkerton ambush, her father was with her. They stood on a ridge above the Rio Grande, deep in the heart of the desert. She could see his face plainly, but he looked older now than he did back then. His sun-bleached brown hair had grayed a touch at the temple. His eyes, the same blue as hers, were ice-cold with disapproval. "I told you not to go into the desert alone with that man. He has no soul."

"I needed the money." She loved her father, but he could be thoughtless sometimes.

"Then go on. You've made it this far." He waved her on

with a sweep of his arm. "Protect yourself. Get what he came for and hide it. And remember, never give up a hostage."

Next, Libby was standing inside the mangled remains of the ship, her leg on fire and bleeding from where she'd been shot. She fought to breathe past the pain. She saw a silver box. She pried it from the wreckage. Then she bolted, running as best she could with her hands full and blood gushing from the wound on her thigh. The Blue man rose from the dead and gave chase behind her. She tripped and he caught her, wrapping those long, hooked, unnatural fingers around her throat, squeezing so tight she couldn't draw air into her lungs.

She awoke as she always did, her heart pounding and her shirt drenched in sweat, with her gun in her hand. Only this time, she knew exactly what had frightened her about the Blue man. She'd had no way of reading his behavior, or anticipating his reactions, as she would any other gunfighter, because his eyes were empty.

Just as her father had warned her to watch out for.

Chapter Eight

It was an unpleasant and unwelcome surprise for Carson to find Judge Roy Rowe sitting in his chair, dusty boots on his desk, smoking a whiskey-dipped cigar taken from a silk-lined box in a secret drawer.

In his White House office, no less.

In a bunker very few people knew even existed.

Carson had no idea how he'd gotten in and he didn't ask. Some things it was best not to question. Judge Rowe, too, was well connected. He and the president were personal friends.

Carson shut the door carefully, with a loud and deliberate click of the lock. It was tantamount to locking himself in a cage with a hungry mountain lion. Since he refused to sit anywhere but his own chair, which was currently occupied, he chose to stand. He waited for Judge Rowe to speak, hoping his nervousness didn't show.

Rowe had the most expressionless eyes Carson had ever

seen on a man. He could fake empathy when he chose, but in reality, a rattlesnake had warmer blood. And the way Rowe was studying him now made him extra cautious.

Rowe removed the cigar from his mouth and examined its smoldering tip. "Why did you send a Special Division marshal to Coyote Bluff?"

"I didn't. Sam Kyote showed up there all on his own." He'd be curious to discover how much Rowe knew about that, too. "He's on an extended sick leave."

"Then you'd know nothing of anyone trying to stir up trouble with regards to the local sheriff's past," the judge said.

Here was yet another connection to Coyote Bluff he hadn't fully considered. Judge Rowe roamed the Territories, dispensing justice, and would have some knowledge of the things that went on. Carson put his hands in the air in a gesture of denial. "I don't know what you're talking about. I have no quarrel with her."

"But you know she's a woman, so you must know who she is." Rowe took a deep puff of the cigar, exhaling its sweet-smelling smoke through his nose. "Her daddy's been dead a few years, and that sometimes makes folks forget he had a long arm. I hear she still has his people looking out for her. They aren't the kind of men anyone should be messing with, either."

"Are you *threatening* me, Rowe?"

"Heavens, no. Merely passing on gossip. In my line of work I hear all kinds of stories. In fact," Rowe's eyelids lowered to narrow slits, "I've heard some tall tales about Sky People during my travels. I thought I might share them with you."

Carson forced his lungs to draw air. "I'm all ears."

"Seems their ship crashed in the Chihuahuan Desert, not far from the Mayden gang's territory. Turns out, that was a prison ship they were on. They're nothing more than cutthroats and thieves, banished from their own world. Before they're loaded on ships on their own world, they're divided up according to their labor skills, handed the technology they need to survive, and then grouped into colonies. Once on board ship, it's survival of the fittest. Or the smartest."

"That's a pretty tall tale. People from other worlds. You might want to be questioning the source. They're most likely heavy drinkers," Carson said.

"My sources are reliable."

"If you say so."

"I do. And one in particular claims that one of the survivors was their pilot. Imagine how tough someone like that has to be, alone on a ship with the worst of his kind. He was supposed to take that ship and go home. The crash trapped him here, too, but he didn't trust the others any more than they trusted him. He swore to them that when their ship went down, a lot of the equipment they needed to build their new colony was either lost in the desert or damaged beyond repair. There's a particular piece of equipment, however, that he claims actually survived the crash. It's small but heavy, stored in pieces in a silver box. And it's mighty powerful."

"Really." Carson feigned boredom. "What does it do?"

Rowe took another draw on the cigar and exhaled. A thin cloud of bluish-gray smoke briefly obscured his face. "Now that I couldn't tell you for sure."

"Forgive me my impatience, but I'm not getting the point you're trying to make." Carson glanced at his watch.

"And while I hate to rush you, I have meetings today."

The cloud of cigar smoke cleared. "That little piece of equipment is valuable to the Sky People, particularly those with mechanical skills who can put it together. So valuable, in fact, they'd do just about anything to get it back. They'd do what looked like favors to the right people. And the whole time, they'd really be doing something for themselves. Something that might not be in anyone's best interests but theirs. Something the Special Division might want to be wary of. Something that, if I were the one doing favors for them, I'd surely be asking myself right now why I know nothing about it."

Unease crawled up Carson's spine. For one long, drawn-out second, panic threatened to follow. Judge Rowe knew he had Sky People working for him. Ones who were good with mechanics.

Then, he came to his senses. The panic subsided and his world realigned. This wasn't information the public would know. If everything Rowe said was true, he hadn't heard these stories in the saloons he liked to frequent. It meant he had Sky People connections, too. That put them on an equal footing.

"Your point is taken," he said.

"I don't think it is. Consider the facts, Whitley. If the Sky People had this equipment already, they'd have used it by now and the Division would know. The whole world likely would, too. And if the Sky People haven't been able to find it, it stands to reason that somebody's found it before they did. Who else besides Sky People know where that ship crash landed? My guess would be some of the old Mayden gang," Rowe answered himself. "They knew everything that happened in the Chihuahuan Desert. You might want to take advantage of having a marshal in Coyote Bluff, particularly one with Marshal Kyote's special abilities, right where Mayden's daughter happens to be."

"I have no idea what you're talking about," Carson said. "Marshal Kyote is a very ordinary man. Exceedingly so."

"Don't play coy, Mr. Whitley. We both know Kyote's been exhibiting an amazing amount of skill in the art of illusion. According to rumor, he practices it faithfully."

Birch had been watching Kyote. This would mean he had kept information from him.

If Judge Rowe spoke the truth.

Carson refused to confirm or deny what he knew, himself. He didn't wish for Rowe to know he wasn't as well informed. And about his own staff, no less.

"Your rumor mill is quite extraordinary. Why are you telling me all of this?"

"Just passing on gossip I thought you should know." Rowe tamped out the stub of cigar in the tray on the desk and swung his feet to the floor. He stood. "If Libby Mayden is in Coyote Bluff, Mayden's men won't be too far away. They'll be looking out for her. Have your marshal see if he can find out from her where that missing piece of equipment might be. Although if your marshal does go after Libby Mayden looking for information on that dandy little silver box, you might want to remember that long arm of her daddy's. If anything happens to her because of it, you're likely the one who'll be wearing the blame."

He brushed past Carson on the way out. The door clicked shut behind him.

Once alone, Carson reclaimed his chair so he could sit

and ponder the situation. There was a harsh and undeniable ring of truth to most of what Judge Rowe had said. The Sky People Carson employed were good with mechanics, although that might merely be a suspicion on Rowe's part, considering the success Carson had experienced with his mining operations and the subsequent patents.

And Rowe had his eye on the presidency, too. No doubt about that.

It was the warnings about Libby Mayden, however, and this mysterious box, that intrigued Carson most. He was willing to bet Rowe was using her to draw Mayden's gang out of hiding so he could get at that box, and he was trying to get Carson to help him. Since Sam Kyote had already established some sort of relationship with her, and having a US federal marshal around her would surely draw the Mayden gang's attention too, Rowe's plan had merit.

But Carson had called Kyote back to Washington. And now Rowe wanted him sent back to Coyote Bluff. Where Birch's men—Sky People, to whom Rowe could also have a connection—were watching him.

Carson tried to decide the best way to proceed. The last thing he wanted was to be of assistance to Judge Rowe.

The second last thing was to be played for a fool.

Sam waited in the reception area outside of the director's office.

Eight days of travel by stagecoach and train…After this meeting with Whitley, he was on his way back to Libby. He'd be eighteen days in total without her. He should have said goodbye.

He hoped she was missing him. She wasn't going to get a chance to forget him. He'd sent telegrams like clockwork at every stop to make certain of that.

He'd taken the lone chair by the door. The outer room was compact and tidy, and windowless because these offices, too, were deep underground. A round, latch-hooked carpet occupied the center of the floor. Someone had painted the walls a pale rose, as if a woman had been meant to sit behind the plain desk. Instead a small, pinch-faced man, obviously bored and without interest in Sam or the world in general, occupied the secretarial space.

After forty-five minutes, Sam's patience had just about worn itself out. He was ready to leave when the inner door opened and Whitley poked his head out.

Carson Whitley was a portly man, not tall and not short, with carefully combed, thinning, colorless hair. He had icy, pale blue eyes that fixed on a man without blinking, giving him a predatory quality. He could pass for a cold-blooded killer, which no doubt explained his success in both politics and silver mining in the Territories. Sam had yet to figure out his real age. A best guess placed him anywhere between forty and sixty.

"This way, Marshal Kyote," he said.

Inside, Whitley's office was larger than the first one, with furnishings of a significantly higher quality. Shelves of leather-bound books lined one wall from floor to ceiling. A wide desk filled the one across from the door. The third held a sideboard well-stocked with liquor, leaving room for two comfortable, overstuffed visitor chairs in front of the desk. The Persian carpet in this room was square, and extended to all four walls.

"Have a seat."

Sam took the one indicated, across from Whitley, who settled into a wide arm chair situated beneath two framed paintings. One was an early rendition of the White House. The second was of an operational silver mine set somewhere in the desert. Sam assumed it to be Whitley's.

"How's your health, Marshal? Improving?"

"Terrible headaches, sir," Sam replied. "They hit without warning."

"No other problems?"

"None at all." At least, nothing to speak of. He tried to think if he'd let anything slip. He hadn't attempted an illusion since he'd boarded the train back in River's Bend.

"I want you assessed by a proper physician. AuCoin is a good scientist, but he's not qualified to give more than a basic physical. These headaches could be something more serious. We wouldn't want you misdiagnosed." The smile on the older man's lips didn't reach his icy, unblinking eyes. "I'd feel responsible if anything unfortunate happened to you."

"Thank you," Sam said.

Whitley's gaze slithered over him, assessing him in a way he didn't like. "Since you're here, I also have some confidential information on the town where you're recuperating. It wasn't anything I wished to put in writing." When he didn't say anything, Whitley continued. "Tell me a little about Coyote Bluff."

Sam shrugged. "It's peaceable enough. The people are friendly and the land is cheap."

Whitley relaxed in his chair as if settling in for a long and casual conversation. "I hear the law in town keeps good order."

A chill settled in. "It appears to be adequate, from what I've seen."

"And I hear that the law is a retired gunfighter by the name of Libby Mayden, who also happens to be the daughter of an infamous outlaw."

"Her name's Libby Mayden," Sam said, "so at least that much is true. I can't speak to the rest of it."

Whitley disregarded the sarcasm. "It's well known that Maxwell Mayden talked as much as he drank, and that he was a heavy drinker. He was also known to consort with people of questionable character."

"If we're talking about the same Maxwell Mayden, then he had a wide circle of wanted men who rode for him. He was shot to death during a failed robbery attempt. It's safe to assume most everyone he consorted with was of questionable character."

"Since I have to spell it out for you, Marshal Kyote," Whitley said, his tone mild but his gaze frigid, "what I'm suggesting to you is that Mayden gave work to Sky People. In return, they gave him information on a box their ship was carrying. That box is of significant interest to the Special Division. Unfortunately, it's been lost. I want it found."

Sam wondered if that box had anything to do with the secrets Libby was keeping from him. "You're remarkably well informed."

Whitley laced his fingers together and rested his hands on his desk. For the first time since Sam entered the room, his eyes showed a flicker of life. "I have eyes everywhere. And don't ever forget it."

That message was certainly clear. Disappearing wasn't

going to be as easy as he'd hoped it might be, not even in the West, if it ever came to that.

"I'm not certain what any of this has to do with Coyote Bluff," he said. "Mayden is dead. When he was alive, he worked out of New Mexico Territory."

Whitley was watching him so closely it made his skin prickle. "Sheriff Mayden has a colorful past of her own. She's killed five men, and those are only the ones we know of for certain. By all accounts, she and her father were close. I find it hard to believe she knows nothing of Sky People, or her father's dealings with them."

"You want me to watch her and report any unusual activity." Sam had no idea what to make of that other than that it couldn't be good.

"I want you to remember that the sheriff in Coyote Bluff has undoubtedly been in contact with Sky People. That her father, a notorious outlaw, worked with them. And I want you to remember, Marshal Kyote, that you are Special Division property, and therefore valuable to us. We wouldn't want anything to happen to you."

His pent-up anger toward the Special Division returned with a slow, simmering burn. He didn't serve Whitley, Louis, or any other man. He served his country.

"I beg your pardon? Are you likening me to a piece of property? Because last I'd heard, slavery was abolished."

Whitley's unblinking stare unnerved Sam even more. "You belong to the Special Division," he repeated. "You swore an oath. A great deal of time and money has been invested in your training. If the physician approves it, you can spend another month in Coyote Bluff. But you're to use caution around the sheriff. You're to report any unusual activity directly to me. If you feel she's in any way connected to Sky People, you're to notify this office. A marshal will then be dispatched to reinforce you. Do you understand me?"

"Completely. Am I free to go?" Sam asked, already rising.

"You are." Whitley's smile was more genuine now, less that of a predator licking its paws after a full meal. "Oh, and Marshal Kyote?"

Sam paused at the door. He half turned, not daring to meet those icy eyes for fear of letting Whitley see what he was thinking. It wasn't flattering to the director. Not at all.

"Yes?"

"I wanted to remind you again of how well connected I am. Try not to forget it."

Sam let himself out. He walked across the reception area with a cursory nod for the secretary, still seated behind the desk, still obviously bored.

He planned to catch the next train back to Nevada Territory. Whitley had made threats. He'd tried too hard to plant seeds of doubt in his head about Libby and he wanted to know why.

No harm would come to her. In this instance, his country came second.

Chapter Nine

Sam had been gone for eighteen days—not that Libby was counting.

The thirteen telegrams he'd sent her, however…

The entire town had counted those. They'd inspired a visit from Pastor Endicott, too, who'd given her a longwinded although well-meant lecture on Jezebels. He'd suggested she should present herself as a role model for young women. Then he'd warned her to think of her father.

That last warning wasn't without merit. It hadn't been intended for her. Sam had no idea the dangers he faced by keeping company with Max Mayden's daughter.

She finished eating her dinner and carried her empty bowl to the kitchen. She worked the hand pump beside the sink, rinsing her bowl and one cooking pot under cold water rather than rekindling the fire in the pot-bellied stove to heat more. Water remained scarce here in the desert, but she'd long ago learned to be resourceful. Her farm's water supply came from an underground spring, pumped to the buildings by a windmill. The spring often went dry in the worst heat of the summer, so a large water reservoir also stood near the outbuildings to catch and contain any rainfall from the cooler months.

After she finished her dishes, she stripped, took a sponge bath with cold water, then dressed in her nightgown. As usual she dropped the bar across her front door, but left the bedroom door ajar so she could listen for unusual sounds. The nightmares had stopped but the panic they induced remained hard to forget.

The new moon had just passed, so when a noise did awaken her, the darkness was thick and complete. Her heart pounded hard in her chest, and at first, befuddled by sleep, she wasn't sure why.

Then she heard it again—what sounded like a boot scraping across the floor in her kitchen—and she remembered that the window sometimes didn't latch.

Carefully, she eased her hand under her pillow for the pistol she kept there. The rifle remained propped by the head of the bed, but for close range, she felt more comfortable with the more familiar walnut grip in her hand. She didn't want to blast a hole in any of her walls.

The bedframe groaned as she inched to the edge of the bed, and Libby froze. So did whoever was in her kitchen. She kept her eyes fixed on the open bedroom door. Even though the night was dark, enough light filtered in from outside for her to be able to detect moving shadows. Raising the barrel of her pistol, her finger tightened on the trigger. As soon as anyone—or anything—darkened her door, she'd shoot. She waited, holding her breath, but nothing moved.

A coyote howled somewhere in the night.

The next thing she knew, the pistol was yanked from her grasp. A heavy weight bowled her backward onto the bed, pinning her against the sagging mattress.

She'd heard and seen nothing.

She didn't waste time or effort on screaming. Instead, she jabbed her thumb as hard as she could at where she thought an eye would be on her assailant. She hit what felt like a cheekbone, and changed her plan of attack. She dug her fingers into flesh, using her thumb to gain a tighter grip on his cheek.

Her assailant swore and she felt him jerk back, and Libby seized her chance. She still couldn't see anything. With no visible target, only a sense of touch to help her, she drove her freed knee upward as hard as she could, hoping to hit a vulnerable spot. Her nightgown and the tangled bedding hampered her so that she couldn't put any real strength behind it, but she thought she connected with the inside of a man's thigh.

"Dammit Libby, cut it out. It's me."

Then Sam was on top of her, safing the pistol she'd cocked before he dropped it onto the bedside table. She'd already recognized his voice, and could make out his shadowy form now as he half-straddled her hips. How dare he slip into her home and try to scare her this way? How dare he send her thirteen telegrams and set the entire town to talking? How dare he, after eighteen days and no further discussion, stroll into her bedroom as if he belonged in it?

Worst of all, how dare he make her miss him so much he was all she could think of?

She shoved the heel of her palm at his nose.

Sam saw the blow coming and managed to deflect the worst of it, so that instead of breaking his nose, she hit his cheekbone. It still hurt like hell, and his eyes watered, but he'd received worse. And he didn't really blame her.

If he'd had any lingering doubts she could take care of herself, they'd just been dispelled. He counted himself lucky that he'd been able to make himself invisible or she'd have shot him long before he ever got as far as her bedroom. All he'd really intended to do tonight was check in on her, to make sure she was safe, but the unlatched window had proved too much of a temptation. He'd missed her unbearably. She hadn't answered even one of his telegrams, and he'd started to think the worst.

He grabbed both her hands and hauled them above her head, trapping her against the mattress and pillows. He could see her quite well despite the pitch black of the room, and he sent out a silent *thank you* to Louis and his experiments. This was one side effect he enjoyed.

Her sun-streaked mass of hair trailed across the bed. Her breasts strained against the bodice of her fine linen nightgown, drawn tight by one of his knees caught on its fabric. He hadn't envisioned her wearing a nightgown. In his dreams, she was naked. He liked this even better. He'd always preferred his gifts wrapped.

"You're angry with me," he said.

"Now, what possible reasons could I have to be angry with you?"

Sam smelled a trap. She'd said *reasons*. Plural. A lot

could happen in the time he'd been gone. She'd had eighteen days to think. And right there was the problem. She was a woman. She'd worried their relationship to death, while for him, the matter was fairly straightforward.

"Are there any right answers to that question?" he asked. "Or can I just start apologizing and making amends?" He shifted his knees, sliding them back so that his body pressed more fully against hers. He didn't dare kiss her yet—he didn't need the bloody lip that action might earn him—so he nuzzled her neck instead.

A small sigh of pleasure escaped her, and Sam knew he'd live to see the sun rise. She turned her head and kissed his cheek.

"Amends," Libby said, sounding adorably sulky. "Unless you'd rather fight first. Because we're going to."

He didn't doubt it, although the warning meant she wouldn't fight dirty. It might even be fun.

"Fighting's not at all what I have on my mind," he said. Already, an erection tested the fly of his trousers.

He released her hands, and Libby's fingers flew straight to the buttons on his shirt. He eased up the hem of her nightgown until its skirt bunched around her hips. This first time tonight was going to be fast. He'd missed her too much. But after this, he'd take his time.

He could at least get his boots off, however.

They hit the floor, one after the other. Then he stood and quickly undressed. The advantage was his in that he could see her quite well, while Libby had to function on touch alone.

He had no problem with that.

She slid her nightdress over her head, then lifted her

unbound mass of curling hair with both hands and let it drop down her narrow back, baring her shoulders and breasts.

She had beautiful breasts, firm, and larger than one might expect based on the clothing she hid them under. Sam sat on the edge of the bed and cupped them in his palms, flicking the tips of his thumbs over her nipples. He bent his head and took first one in his mouth, then the other, letting his tongue take up where his thumb left off. Libby's fingers knotted in his hair as she held his head, the breathy sounds she emitted leaving him painfully hard.

He had to have her.

He pressed her into the pillows and nudged her thighs apart with one knee. He positioned himself at her cleft, then hesitated, wondering if she was ready, remembering that this was still new for her.

"Please," she whispered, the word thick with need, and Sam, no longer able to think, thrust his erection deep inside her. Her fingers, stroking the curves of his backside, bit into his flesh as she moaned in pleasure.

There was nothing more erotic to Sam than the soft sounds coming from Libby as he made love to her. They curled around his brain, leaving him dizzy with desire for her.

He kept his strokes gentle at first, mindful of her inexperience, but her hips rose eagerly with each of his movements, her whispered words urging him to increase the tempo. Sam pressed his face into her throat and hair as she came, enjoying the unbelievable sensations it created for him. The tiny muscles controlling her orgasm spasmed around him, clenching him tight, and he let out a cry of his own as his release exploded from him.

Afterward, he didn't withdraw but held her tight in his arms, knowing it wouldn't be long before they were both ready again, and next time, he intended to be much more thorough in his lovemaking.

"I had no idea what I was missing all these years," Libby murmured into his shoulder. Contentment and languor drifted off her.

Sam wanted to laugh. He'd had no idea either, because this was so far from anything he'd ever experienced, even he was surprised by it.

He had to rethink his strategy. From the moment he'd met her, he'd been rushing her too fast. He'd seen something he wanted, and as he always did, he went after it without thought for the consequences.

But Libby was no ordinary woman. He couldn't expect her to act like one, nor did he want her to. He'd let the fact that he wanted her so much cloud his good sense. He held her in his arms, liking the feel of their physical connection and the soft scent of her hair and skin. He still wanted to marry her, and he intended to, but she deserved to be courted. That meant doing so in a manner of her choosing, not his.

There were two issues regarding this courtship on which Sam would not bend, however. One of them was that it would lead to marriage. The second was that a pregnancy would bring about that marriage a great deal faster.

There was a third issue as well. For his own peace of mind, he had to know what her involvement with the Sky People had been. He didn't want for anything Whitley had said to be true. He had a bad feeling it might be.

The first rays of the morning sun saw Sam sprawled on her bed as if he belonged and Libby experiencing a strong sense of déjà vu.

She flushed to the tips of her bare toes. She hadn't intended to allow him to spend the whole night again but asking him to leave hadn't once crossed her mind. She'd spent far too much of the night encouraging him to make love to her. Now she'd have to deal with his expectations. And they still had a fight to get past.

Sam stretched, rolled over, and without opening his eyes, kissed her bare stomach. Desire crawled up the insides of Libby's thighs in response, almost making her forget how tired she was and that she was angry with him.

The clock on the bedside table ticked into the otherwise silent room, and she checked the time. It was still early.

She pushed at Sam's shoulder.

He sighed and peeled open one of those, gorgeous, gold-flecked eyes to look at her. "We're going to have that fight now, aren't we?"

"I'm willing to concede that we're in a relationship," Libby said, diving right in. "But you don't get to dictate the terms of it to me."

Sam slid a hand from her knee to her hip, taking his time, and she sucked in a breath.

"Agreed," he replied. "But then you don't get to dictate any terms to me, either."

She hadn't expected a compromise, but since she hadn't anticipated him agreeing to anything, was willing to concede it seemed fair.

"How about if we both get to dictate an equal amount of the terms? But they can't conflict," she added hastily when he started to smile. "If they do, we'll have to negotiate."

"Tell me what you want, then I'll tell you what my expectations are going to be," he said.

Speaking first made her feel in control, and gave her more courage than she might have expected, given that she was naked and feeling more than a little exposed. She turned to her side so she could see him better and crooked her elbow under her head, snuggling deeper into the blankets. The room was chilly first thing in the morning.

Both of his eyes were open now and regarding her with patient anticipation. A stubble of blond whiskers shadowed his chin and jaw, and helped explain the faint raw, burning sensation she had over certain sensitive areas of her skin.

"I don't want anyone to know we're seeing each other at night," she began. He said nothing, only watched her with increasing interest, so she took a deep breath and plunged onward. "I don't want us to be exclusive. I don't want to talk about marriage. And I don't want you hovering around me when I'm doing my job. I'm used to taking care of myself and I like it that way."

The muscles worked at the corners of his mouth. Whether from amusement or because he was irritated with her, Libby couldn't be certain.

He didn't sound irritated, though, as he reviewed her demands one by one. "I won't tell a soul," he replied, "although what people determine on their own is beyond my control. As far as exclusivity, for my part, I don't plan on warming other beds. We won't talk about marriage unless there's a possibility of a baby, in which case we won't need to talk about it until we're standing in front of a preacher. You might want to think about babies if you do decide to become more adventurous though," he added, his eyes darkening as they rested on her. "While I'd like to know for certain I'm the father, I won't be the first man to claim one that isn't his. And as for you doing your job, I'll be *hovering around*, as you put it, for anything that falls under federal jurisdiction. Let's just agree that I won't interfere in your job if you don't interfere in mine. But for simple, professional courtesy, I'll be spending most nights with you so we can share information." He ran a finger along her bare shoulder, sending a second wind straight to her tired inner muscles. He smiled at her like a cat cornering a mouse. "I hope that doesn't prove too exclusive for you. You being so adventurous and all. But duty comes first."

Libby could think of nothing to say.

Sam leaned over and kissed her, shot a glance at the clock, then scrambled over her to climb out of bed. She watched him as he dressed, still speechless.

Working the last button into the placket of his shirtfront, he bent over to kiss her again. Cocky triumph spread across his smug, handsome face and melted the gold in his eyes.

"See you tonight, darlin'," he said. "I'll be wanting to talk business so you'd best be alone."

Chapter Ten

Sam pounded the last fencepost in place and set down the post maul, wiped his forehead with his rolled-up sleeve, and surveyed his handiwork. At the rate he was going, he'd have his paddock finished in a couple of years.

Sooner or later he'd have to give some serious thought to his future with the Special Division. Right now he chose to enjoy the solitude. The sky above yawned a deep, brilliant blue, unbroken for miles, with not a cloud in sight. The morning remained young, the heat of the sun not yet at full strength, but it was soon going to be time to exchange chores for something less strenuous.

A tiny dark shape appeared on the horizon, growing larger by the minute. Dust kicked up around it. Sam hoped for a moment it might be Libby, come to pay him a visit. The possibility of a midmorning diversion threw out all worry over any work needing to be done. Keeping her busy and satisfied had become his number one priority.

The lone rider wasn't Libby. A man, dressed all in black, sat tall in the saddle.

Sam reached for the gun holster, hanging from one of the posts he'd already set, and strapped it on. He wasn't anticipating trouble, but he hadn't had a good run of luck lately and in these parts, based on recent events, a man had to be careful.

He mustn't forget what a valuable Division resource he'd become.

That statement still festered. He hadn't decided yet what he planned to do about it, but he planned to do something. Sam was nobody's property. And he wasn't a piece in a game to be moved with the nudge of a finger.

The rider turned out to be Coyote Bluff's preacher, identifiable by his square-toed boots and stiff white collar. A rifle scabbard hung from the side of his saddle, near a black-booted foot and his right hand, showing he didn't place all of his faith in the Lord. He appeared to be close to Sam's age, another surprise. These isolated parts of the Territories tended to attract either young families seeking fortune, or rough men avoiding the long arm of the law, not young men needing wives.

Sam could only guess at what he'd done to attract the attention of God and one of His servants. He hoped it had nothing to do with his nights spent at Libby's. She'd kill him for sure.

"Good morning, Marshal," the preacher called out while still a few hundred feet away. "I'm Pastor Wade Endicott. Your place is on this week's rounds so I thought I'd drop in and introduce myself."

Sam shielded his eyes from the sun as he looked up at

the mounted man. As tempting as it was to try and find out the real reason behind Pastor Endicott's visit, he didn't quite dare. His ability with illusions was another rumor he didn't need spreading around Coyote Bluff.

"Can I offer you a cup of coffee?" he asked instead.

The preacher declined. He had bright, friendly eyes and an easy smile, and gave off the impression of a well-educated, intelligent man. Sam decided not too much got past him. Judging by the accent he'd be curious to know how many years Pastor Endicott had spent in the West, but it was rude to ask a question that was none of his business on such short acquaintance.

"I've been meaning to get to church," Sam said, "but what with one thing and another…" He waved a hand around the yard at the general state of disrepair. The outbuildings and house needed fresh paint, the barn had seen better days, and most of the paddock fencing had either fallen down or sagged to the ground.

Endicott grinned, showing a set of white teeth with a slight gap in the front. Fine lines puckered the corners of his eyes, illustrating a natural inclination towards good humor. The brown hue of his skin alluded to a great deal of time spent outdoors. Sam decided he liked him.

"That's not why I'm here," Endicott said, "although I do hope you'll join us in church in the near future. Sunday mornings we congregate in the saloon. While the location helps raise attendance, I'm forced to work harder to keep everyone awake and attentive. There's the added disadvantage of finding the appropriate sermon for everyone." His smile widened. "If you'd prefer, I offer a second service later in the day for the sober, delicate, and unarmed. Mae

Miller provides the use of her parlor and serves tea after." The creases around his eyes deepened. "Her daughter is an exceptional cook."

"I believe I've heard that mentioned."

"My reason for stopping in unannounced has more to do with the congregation's activities after the service," Endicott continued. "Some of the men were wondering if you'd be interested in joining our monthly baseball league. I saw you play in Boston about seven years ago. We could use a good pitcher."

"I figured you for an Easterner," Sam said, "but I'd never have guessed a Bostonian."

"I'm originally from New York City." Endicott's horse twitched its tail, shaking off flies. That was all he said on the matter, Leaving Sam's curiosity as to his background unsatisfied. "Some of the men are good. Others could use some pointers. Knickerbocker rules, more or less. It's all in good fun."

The thought of Sunday afternoon games was tempting. Sam had once played with a minor league, and had toyed with the idea of going professional, but opted to continue his education instead. He'd never lost his love of the game. He simply hadn't cared for the politics that went with professional play.

Becoming more involved in the community might be a good idea, too. Someday he'd like to live in Coyote Bluff year round.

"Turnabout's fair play, Marshal," Endicott added. "The men tend to be a tight knit group. If you were in need of a hand with some painting or fencing, say, or any other repairs, they'd be more than willing to lend a hand in return."

Sam continued to hesitate only because of the obligation involved. He had no problem with reciprocating favors, but the nature of his work meant he sometimes disappeared without warning for extended periods of time. That would leave their team deprived of its pitcher, and some farmer short a pair of spare hands. "Are there enough players around here to form two teams?"

"We make do. For instance, the sheriff is base runner for Harley Temple. Harley's a good man with a bat. He's hit more home runs than everyone else combined, but his wooden leg means running is out. Once a year we organize a tournament with a few other towns."

Sam heard one thing. "Sheriff Mayden plays in a men's league?"

"I know it's unusual, but the sheriff's not your average woman."

Sam curbed his tongue. The assessment was fair. The fact that she played meant she either felt comfortable or obligated. He wondered which it might be. "I hear she's independent."

Endicott frowned. "Careful where you say that, Marshal. Sheriff Mayden's reputation is above reproach in these parts. Her past is her own business and she keeps it to herself. She's a true Western woman, born and raised, and she's tougher than most of the men. She's faster than them, too. Harley doesn't get those home runs on one leg. The players all stay respectful."

"No disrespect intended," Sam said. If she genuinely liked the game, and wasn't simply helping this one-legged Harley out of a sense of obligation, he might even get a chance to impress her. And he'd get to watch her run bases.

He'd wager that was as much fun as watching her chase Mary Lou Bennett. "I'd like to get back into practice."

Endicott touched the brim of his hat. "Excellent. It's been a pleasure meeting you, Marshal. The men are anxious to get to know you. We're all real happy to have a lawman in the area."

"You have a sheriff," Sam pointed out.

The other man's expression went blank. Then his face cleared. "Sheriff Mayden handles the paperwork, since Pete Gaster can't read. And it's nice to have a woman in charge of the jail. William Bennett's wife is the only real criminal around Coyote Bluff and Sheriff Mayden keeps things respectable. But Judge Roy Rowe is the real law in these parts. Fear of him is what keeps outlaws and bandits away. He's got a long arm."

Sam watched Endicott ride away, more than a little unsettled by the warning. He'd heard stories of Roy Rowe. The judge was a legend in the West. Most of his counterparts didn't dare travel the empty distances to tiny outposts like Coyote Bluff, dispensing justice. The ones who did rarely survived more than a month. Rowe, on the other hand, went where he pleased. It was rumored he had the ear of the President himself.

Judge Rowe's reputation wasn't entirely to blame for Sam's sudden concern, however. He had a sneaking suspicion Libby wasn't going to be too happy about him playing baseball. She could be peculiar when it came to him encroaching on her public territory. If the men started to treat him as another arm of the law in Coyote Bluff, she might view that as him interfering.

Sam liked keeping calm, practical Libby on her toes.

More than that, he liked making her happy.

Because she made him happy, too.

One of the less enthralling duties of being a small town sheriff involved monitoring local pest control, but still, it was a task Libby enjoyed.

She spent the morning riding the range of the Double U, a good-sized ranch on the opposite side of Coyote Bluff from hers, counting pocket gopher holes in the bushes over a five mile stretch of desert. By the time she reached thirty, her mind had wandered off to greener pastures.

See you tonight, darlin'.

Sam Kyote, she decided, more than lived up to his namesake's trickster reputation. He could talk circles around her. She freed her boot from the stirrup to kick at a creosote bush, careful to watch out for snakes. Right when she thought she'd won an argument, it all fell apart.

What captured her thoughts most as her horse plodded along, its hooves sending up dry puffs of dust, was the way Sam made her laugh. As much as he frustrated her, too, she liked having him around more than she'd expected. She also liked being seen as a woman.

But when it came to their negotiations, she didn't quite trust him. She suspected all his talk about babies was so much hot air, and his way of trying to persuade her to do something he wanted. Mary Lou and William had been married nine years and had no children to show for it.

Libby bit her lower lip. On the other hand, Greta Rosenberg had three, with a fourth on the way.

The sun burned through her linen duster, beating uncomfortably hot against her back. A few of the town's public women went to church Sunday mornings. Libby thought she might find a way to ask them some indelicate questions. For the most part, the women avoided her, which Libby assumed was largely due to a fear of being fined for practicing their trade inside town limits, but as a courtesy from one working woman to another, she'd always left them alone.

But she didn't care to hear any more uncomfortable lectures from Pastor Endicott. Since she wasn't sinning alone, it hardly seemed fair. If Sam's talk about babies was true, then she was the one who stood to pay the higher price.

The path she followed took her through a wide wash draped with overgrown desert willow, providing a welcome respite from the scorching rays of sun.

At the end of the wash, two riders blocked her way. They had their backs to her, and appeared to be engaged in a heated discussion. Based on the way they sat their horses, she'd have to say they were strangers to her.

She reined in her mount, cautious and undecided. Sheriff or not, she was a woman alone. She could turn back and choose another route.

Then stubborn pride reared its head. She asked herself if she was nervous because of her recent run-in with Sky People. If so, her daddy had taught her better than that. She'd grown up around the roughest of men. She had a rifle in her saddle holster, a pistol on both hips, and a derringer up the sleeve of her duster. She could handle herself.

She squared her shoulders, lifted her chin, and urged her horse forward through the wash. Maxwell Mayden's daughter was no coward. Besides, not every stranger she met would turn out to be one of the Sky People. The odds were against it.

When she came within shooting range, she called out a greeting so as not to startle them.

Both men turned at the same time. Two heads bobbed in polite acknowledgment.

"Ma'am," one of them said.

As she drew up beside them, she took mental notes. With camping gear, panniers, and ragged bedrolls strapped to their drooping mounts, they looked like typical cowboys searching for work. The one rifle they carried was more appropriate for shooting squirrels and small game than for protection.

They were so young. The thought filled her with dismay. If the oldest was sixteen, she'd be shocked. From their faces, she guessed them to be brothers. Possibly cousins. They looked hungry, too. The younger boy was all long bony wrists, shiny cheekbones, and big eyes.

Her heart twisted with pity. The last thin remnants of her fear evaporated in the dry desert air, even though it was clear they were up to no good. She'd seen too many boys like this end up riding with men like her father simply because they were starving and desperate. These two weren't at that point yet, but she'd say they were close.

They tipped their hats as they moved their horses to one side of the wash so she could ride past.

"You gentlemen looking for honest work?" she asked.

They said they were, and even though their eyes never met hers when they spoke, she chose to give them the benefit of the doubt. She directed them back in the direction she'd come from, toward the Double U Ranch, and told them to give the foreman her name.

As she continued on her way, making a circuit of the ranch, the skin between her shoulder blades prickled. They were watching her. She didn't turn around again to see what they did next, or if they rode off. That would be asking for trouble. She'd rather risk a bullet in the back than insult them by calling their honor into question.

Especially since their honor was questionable. She felt confident they hadn't come all the way to Coyote Bluff, which was next door to nowhere, to find work on any ranch. The local mines weren't all that profitable, either. The best claims had been worked out years ago. The Rosenbergs struggled to make ends meet on theirs and had brought in cattle to supplement their income.

Those boys had come to an isolated town for a different purpose, and that it involved making fast money went without saying. She thought of that poorly executed stagecoach robbery attempt.

And she thought outlaws had to start somewhere.

That night, as she sat on her front porch with Sam's arms and legs around her, she decided the best part of being an adventuress came after the actual act. It was equally intimate and offered a great deal of personal contentment.

Sam lounged on the top step, wearing nothing but his long johns, all bare-chested and beautiful, while she nestled between his bent knees, dressed in his shirt. His chin rested on the top of her head, and she rubbed his thighs with the palms of her hands. They gazed across a desert clad in a sparkling blanket of black velvet sky, quietly enjoying each other's company. She tracked her fingers down the length of Sam's leg to the top of his foot.

"I never noticed before how beautiful a man's feet are," she said.

She felt the laughter bubble up in his chest, then its soft rumble as it poured out past his lips to tickle her ear. "Maybe it's just my feet you find beautiful. Maybe they're special."

"I'm sure that's it." Sam tugged her hair. She rolled her palms over his knees, back and forth, as she stared at the moonless sky.

Her thoughts drifted. The two boys she'd met that morning continued to trouble her.

"What are you thinking about?" he asked. "Is something wrong?"

"Can I ask you a question?" She tilted her head to the side and glanced up at him. "Out of that professional courtesy you seem to have such a fondness for?"

At once, he was alert and all business. "You can ask me anything."

"Were you on the stagecoach when someone took a couple of shots at it?"

"I was."

She felt the shift in his muscles. The way they tightened. If she listened only to his voice, she'd have heard nothing unusual. It was amazing, however, how much she could tell about him when they were touching this way, with such intimacy—as if they were speaking a completely new kind of language. He'd answered her honestly, but with a great deal of caution, and she wondered what he didn't want her to know.

What he hadn't put into words.

Her heart lodged in her throat as her head leaped to a logical conclusion. He'd been in danger. That was what he was trying to hide. It was how much she was bothered by it that really took her by surprise. Sam was a federal marshal. His job was inherently dangerous. Her whole life, she'd dealt with the knowledge that people she cared about might not come back. Many of them hadn't.

It was different with Sam in a way she couldn't put into words and wasn't sure she should try and figure out. She was happy with the way things were between them and saw no reason to borrow trouble.

Not unless trouble was staring them right in the face.

"What was your opinion on it?" she asked, turning back to her original question. "Was it a simple robbery attempt?"

He took a minute to think it over. The wind curled around them, cool once the sun went down, and his arms tightened around her to add warmth when she shivered. The tension in him dissipated.

"That's the likeliest explanation," he finally said. "It wasn't professional by any means. Wrong weapon, for one thing. And whoever was shooting didn't want to be seen. Either that or they were afraid of getting shot at in return. The only thing they got right was the location, and even then, only if they were trying to protect themselves. They were too close to town. But that was three weeks ago. Why are you asking about it now?"

She told him of the boys she'd met that morning, in a place they had no reason to be. Sam's mention of the wrong weapon being used added to her list of concerns. They'd had that squirrel gun.

Sam leaned back. He settled his hands on her bare shoulders beneath the collar of the white cotton shirt of his that she wore. His warm fingers tightened, but in a gentle, possessive manner that made her heart skip a beat, then quicken its pace.

"You took a chance, Libby. I don't like that. You should have left them alone. What if they'd been Sky People?"

It was hard to be annoyed with him for being genuinely concerned when his thumbs were rubbing in sensual, deliberate circles against her shoulder blades. She had no urge to ask him to stop. Not on either account. Instead, she chose to point out the obvious.

"I was doing my job."

"You could do it with a bit more caution. Next time you come across strangers in a place they have no business being, shoot first and ask questions later."

"I can't kill everyone who wanders into town unannounced," she replied. "If I did, you'd be dead, too."

He kissed the curve of her throat, then ran the tip of his tongue up the lobe of her ear, making her shiver in a way that had nothing to do with the cold. "Go ahead and think that, sweetheart. After all, there's no harm in dreaming."

"To answer your question," she said, fighting off the distraction he was creating with little success, "they weren't Sky People. They were a pair of hungry boys who were up to no good. When I first caught sight of them, they seemed to be arguing."

"They might have been rustling. That would explain what they were doing on Double U land."

The thought had occurred to her. "Maybe, but they'd have to drive the cattle a long distance in order to sell them, and

I'd think that would be a lot of work for two inexperienced boys. Besides, the West is settling more every day. Coyote Bluff is hardly prime real estate, but it's not the worst spot to start out, either." She sighed, and dropped her head back to rest against his chest. "I can't think of any other reason for two boys to be here other than that they're already in trouble with the law and in need of a place to hide. I don't want to have to kill them, and I'm afraid that's where they're headed. They're hungry and desperate, and maybe a little lazy. They think stealing is easy money, and don't understand it's also high risk. I sent them to the Double U to find out how hard they're willing to work for honest pay."

His hands fell from her shoulders. His arms encircled her waist. When he spoke, his words were soft and warm in her ear.

"You, Libby Mayden, are a good and kind person. You've already done more for them than their own families likely did, or ever will. You don't need to take on responsibility for them. Besides," he added, "it's my understanding most people with criminal intent know to stay out of this area. Rumor has it that Judge Roy Rowe has Coyote Bluff locked down fairly tight."

"Judge Roy commands respect, but to claim he has Coyote Bluff locked down is an exaggeration."

"I'm not sure I agree." Sam's words rolled out into the quiet night, slow and thoughtful. "He's famous in Washington. He's on first name basis with the new president. He'll no doubt end up in the Senate, and maybe even sit as president himself someday. There's got to be more to him than an ability to inspire respect."

Judge Roy had never breathed a word of any of this

to her. She wasn't sure how she felt about it either. "I had no idea he was so ambitious." She should have known it, however. He'd never done anything by halves.

"Most men have ambitions and a taste of power tends to feed it." Wrapping a thick tress of her hair around one of his fingers, he gave a gentle tug. "How well do you know him?"

She'd thought she'd known him better than this. She'd seen a side of him most people had no idea existed, although she couldn't say that to Sam without betraying his confidence.

But lying to Sam also felt like a betrayal, one Libby liked even less.

"Do you want me to keep an eye on those boys for you?" he asked. "Maybe go out and ask them if they know anything about a stagecoach robbery attempt? Put a little more fear of the law into them if they don't have enough already?"

She'd asked for his opinion because she'd wanted it, but she knew him well enough by now to be careful of how much involvement in her own work she gave him. If she didn't enforce the boundaries between them, he'd forget they existed.

"Thank you for the offer, but I'll take care of matters affecting Coyote Bluff. It's what I get paid for."

His arms tightened. "I understand."

The best part, she thought, was that he really did. Despite her past reputation as a gunfighter, he knew how hard it was for her to be taken seriously by people who'd never seen her in action.

She shifted around in his arms and lifted her face so she could look in his eyes, but it was too dark for her to see the little gold flecks that fascinated her. He dropped a light kiss on her mouth.

"Do you really play baseball?" he asked.

"No. I run the bases for Harley Temple."

She must have sounded more sour about it than she'd intended, because he laughed out loud—a rich sound that drifted across the yard, sparking a soft whicker of response from his horse in the barn.

"Do you mind that Pastor Endicott stopped by my place today to ask me to join their league?"

"Why should I mind?" She drummed her fingertips against his knee. "Because you got asked to play baseball, while I got a lecture on circumspection, Jezebels, and leading men into sin?"

"Did you really?" He managed to sound annoyed, fascinated, and amused all at once.

"It's not funny."

"Of course it's not." He was quick to try and placate her. "But we can do something about those lectures real quick. All you have to do is marry me."

Coyote Bluff had too many secrets that weren't hers to share. She couldn't put him in that position. He was a federal marshal. And she'd seen what all the lies her father told had done to her mother. She'd died hating him.

The last remnants of her earlier contentment vanished. "I like my independence."

"Then I guess you'll have to get used to the lectures, Sheriff Jezebel," he replied.

Chapter Eleven

From his position in the nest of twisted bed sheets, his hands clasped behind his head, Sam watched the show with enjoyment as Libby slid her long legs into a clean pair of trousers. Speckles of dust floated aimlessly in the warm morning sun that caught the streaks of gold in her mass of glossy brown hair.

He couldn't say he cared for the preacher questioning her morals, but for different reasons than hers. Call him suspicious, but he found it odd how Endicott had warned him that Libby's reputation was beyond reproach, yet given her a different message than that. It made him wonder if maybe Endicott was more interested in the sheriff as a woman than he'd let on.

"Where are you off to in such a rush?" he asked.

Her fingers halted in the act of fastening the buttons on her blouse. Other than undergarments, it was the only piece of woman's clothing he'd seen her wear.

He frowned. Libby should have pretty things. Her father had a lot to be ashamed for, but Sam figured this was the worst. He liked her just as she was, trousers and all, but she'd never had the opportunity to be more feminine.

Then again, if she'd been any different, someone else would have found the courage to grab her before he had.

"Church," Libby said, in answer to his question. She tugged her hair free of her collar, picked up a brush from the top of the commode, and began to work it into its usual single braid.

The Sunday morning service.

At the saloon.

Sam pushed back the sheets, and stark naked, surged out of bed. "That's right. I almost forgot. Pastor Endicott expects me. We can ride in together."

Libby played with the long-handled brush, a sure sign she was about to offer a contrary opinion. Sam waited with eager anticipation for the upcoming debate. She was fun to get riled.

"We can't do that," she said.

"Why not? We're neighbors. No one will think twice."

She set the brush back on the commode with a bit too much force. "Have you ever heard of the word discreet?"

He waggled his eyebrows. "I don't suppose you want to come back to bed for a bit and explain it to me?"

"We'll both be late if I do. You're remarkably hardheaded when it comes to learning lessons." Her blue eyes sparkled with a mixture of exasperation, good humor, and regret.

It was the regret that touched him the most. She wanted to, but she hadn't forgotten the things the pastor had said. Maybe he should have a frank, man-to-man discussion with

Endicott—one that plainly stated the pastor should mind his own business and let Sam deal with Libby's adventurous ways on his own.

Or he could respect Libby's wishes and let her ride into town by herself.

He took her face in his hands and kissed her. "I'm messing with you, sweetheart. I'll see you in church."

He gave her a twenty-minute head start.

The morning air had a fresh bite to it, although by the time he tied his horse to the hitching post outside the saloon, the day promised to be sunny and hot.

The Evening Lily was a long, low, rough-looking building with a false front. Batwing doors squeaked on hinges gone dry in the desert heat. He pushed through the doors, not knowing what to expect, but certain it would be worth a morning's entertainment.

The interior was gloomy, with walls built of shaved and whitewashed pine planks. It appeared to Sam as if gas lighting had recently been installed. A pump organ in one corner, and a cleared floor space, indicated the presence of Friday night dance girls, while crude stairs leading to an upper story suggested the girls could also be rented out by the hour.

The tables had been pushed to one side, and the chairs lined into neat rows on the dance floor. Most of the seats at the back, which in this case meant near the door, were already occupied. He spied Libby straight away, in the very last seat and to the right of the room.

A pulpit, sticking out like a sore thumb in its hedonistic surroundings, had been set in place near the organ. The organist, looking as if he'd had a long night, perched on a stool. He had suspicious stains on the puffed sleeve of his grimy white shirt.

Sam did a quick scan of the rest of the room. If he read it right, the mood was more sullen than God-fearing Christian. Half of the congregation—about fifty, in total—appeared in worse shape than the organist. Some slouched in their chairs, three slow blinks from actual unconsciousness. The place smelled of stale beer and sour whiskey, and he doubted if it could be blamed entirely on shoddy housekeeping.

Endicott must be a lively and highly entertaining speaker, indeed.

Sam would have preferred to take the empty seat beside Libby. Instead he removed his hat, nodded to her and several ladies he suspected might be those dance girls, and worked his way to the front of the room. He chose a seat to the far left, so if he turned slightly, he could watch out for Libby as well as see the whole room.

As he waited for the service to start, he felt every eye in the room boring into him. US federal marshals weren't high on the popularity scale and Sam's shoulder blades twitched. He wondered how many in the congregation were armed. Libby, beyond a doubt, but she was the sheriff. Most saloon keepers in the region didn't allow guns inside their establishments other than the shotguns they kept under the bar, but the odds were small comfort.

Wade Endicott, serene in wire-framed reading spectacles, dressed in the usual black and clutching his bible, entered the makeshift church through the front doors. The mood shifted from sullen to one of expectancy as everyone stood and waited for him to walk to the pulpit. Endicott took his time, which built on the suspense, and Sam began to suspect he was in the presence of a truly great entertainer.

Endicott reached the pulpit and nodded to the organist to begin. Music groaned out of the old instrument. Sam recognized a hymn from his childhood. He hadn't heard it in years. There weren't any hymnals so not everyone sang, which meant one voice at the back of the congregation stood out from the others—Libby's, sweet and clear.

Well, well.

While captivated by her singing abilities, Sam was far more impressed that Maxwell Mayden's daughter knew all the words to an obscure hymn. It would give him something to ponder on to keep him awake during the sermon if Endicott didn't live up to expectations.

"Hearers, I'd like to speak to you today on the weaknesses of the flesh."

As it turned out, Sam didn't need any help staying awake. Endicott proved an even better entertainer than he could have hoped for. He was willing to hazard a guess that the speech Libby'd endured hadn't been entirely for her benefit either, but that the pastor had been rehearsing to judge its effect. This morning, he attributed much of the blame for loose morals to the men who couldn't resist the lure of said fallen women.

The congregation shifted uncomfortably in their chairs for the next hour. Sam kept his head down and fought not to look over his shoulder at Libby to see her reaction. This explained why so many men, who under other circumstances would be at home sleeping off an ill-spent Saturday night, had chosen to stay for church. Endicott selected his topics well. This one was guaranteed to stir up trouble.

The sermon ended, and after two more hymns and a prayer, the service was over. Sam rose, already searching for

Libby through the throng of departing worshippers, when a lean, bow-legged cowboy pushed his way upstream to where Endicott stood. He had a scrubby jaw and bloodshot eyes. He was young, maybe nineteen.

He planted a palm on Endicott's chest and gave him a light shove. "Who do you think you are, spouting off about another man's business in public like that? Making me the laughing stock of the town?"

Libby had moved up the far side of the room, out of the exodus down the center. She came up behind the young cowboy, edging a bit to one side so he could take note of her presence but she wasn't within striking range. Sam moved ahead a few feet, ready to leap in and protect her if he was needed.

"Behave yourself, Cash," she said, sounding like some prim schoolteacher, all scolding and calm. "The pastor wasn't talking about you."

"No? Who was he talking about, then?" Cash demanded of her.

She'd succeeded in diverting his attention off the preacher, but Sam couldn't say he cared for where the young cowboy named Cash now turned it.

She started to respond. She stopped. Then she faced Endicott, hands on her hips. "Shame on you, Pastor. Calling a young man out in public like that."

Cash shoved the pastor again, forcing him to take a step back.

Sam decided it was time to intervene. He strode forward, ready to wrestle the cowboy to the floor if he had to, but Endicott caught his eye and waved a hand for him to stay back.

"There will be no fighting in a house of God," Endicott said to the cowboy. "If you have a problem with the sermon, and take exception to a message you clearly needed to hear, then we'll take it outside for further clarification."

"This is a saloon," Cash said. "I was fighting in here last night."

"Today it's a church. We take our disagreement outside."

Sam didn't believe he'd ever seen a preacher challenge a man to a fight, before. He looked to Libby for guidance. She shrugged her shoulders as if to say *Leave them alone*.

With Endicott in the lead and Cash right behind him, and Libby and Sam bringing up the rear, they filed outside.

Libby perched on the hitching post. Sam sat down beside her. A small crowd had begun to gather, although on a Sunday morning, it was mostly members of the congregation who weren't in as great a hurry to get home and back to bed as they'd been only moments before.

To Sam, this didn't feel right. It smelled sacrilegious.

"Shouldn't we be doing something to stop this?" he muttered to Libby. "What with you being the sheriff, and me a marshal? Endicott's a man of God. It hardly feels right to sit here and do nothing."

"I could sell tickets and raise money, but most of these people spent what they had on them in the saloon last night. Besides, Pastor Endicott can take care of himself."

Sam confessed to a high level of skepticism. Traveling preachers sometimes had to defend themselves, but it was usually with a pistol, and from thieves, not a parishioner wrestling what looked to be a fierce hangover. "Have you seen Endicott fight before?"

She wasn't looking at Sam. She was more interested in

watching the two men strip off their shirts. Her cheeks dimpled as she sent Sam a sidelong, chiding glance. "Pay attention to details, Marshal. Take a good look at his knuckles."

Now that she'd pointed them out to him, he could see she was right. The preacher's knuckles were unusually large, scarred, and heavily calloused. His chest, too, now that he'd taken off his shirt and stood exposed in broad daylight, was broader than one might expect of a preacher, and bore numerous faint, yet unmistakable, marks.

Sam grinned. Endicott was, or had been at some point not too far in the past, a bare-knuckles brawler. Best church service he'd attended in years.

"Are we agreed I can step in if it looks like he's going to beat that young fool to death?" he asked.

"The pastor doesn't carry himself like a killer," she replied. "He'll teach Cash a lesson." She caught the inside of her lip in her teeth, looked a little worried, then seemed to decide it was better to err on the side of caution. "Although Cash can be pretty dumb. We'll step in if it takes him too long to catch on."

The fight was short, but entertaining enough while it lasted.

Endicott danced, light and graceful on his feet, easily dodging the sturdier blows but taking a few of the weaker ones, letting Cash wear himself out with his swinging. Sweat dripped off the cowboy's chin. His face had gone red as a beet, and the hangover couldn't be helping his cause.

Finally, Endicott took pity on him. A hard jab to the bridge of the nose, then a follow-up to the temple, and the cowboy sank to his knees, the fight over. Sam watched Cash's eyes roll back in his head before he fell backwards to sprawl in the dusty street.

Someone doused him with a bucket of water. He sat up, spluttering, but otherwise appeared in remarkably good cheer. Endicott helped him to his feet. Once the cowboy was steady, Endicott delivered him a blistering lecture on temperance.

The cowboy rubbed the side of his head. "This don't seem right," he complained. "You're a man of God."

"And God just sent you a message. Perhaps you should heed it." Endicott reached for his shirt. One of the parishioners had been holding it for him, and he nodded his thanks as he eased his arms in the sleeves and began fastening the buttons.

"This," Sam said to Libby, "was worth the ride into town. I'll be coming to church every Sunday morning from now on."

She started to lean toward him, to say something in response, withering, no doubt, when she caught sight of something behind him. Sam turned to find her deputy, Pete Gaster, heading down the street from the jailhouse toward them. He wore his badge and his guns, so Sam assumed he was on duty.

Rather than confront the combatants to find out what was going on, he strolled up to Libby and Sam where they perched on the hitching post.

"Well, don't you two look cozy," Pete drawled, his gaze drifting back and forth, noting the short distance between them. "And it ain't even a full moon."

"What's the full moon got to do with anything?" Sam asked.

Libby's elbow caught him in the ribs. "Don't ask questions you don't want to know the answer to."

Pete's grizzled face creased into a wide, knowing grin, exhibiting his eagerness to explain. "Legend has it, when a pale moon walks in the night sky Coyote Trickster wins the Maiden he desires." He twitched a finger from Libby to Sam. "Get it? Kyote? Mayden?"

Based on the sermon the pastor had recently dispensed with such eloquence, Sam decided the most circumspect thing to do was treat those remarks as a joke. "Do you have any sisters?" he asked Libby. "I wouldn't want to end up with the wrong Mayden."

Her face gave away nothing of what she was thinking, but when Sam looked in her eyes, he knew she'd lost her sense of humor right about the same time Pete opened his mouth. She had the cool, unblinking stare of a cool-tempered gunfighter down to perfection. He suspected he'd have to use the window tonight if he wanted to sleep in her bed, because her front door would no doubt be locked.

He would if he had to. Because there was nothing he loved more than seeing that cool gaze melt, replaced with bright licks of heat.

"I think I have a few cousins in England," she said, her voice as chilly as her eyes. "You might want to take a long trip and find out. Otherwise, you'll end up with no Mayden at all and Pete will be disappointed."

Behind Pete, Cash addressed Endicott. "My apologies, Pastor," he said. "I guess I jumped the gun a bit on who your sermon was truly intended for."

Endicott's blond hair gleamed in the sun as he bent his head and concentrated on beating the dust off the legs of his trousers with what appeared to Sam to be unnecessary force. "Careful, Mister Robson. You've already had one beating today. If you cast aspersions on a lady's honor, you may yet receive another."

"I wasn't talking about no lady," Cash protested. "I was talking about the sheriff and the marshal."

"If you want to shoot him," Sam said to Libby, "I'll look the other way."

"There's no need, Marshal Kyote." She leaped off the hitching post. "All I'm hearing is a couple of fools flapping their lips, spouting nonsense."

She strode off, pushing her way through the remaining bystanders, her head held high. He watched the pretty sway of her hips, her gun belt hanging low and bouncing with each stride as she stalked up the street. Her braid of hair formed a neat, dividing line down the straight length of her ramrod-stiff spine.

He wished he hadn't fixed the latch on that window. Getting into her bed tonight was looking less and less like a foregone conclusion. Maybe he should start with trying to get back in her good graces. He hadn't started any of this, but he hadn't stopped it, either.

He noticed all the other men were watching Libby, too. They might not know what to make of her, but no matter what she might think, they weren't immune to the fact she was a woman. It gave him an unpleasant little jolt, and served as a reminder that, Pete's legend or not, this particular Kyote hadn't yet won any Mayden.

"What's she so mad about?" Cash asked, of no one in particular.

Libby spent the rest of the morning at the jail, waiting for the second church service to end and the afternoon ball game to begin.

While she knew not to pay men being boys any mind, she'd expected better from Sam. She didn't know what better might be, which put her in a bad humor, and since she'd never been prone to moodiness before, she blamed him for it. She didn't want him seeing her the same way the entire town already did. She wasn't one of the boys, but she wasn't one of the women either, and the ball game that afternoon wouldn't cast a more favorable impression as to her overall femininity.

As well as the base runner for one-legged Harley Temple, she also served as Coyote Bluff's umpire. She was one of the few people who could read and write, and therefore able to keep the club's records, so the town treated it as part of her duties as sheriff.

Not only that, she was familiar with the Knickerbocker rules gaining in popularity among enthusiasts such as Pastor Endicott. Baseball had long been considered a gentleman's sport, which meant Libby's father — the disinherited younger brother of a British duke — had insisted his gang learn to play.

Libby showed up ten minutes early at the field a group of men had cleared on the outskirts of town. Pastor Endicott was a stickler for the rules, and they clearly stated members had to be punctual.

While the infield had been carefully swept clean, the outfield retained a lot of its natural rough patches. They'd implemented a single-bounce rule. The ball could hit a rock or clump of dirt, maybe a new shrub or stump, and still be considered in play.

Libby wasn't the first to arrive. Prim Bess Miller, pretty and plump, the daughter of the Millers who ran the mercantile, already waited in the shade of a stand of cottonwoods at the edge of the ball field. Her long brown ringlets were tied up with pink ribbons that made her look younger than her sixteen years. Libby was somewhat surprised to see her, especially alone. She'd always seemed so shy around men. Probably because her mother, while no doubt well-intentioned, tried too hard to draw their attention to her.

Libby walked over to the shade to join her.

"Good afternoon, Bess," she said. "Come to watch the baseball game?"

The girl made a face. "Sorry Sheriff, I know you like it and all, but I don't see the sense in running around in this heat." She looked at her hands, then at Libby. Her round cheeks shone a bright pink that matched her hair ribbons. "I came to ask a favor of you."

"Of me?" Now Libby was truly surprised. She and Bess barely knew each other and had little in common.

"I'll find a way to repay you. Truly. But I thought…what with the legend and all…" Bess's voice trailed off.

Libby was lost. "What legend?"

"The one about you and Marshal Kyote."

Bess looked so hopeful, with a touch of fear lurking in the depths of her pretty blue eyes, that Libby didn't have the heart to tell her Pete's legend was a joke. One only he thought was funny. Instead, she decided she'd do what she could to help ease the girl's mind, because it was obvious something important was troubling her. She'd never have approached Libby otherwise.

"You're going to have to explain," Libby said. "I can't even imagine what this is about."

"My mother is determined the marshal would make me a good husband."

She didn't know what to say to that. The thought of Sam with Bess was beyond her imagination's capacity. Then again, she had to concede that the thought of Sam with her seemed equally far-fetched, yet they were spending their nights together, so stranger things had happened.

"I'm not sure how I can help," she said carefully.

Bess's eyes brightened with hope. "You aren't all that old yet. And you're real pretty. You and the marshal are both interested in the law, so you have that in common. You could catch his interest if you tried."

"You want me to make a play for the marshal?" Libby asked, not sure she was hearing her right. Then, her sense of humor took over. "What's wrong with him that you don't want him?"

"He scares me." Bess's voice dropped to a whisper and she glanced around. A few of the league members had begun to arrive, so she spoke in a rush, clearly not wanting to be overheard. "Besides, I already have someone who wants to marry me."

That gave Libby a bad feeling. If Bess didn't want her mother to know about him, then whoever her beau was, he had to be trouble. Mae Miller was a decent woman who loved her daughter. Libby didn't believe she'd stop Bess from marrying a man she'd chosen for herself unless she had good reason to object. "Mind if I ask who he is?"

Bess's expression grew dreamy. "Cash Robson."

Libby's bad feeling worsened. Somehow she doubted if

Cash's objection to Pastor Endicott's sermon that morning had anything to do with sweet little Bess Miller. Maybe she should speak with Mae Miller about Cash.

Then again, any interference on Libby's part would only shine too much light on the problem. For all she knew, Cash and Bess might make a perfect match. Maybe Bess was what he needed to settle him down.

Her lips twitched. For that matter, Bess and Sam might make a good match, too.

"I'm sorry," she said. "I can't help you. Marshal Kyote and I have a strictly professional working relationship. Anything personal between us is out of the question. It wouldn't be proper."

Tears filled Bess's eyes. "But I thought…"

"You thought wrong."

"I don't want to marry the marshal."

The girl seemed equal parts terrified and crushed, and Libby couldn't be so cold-hearted as to not offer some small ray of hope. "There, now. Don't fret. These things have a way of working themselves out. Besides, you shouldn't be so afraid of Marshal Kyote. From what I've seen he's not unkind."

On that note of encouragement Pastor Endicott arrived, ending the conversation. He began pacing off the bases according to the rules, from home plate to second, then first to third. That meant the game would start in a few minutes, and there was no sign of Sam.

He was getting himself into all kinds of trouble today.

He rode up ten minutes late, dismounted, and walked his horse over to where Bess was sitting. The girl's round face went pale. Libby watched from the corner of her eye, not wanting to stare but curious to see what would happen next.

Bess looked around as if seeking a place to hide, or an avenue of escape. Sam paid her no mind at all, other than a tip of his hat and brief nod of his head in her general direction, as he hitched his horse.

Libby couldn't hold back her smile any longer. That was no way for him to be treating his future bride. He sure wasn't marrying for love.

As the men went through their warm-up drills, Libby watched Sam with the same unabashed interest as everyone else. That he was an experienced hurler was without dispute, but in her opinion, he was holding back. That came as no grand revelation. Sam was a showman at heart. He'd save his tricks for the right moment.

"Let's get this game started," the pastor called out.

She took her position behind the catcher and home plate. Sam stepped up to the mound. He winked at her, flipping his tawny hair from his forehead. The sun caught the strange gold flecks in his eyes so that they seemed to glint.

That could also be her imagination. Libby'd gotten fanciful lately. She blamed him for that, too.

Sam lobbed the first pitch underhand, according to the rules. The striker swung, missing the ball by a mile. The catcher fumbled and dropped it.

Libby was impressed. The striker at the plate was no Harley Temple, but he was still one of the town's better players.

Now that he'd taken the striker's measure, Sam's next pitch had more weight behind it. It came in fast and low, but within bounds, and Libby knew what was coming. The catcher threw himself out of the ball's path. She shifted sideways in an effort to avoid it, but it struck her hip hard.

Sam jogged toward home plate, his face tight with concern. Pastor Endicott did, too. Libby waved them both off, embarrassed by the attention.

"It's nothing," she said. Both men looked at her, then at each other, uncertain what to do next. She could see that Sam in particular was reluctant to return to the mound without some sort of reassurance. "Marshal Kyote, that's an impressive arm you have on you."

Sam's golden-green eyes promised he'd be doing a more thorough investigation of her later. Libby's toes curled in her boots. It was impossible to feel like one of the boys when he looked at her in a way that made her insides turn all hot and soft.

Pastor Endicott nudged the shame-faced catcher with an elbow. "I had no idea your fingers were so delicate. Would you like someone else to take over your position?"

The catcher tossed the ball he'd retrieved in his palm, ignoring the jibe. "My apologies, Sheriff. The marshal surprised me, is all. Next time, I'll be better prepared."

After that, the game progressed well.

Harley Temple limped to the plate. His wooden leg scuffed through the dirt a half-step behind him. At over six and a half feet, he was a giant. He had a full head of black hair. It also covered his broad face, and sprouted from the backs of his hands and fingers. His biceps were as big around as the pipe on Libby's wood stove. His chest was as wide as her horse's. It was rumored he'd lost his leg while working on the railroad. He wasn't much of a talker, and no one was bold enough to inquire, so it was impossible for anyone to say for certain.

Libby had offered to run bases for him when she'd realized he'd sometimes come out to watch the practices, but never played. The rules didn't forbid it, and once everyone saw what he could do with a bat and a well-hurled ball, he was in.

Harley tapped the bat against his enormous black boot. Libby rolled up her sleeves and got into position a few steps from the plate, so Harley didn't hit her by accident when he swung.

Sam and the catcher had reached a mutual understanding. He hurled the first pitch faster than the last ones, but not so hard that the catcher couldn't handle the ball with his bare hands. Harley, however, had been watching Sam closely and was ready. The pitch came in a bit to the outside, and while Libby might not have allowed it as legal, she was a runner right now and not an umpire. They operated on the honor system, and the pitcher was responsible for calling it.

Besides, Harley's reach was impressive. So was his speed. He caught the ball with the tip of the bat, sending it fast and low straight down the pitch.

Libby took off like a rabbit as soon as she heard the crack of the bat. She approached first base at full speed, saw no one coming at her, and didn't slow down. She rounded the base and headed for second.

From the corner of her left eye, she spotted a fast-moving blur. Sam had the ball, and rather than give it up to the second baseman, he was pursuing Libby himself, planning to cut her off before she could reach safety.

She judged the distance between Sam and second base, and the space she had left to run. She never slowed, but instead, dropped onto her right calf and thigh in a long slide, folding her left leg and throwing her hands high as she did. She kept her attention focused on touching the base with her foot. Nothing else mattered. Either he caught her or he didn't.

She felt her foot connect with Sam's ankle at the same time he reached second, knocking him off balance as she finished the slide. He threw his arms up, just as she'd hoped. He windmilled in slow motion, unable to regain his footing, and toppled on top of Libby, knocking the air from her lungs with his weight.

He brought his arms down on either side of her face. His chin connected with her forehead and she heard the faint click of his teeth striking together.

He grinned down at her, the gold flecks in his eyes sparkling. He touched the ball to her collarbone, just below her jaw where he knew it was sensitive, and Libby's toes burst into flames. "You're out, Sheriff Mayden."

"In your dreams, Marshal Kyote," she wheezed back. "If you check, you'll find my boot's on second base."

Sam didn't budge. "We'll have to consult the umpire. Oh, wait. That would be you." His grin widened, and now Libby couldn't breathe for a whole different reason. "How are you planning to call it from this position?"

His face so close to hers he could kiss her if he chose, and with him smiling at her as if she were the only other person in the world, some of her earlier irritation with him slipped away. It was hard to pretend she didn't know every inch of his body already when the familiar, sun-heated scent of his skin made her dizzy with a desire for more adventure.

The fact of the matter was, Libby had gotten herself too attached. She liked everything about Sam Kyote. The way he smiled. The way he smelled. How he touched her, like she was pure gold.

Libby was anything but.

Her heart started to pound, but this time, with panic. She knew a lot about baseball, but the game Sam was playing was out of her league. She put her hands on his chest and tried to push him off her, but he was heavy and she didn't have all her breath back. "So far we've used the honor system for questionable plays, but if you're going to be a regular member, I can see we'll be revisiting the actual rules."

A shadow fell across them.

"I'd say she's safe," the second baseman interrupted, bending to peer down at them with his hands braced on his thighs. "But we can consult with the pastor, if you'd like another opinion. He seems mighty interested in what's delaying the game over here, Marshal Kyote."

"Safe it is, then," Sam said, but his eyes promised Libby something else altogether.

He helped her to her feet. She took the base, her thoughts all snarled in her head.

The game ended an hour later. Several of the men stopped to talk with Sam.

As Libby walked off the field alone, Bess approached her.

"Thank you, Sheriff Mayden!" she cried, throwing her plump arms around Libby and hugging her with youthful exuberance. "I knew I could count on you!"

Chapter Twelve

Sam rode his horse at an easy pace on the way out of town, waiting for Libby to catch up so they could ride home together.

Once out of sight of the ball field, he dismounted and gathered a small posy of brightly colored wildflowers growing amid the rocks and desert scrub. It wasn't much, but after Cash's comments that morning, he thought a small peace offering might be in order.

He watched her approach, sitting tall and graceful in the saddle, and marveled at his good fortune that she'd decided to be adventurous with him.

She reined in when she reached him.

Confusion, and a charming pink blush, flushed her cheeks as he handed the flowers to her. She looked even more beautiful when she was flustered, and he was glad he'd thought of the tiny gesture, because she seemed so pleased by it.

Her horse shied at a shadow, dancing a few steps to the side, and he caught its bridle to steady it as Libby grabbed for her hat with the hand clutching the posy.

"What are these for?" she asked, examining the pink and yellow petals once her hat was secure and her mount under control.

"For protecting my honor this morning," Sam said. "My reputation will be ruined if anyone discovers I'm keeping company with the most beautiful woman in town."

"It certainly will," Libby agreed. "Since you're practically engaged to Bess Miller."

He almost fell over. "I'm what?"

"You make a lovely couple," she added. Fun slipped into her too-serious eyes, warming the ocean blue of their depths.

"Have I ever spoken to her?" He searched his memory and came up empty.

"You lifted your hat to her at the ball field, right before the game. You might have said something."

"Now it makes sense. I can see how a polite greeting in public might have been misconstrued as a marriage proposal. I'll be expecting her daddy to show up at my spread tonight with the preacher and a shotgun in tow." Sam smiled up at Libby. "Unless I can hide out at your place."

She didn't say yes. She didn't say no, either. Long, gold-tipped lashes dropped over her eyes like a curtain coming down at intermission. Sam got the sense that something was troubling her and he didn't think it was his supposed engagement.

"Bess fancies herself in love with a cowboy," she said.

He pressed a hand to his heart. "It'll be a sacrifice, but I'm willing to step aside for the happy couple."

"The cowboy's Cash Robson."

He winced. "Dang. Jilted for Cash Robson. That's hard on the ego."

Libby studied her flowers. "She asked me if I'd keep company with you. She thinks people will believe you're courting me because of that ridiculous legend Pete spouts on about."

"The one with the walking moon? Why didn't you tell me about this intriguing local legend before this? It would have saved us both a lot of time and inconvenience, seeing as how we're destined to be together."

"Pete made that legend up. It's an unfortunate play on our names. And now, thanks to your little display at the ball game, Bess thinks I'm doing her a favor by encouraging you so that she can be with Cash."

Sam folded his arms across his chest. "I'm beginning to feel used. You ladies are trifling with my affections."

"Would you be serious? Bess is going to get herself into trouble." She bit her lip, looking worried. "Pastor Endicott was right. I'm not a good role model for young women."

"What Bess does with Cash has nothing to do with you. And Pastor Endicott found an excuse to speak with you in a professional capacity is all, by giving you a lecture on morals, because he wants you for himself." Libby started to laugh, but by now, Sam wasn't amused. "I'm serious. You think the men around here see you as one of them. What they see is a beautiful woman who doesn't need a man to take care of her. They've got nothing to offer you. They're intimidated by you, and they know you're too good for them, so they try to diminish you. Endicott's not intimidated, but he wants you to believe he'd be doing you a favor by courting you, so he's playing his cards with more care. He suspects he's lost the first hand to me, but believes he's still got money left in the pot."

Libby's eyes had gone wide. "Are you *jealous*?"

She sounded as if she couldn't quite believe it, which riled Sam even more. He knew what Endicott's game was, and it wasn't baseball.

"Damn straight I am." And he wasn't used to the feeling. "You're an exercise in frustration. You refuse to make a commitment to me even though I asked you to marry me. Why wouldn't I be jealous when another man expresses an interest in you?"

"I'm saving you from making a grievous mistake. You don't know anything about me."

"Then why don't you tell me what I need to know."

"The fact that I grew up with the Mayden gang isn't enough?"

It really wasn't. She was hiding something.

Sam debated with himself. If he wanted her to be honest with him, then he should be open with her. Whatever her father had done, he didn't believe she had dealings with Sky People. Not back then, and not now. Besides, what good were his talents to him if he couldn't put them to use?

"I want to show you something," he said. "I think you'll be impressed." He lifted his hands, silently inviting her to let him help her from the saddle.

She slid off her horse and into his arms. "There's no need, Marshal," she said, the tongue-like lick of her breath on his throat sending shivers straight through him. The brim of her hat brushed his cheek as she tipped her head back to look at him. "While I agree it's impressive, I've seen it already."

Sam chuckled softly. "We can save that for later. This is something else you've already seen, but I've never fully explained it to you."

He told her about the nanoparticles injected into his blood, and where they'd come from. He waited for the questions. She didn't ask any. In typical Libby fashion, she rolled his words around in her head before expressing either skepticism or belief.

Then, "Show me," she said.

They were all alone with nothing but the fading blue sky and a slight breeze for company. The next homestead was Sam's. Coyote Bluff was a tiny ripple of rooftops on the opposite horizon. Between them, the desert was miles of wide open space.

He'd spent some time thinking about the perfect illusion for Libby. She was practical. No nonsense. So he thought he'd give her the opposite. She wasn't used to pretty things or fine gestures. That didn't mean she couldn't appreciate them. It was hard for her to miss something she'd never had.

He'd courted her backwards. Now, he wanted to offer her romance.

"Close your eyes."

Her long lashes, the ones that tickled his cheek when she slept in his arms with her face pressed to his, fluttered shut. She still held the flowers he'd given her, bright pinks and yellows against the dusty white of her blouse. Dirt coated the leg of her trousers where she'd slid into second base. He took her hand in his and squeezed her fingers. A smile of anticipation lifted the corners of her mouth, but she kept her eyes closed. Sam swallowed hard.

Pastor Endicott could find an adventuress in some other

town. Libby was his.

He concentrated on setting the illusion in place, making sure all of the details were right. Then he stood behind Libby with his arms wrapped around her waist so he was looking over her shoulder.

He'd outdone himself. The headache was minor, and a small price to pay.

"My expectations are suitably high," she said, although she sounded more indulgent than curious.

Sam had reasonable confidence she'd change her mind in a moment. Still, he was nervous. He wasn't certain what Libby would like, only what she deserved, and he might have made a mistake. "You can open your eyes now."

Libby did. She gasped.

Except for the deepening sky, the desert was gone. He'd hung gaslight chandeliers, crafted of thousands and thousands of tiny crystals, from the sky, that shimmered and sparkled as they twisted and turned. Imaginary walls had been strung with long strands of thousands more glittering gems. An enormous dance floor was empty except for two lone figures.

At the very center, he'd created an illusion of Libby. He'd dressed her in a fine ball gown of a deep, dusky rose, although he'd kept the skirt less full than was fashionable because he'd like for his illusion to be capable of holding her close. She wore her hair bundled high on her head in a complicated mass of curls, exposing the length of her neck and her bare shoulders. A silky pair of gloves covered her arms to the elbow. She looked beautiful, although in his opinion, no more so than usual. The object was to please her, not him, however. He would have left her hair long and loose, and dressed her in one of his shirts, with her legs bare. Or dressed her in nothing at all.

At the far end of the room, he'd created an illusion of himself. He was dressed in a black top hat and tails, and he carried a long-stemmed red rose.

At the edge of the illusion, where he watched with the real Libby, he tightened his arms around her and breathed in the familiar, fresh scent of her. Even though she'd been running bases and standing in the heat all afternoon, she managed to smell feminine, like sunshine, not sweaty the way he no doubt did.

Illusion Sam crossed the length of the gleaming dance floor to where Libby, in her pretty pink dress, awaited him. Music began, swelling until it filled the room with the strains of a round dance that wasn't too quick. Sam bowed, held out the rose, and waited for Libby to accept both it and his hand. She stepped into his arms, and he spun her around the entire room beneath the sky and the sparkling rays of the crystal lights. They passed so close to the real Sam and Libby that he swore he felt the brush of the breeze from her swirling skirts.

Libby watched the illusion without saying a word. He hoped it was delight that was leaving her speechless. Otherwise, her silence didn't bode well.

The dance ended, the final notes of music dying away. The light from the gas-lit chandeliers dimmed. Illusion Sam took a step back but kept his hold on Libby's hands as he gazed at her, everything the real Sam felt for her shining through his eyes.

The illusion faded away with the last of the music. The desert returned, wide and empty and as silent as Libby, still in his arms with her back pressed to his chest. He kissed the soft curve of her throat and continued to hold her, giving her time to absorb what she'd seen.

Then he shifted her in his arms, turning her so that they faced each other. His heart pounded like crazy. She clutched the posy he'd given her in one hand. He took her free hand in his as he got down on one knee before her. "Libby Mayden, will you marry me?"

She gripped his fingers so tight he figured she'd leave imprints. Her gaze remained serious, never wavering from his. She didn't ask any of the million questions he'd assumed she would have.

Slowly, she withdrew her hand from his clasp. "I think it might be best if you and I spend time apart."

Carson never went into Washington's Hell's Bottom district. After the end of the war it had been settled by soldiers with nothing left to do except fight for the sake of it. Murderers, thieves, and drunks now called it home.

It was also the perfect place to hide in DC for anyone not wanting others to know of their presence. So while Carson never went in, he sometimes arranged for others to come out.

He walked to a drinking establishment at the edge of the district, not too far from the White House but close enough to Hell's Bottom that no one of importance would see him. The evening air reeked of urine and vomit. He handed a young boy on the street corner a few coins and a message, and sent him off to deliver it. Then he went inside and found a small booth buried in the shadows at the back, hidden by the bar and well away from the door.

If he didn't need to make contact with Birch he wouldn't be here. But Judge Rowe had stayed in Washington, so he'd been forced to stay, too.

He'd been patient long enough. Kyote had been back in Coyote Bluff for at least a week now, and so far, he'd not sent any word. Carson wanted to know what was happening. If Kyote had learned anything from Libby Mayden. If this box Rowe had spoken of truly existed.

It was time to put a little pressure on the outlaws who'd once ridden with Mayden. Judge Rowe had made it clear that going after Mayden's daughter might bring them out of hiding. That's what Carson planned to do next. Have Birch push them a little. If Libby Mayden died in the process it was nothing to him. She was a retired gunfighter. No one would care.

But a dead marshal would raise too many questions. That had to be handled with care. Replacing Sam wouldn't be easy. Being in Washington created communication problems. He couldn't contact Birch by telegraph to give him instructions without the entire world knowing about it.

So he waited thirty-seven minutes for his message to be answered.

The man who responded was tall and thin, and he had to duck his bald head when he entered the bar. He had the pale skin of a cadaver. He didn't look right or left, but headed straight for the table where Carson was sitting. He was unlike the Sky men Carson normally dealt with, however, which was why he'd survived for so long in Hell's Bottom. He had no soul. No conscience. His frigid, unblinking gaze left no doubt that he'd kill a man on the spot, with no warning or provocation. Everywhere he went people automatically stepped out of his way. No one dared challenge him.

And Carson wondered if maybe—just maybe—he had dealings with Judge Roy Rowe, too.

The man squeezed his lanky frame onto the narrow bench across the table from Carson. He reached up and yanked a curtain across the booth to give them more privacy, and the already confined space became claustrophobic.

He fixed those empty, unblinking eyes on Carson. "What do you want?"

"I need you to get a message to Jace Birch and his men for me."

Those eyes, with the overly dilated pupils showing more black than white, never wavered. "Send a telegram. Use smoke signals. I'm not your messenger service."

Carson knew his worth or he wouldn't have come. "I supply you with a level of protection you'd never get from anyone else."

"You've profited from it, too." The Sky man leaned forward, shrinking the already confined space and consuming the breathable air. "Make no mistake, Mister Whitley. No one is irreplaceable."

"Perhaps not irreplaceable," Carson conceded. "Simply well-connected and conveniently situated." He nudged a shiny new marshal's badge across the table's scarred, sticky surface with his fingertips. "I need this delivered along with my message. Marshal Birch has been deputized."

That should put a little pressure on someone.

Chapter Thirteen

It had been two weeks. Libby was no closer to resolving her conflict as to where her loyalties resided.

Her difficulties had nothing to do with what had been done to Sam. That was between him and his government. She knew as well as he did that Sky People were out there, and it stood to reason that the government would want to take measures against them. That same government would care nothing about the wellbeing of one man.

But Sam was a federal marshal. If he ever discovered Coyote Bluff was a haven for Max Mayden's old gang, and that Judge Roy played a significant role in their relocation, there was no telling what the results might be. His government had no loyalty to him as an individual. He, however, had sworn loyalty to it as an institution.

Hence her conundrum. Coyote Bluff needed a sheriff it could trust. A marshal like Sam deserved a wife he could trust, too.

"Good morning, Sheriff."

She looked up from the stack of mail on her desk to find Pastor Endicott standing in front of her. The door was propped open to let air circulate through. She'd been lost in her thoughts and hadn't noticed his entrance. "Good morning, Pastor."

They chatted a little about baseball, the weather, and church attendance on Sundays before he came around to the real purpose of his visit.

"Bess Miller tells me you and Sam Kyote are courting."

Lying to a preacher felt wrong, but going into a detailed explanation wouldn't be right either, especially with one who had the ear of Judge Roy, so she was stuck telling half-truths. To everyone. Besides, she and Sam weren't seeing each other right now, and she had no idea whether or not the situation was permanent. He could be stubborn. And she wasn't changing her mind.

She chose her words with care. "Bess is mistaken. Marshal Kyote and I barely know each other."

"I told her there had to be a misunderstanding."

Pastor Endicott sounded smug, and certain of his facts, and it annoyed Libby. For the life of her, she couldn't imagine why Sam might be jealous of him. She liked the pastor. Endicott was friendly and personable, even if somewhat judgmental, and his ability to fight gave him a layer of complexity most people would never suspect. He liked baseball. He was also quite handsome—tall, blond, and rugged. Fearless, too.

But Libby didn't have the slightest desire to be adventurous with him, and he gave her no reason to believe he would want her to try. He didn't look at her the way Sam did, with promise and heat. There wasn't a spark of male interest in Pastor Endicott's eyes.

Although today, she saw plenty of speculation.

"Can I help you with something?" she asked. "Do you require my services?"

"I'm here to offer mine. I'd like to speak frankly and in confidence with you, in my capacity as pastor."

Libby braced herself for another lecture on Jezebels. "I assure you, I listened quite carefully to your sermon last Sunday, and also when you spoke to me frankly and in confidence prior to that."

"I find I have reason to retract at least part of that message. I would like to request a small favor of you. I'm not asking you to do anything immoral," he added hastily. His face reddened.

"Since you say it isn't immoral…" she murmured, curious. That covered a lot of territory. She wondered what could be making Pastor Endicott blush like a schoolgirl. He'd removed his shirt in front of her without a second's hesitation. Of course, the only man around these parts who viewed her as a woman was Sam.

"Mae Miller believes that Bess is seeing someone on the sly who she considers unsuitable. I'm telling you this with her permission, and in the strictest confidence," he added. "You and the marshal are neighbors. You seem to have a mutually congenial acquaintance. You have a love of baseball in common. Mae thought you might encourage his attentions toward Bess in the hopes she'll come to see how a gentleman should treat a lady and it'll spark her common sense. The marshal is an excellent option for her."

"What if the marshal isn't interested in Bess?"

Pastor Endicott seemed taken aback by the possibility. "Oh, I'm quite certain he is. Mae is convinced of it."

Then Mae Miller had gone mad. How unfortunate. She'd always seemed like a lovely woman, even if too involved in her daughter's life. Then Libby remembered Cash Robson and decided a little parental involvement wasn't amiss.

"I'll think on it," she said.

Pastor Endicott hadn't been gone more than ten minutes before a second shadow darkened her door. She expected it to be him again, returning with something he'd forgotten to say. When she looked up, however, she found a tall man with cold, expressionless eyes watching her. He held his hat in his hands. A shiny badge was pinned to his shirt and he carried a Peacemaker.

"Good afternoon, Ma'am," he said. "My name's US Federal Marshal Jace Birch. I'm investigating unusual activity in the area."

A second marshal had been sent. She wondered how frequent the Sky People sightings had become. How widespread. And why they were happening now, after so many years.

Why Coyote Bluff?

She introduced herself in return. "What kind of unusual activity are you referring to?"

The marshal toyed with his hat. "I'm not at liberty to discuss it, ma'am. Suffice it to say, anything that can't be easily explained."

He was Special Division then, same as Sam. Her heart began to race. Why would they send two of their marshals to the same area? What special talents did this man possess?

"We already have a marshal around here," she said.

"Coyote Bluff is a quiet town. I'm surprised anyone would see the need for a third lawman."

"There's no active marshal in Coyote Bluff at this time."

Birch sounded definite. She knew that was untrue.

"Sam Kyote bought a spread a few miles outside of town."

"Marshal Kyote has been suspended from duty. In order to be reinstated, he'll need to meet a list of requirements. I'll be discussing those with him later on when I take a ride out to his place. Which brings me back to my original purpose for stopping here to speak with you," Birch continued. "From now on, any reports of unusual activity are to be made to me."

That cold gaze made her shiver. "While I thank you for your interest in Coyote Bluff," she said, "I serve as the law here. I'm capable of making my own decisions as to when federal involvement in its affairs is required."

"I'm aware of your reputation, Sheriff Mayden. Certainly, any help you wish to provide will be welcome. But this is a federal matter."

"I'm not convinced that all the unusual activity in Coyote Bluff falls under federal jurisdiction. Some of the residents can be quite colorful. I'd think you'd need to be a touch more specific."

Marshal Birch gave her a thin, unsettling smile. He settled his hat on his head. "Good afternoon, Sheriff."

She went to the door and watched him as he rode the length of the town's one street, then headed for the trail that led into the desert toward Sam's place.

Pete Gaster strolled the boardwalk in the direction of the jail, a home-rolled cigarette caught between his teeth and lower lip. He half-turned as he, too, watched the new marshal ride off. His eyes narrowed. "Who was that?"

"You've never seen him before?" Libby asked, surprised.

"First time I laid eyes on him, this very second."

If Pete, the town gossip, knew nothing about him, that meant he hadn't been in town long—yet Marshal Birch had known in which direction to ride to find Sam's homestead.

It might be nothing.

To Libby, however, that qualified as unusual activity.

Sam leaned into the shaft of the crowbar and pried another rotted board off the doorstep.

He'd been respectful, giving Libby the distance she believed she needed, but since she hadn't said a flat out no to marriage, he viewed this as nothing more than a minor setback. He understood reservation. He'd had cold feet himself more than once when a woman got more serious than he did but things were different between him and Libby. Her refusal to marry him was plain stubbornness on her part.

And worry over Endicott taking advantage of his absence continued to nag him. The preacher was no fool. He'd already taken note that Libby was something special. He'd move in when he decided the timing was right.

The shadow of a horse and rider appeared on the horizon. Another damaged board groaned free as Sam waited to see who was coming to visit.

The tall, thin man in the saddle, with legs too long for his horse, was a stranger. As Sam descended the front steps to greet him, he spotted the gleaming badge pinned to the faded red shirt and knew at once why he was here. Whitley had run out of patience.

"Good day," the stranger said, touching the brim of his hat with his fingertips. "My name's Jace Birch. I'm your new partner."

No telegram had been sent to prepare him. Sam found that peculiar.

He leaned on his crowbar, wiping his face on his sleeve. "You've been misinformed. I'm here on sick leave, not in an official capacity. I'm in no need of a partner."

"Seems your sick leave's been canceled. Washington's been getting reports of strange happenings around here. Gunfire at night. Dead bodies that don't look quite right." Birch dismounted, wrapping the reins around the horn of his bay's saddle. "A tightlipped sheriff who has a questionable past and maybe doesn't adhere to the law as strict as she should," he added.

Mention of Libby raised the hair on the back of Sam's neck. He hadn't forgotten Whitley's words or the way he'd tried to plant doubts about her.

"This is the West. There's plenty of gunfire at night. People shoot at all kinds of critters too close to their property, two-legged and four. And while I'm not sure what you mean about dead bodies looking right or wrong, I'd have to guess a lot would depend on how they died. It also seems to me Sheriff Mayden's as law abiding as anyone else in these parts. This isn't the East, after all. Out here they don't play by civilized rules."

Birch's expression never changed. It was as if he had no emotion. "Speaking of civilized. There've also been reports of outlaws hiding out here."

"In Coyote Bluff?" Sam started to laugh. "If that's true,

then they've turned over a new leaf. They aren't a bother to anyone. This is Judge Roy Rowe's territory. He's not known for his tolerance."

"No. He's not. But it's claimed he'll give a man one second chance—as long as he's running."

"That's not much of a chance. Out here he'd have nowhere to run but the desert."

"He wouldn't, would he?" Birch mused. His eyes remained flat and cold. Lifeless. They gave Sam chills despite the searing heat of the sun. "A man would need a guide. Someone who knows that desert. Something to think about, isn't it?"

He was being sent a message. Several, if he was reading them right. There were too many allusions to things he'd been warned of or told. Louis had said that Sky People were making friends with powerful men in Washington. At the time, Sam hadn't believed much of what Louis was saying because he'd been too angry. He believed a lot more of it now.

And it made him angrier still because Libby'd gotten caught up in it, too. She'd told him she'd acted as a guide and taken one of the Sky People into the desert. She'd told no one else. He'd bet his life savings on that. So Birch bringing it up now couldn't be good.

He considered his next move. Birch was pushing him. Trying to see what would make him react. Sam couldn't simply stand here and do nothing, but if he killed a federal marshal doing his duty, he'd be hard-pressed to convince anyone he was defending himself. He had to figure out what Birch was up to before he did anything he couldn't undo.

He met Birch's eyes. He tried to project an illusion from

the other man's thoughts in an attempt to find out what he was planning. He came up empty-handed. Despite the dry heat, he started to sweat. Jace Birch was no ordinary marshal—not even for the Special Division.

Wounding him was the next plan of action. A man could survive with one kidney. If the shot turned out to be fatal, then at least one of Sam's questions would be confirmed.

And a whole bunch about the Special Division would be raised.

He had no weapon of his own on him, however. He needed to learn to start keeping one close at hand at all times. That was a western habit he hadn't yet consistently formed. That left him the gun in Birch's holster. He'd have to distract him in order to get it from him.

"Why don't we go in the house and have a cup of coffee so we can discuss your orders from Washington?" he suggested.

He turned as if heading inside. At the same time, a blanket of darkness fell over the yard. He stooped, grabbed up the crowbar he'd let drop to the ground, and struck out with it, catching Birch in the side of the head. Birch staggered a few steps, then regained his balance, shaking it off. Sam threw the crowbar aside and tackled him around the waist, trying to get him to the ground, grappling with him for the gun.

Birch, however, was surprisingly strong.

Sam jammed a fist into his groin, a place he figured was sensitive no matter how a man's inner parts were arranged, and gouged at one of his eyes with a thumb. He got hold of his hand but couldn't wrench the Peacemaker from his grip. He brought his knee down on Birch's gangly wrist and heard a snap as something inside it broke. Birch let out a grunt of pain. Sam snatched the Peacemaker from the dirt, rammed the barrel into Birch's right kidney, and pulled the trigger. Birch's body jerked beneath him, then went still.

And Birch began to change shape. He lengthened. His skin cooled to the touch. He took on a blue color, visible to Sam despite the blackness he'd brought down around them.

Shaking, Sam lurched to his feet. He wiped the sweat from his brow with the back of his hand and breathed deeply, in and out, in and out. His ability to use illusions wasn't much of a weapon, but if used right it made a powerful distraction. Even so, that hadn't been as easy as he would have liked. He'd gotten lucky because he'd caught Birch by surprise. It gave him a firsthand appreciation of the danger Libby had faced, alone in the desert with one of these creatures.

His head was aching with fierce pinpricks of fire. He peeled back the layers of darkness and contemplated the position of the sun. Hours remained until sunset. Birch might not have been working alone, so a trip into town to check on Libby was in order. The pain in his head was slow to recede. He'd never noticed before, but when he created illusions for Libby the headaches never seemed to last very long and they weren't as strong.

He grabbed the dead Sky man by the heels and dragged him into the barn, then unsaddled the horse and set it free in the newly repaired paddock.

An hour later, he rode his own horse into Coyote Bluff. He left it hitched in the shade of the mercantile. He wasn't fool enough to head straight for the jailhouse, not with Libby still not speaking to him, so he aimed for the saloon instead. That was the best place to learn things.

Today the saloon sat almost empty, except for a few locals, the bartender, three strangers, and Sam. The strangers interested him the most. Two of them occupied one table. They were young, and appeared to be cowhands, and he was willing to bet if he asked a few questions, he'd discover they'd recently been let go from the Double U ranch. They fit Libby's description of the men she'd encountered, and they carried what appeared to be their worldly possessions with them. The third man stood at the bar, a foot on the rail and an arm on the counter. He seemed to be alone and involved in a disagreement of some sort with the bartender. Sam's gut tightened. Any or all of these strangers could be Sky People. He didn't dare look in their eyes. Not here. Not in public.

The bartender's name was Eldon. He was addressing the man in the sweat-stained shirt at the bar. "I'm not going to say this again. This is a peaceful town. We don't like strangers poking around causing trouble. I'm not serving you until you check those fancy-handled pistols of yours in with the sheriff over at the jailhouse."

The man gestured to Sam, who'd stepped to the side of the doors but not ventured much farther inside. "He's wearing a gun."

Although no business owner in Coyote Bluff had yet asked Sam to give up his gun, by rights, they could if they wanted. A lot of western towns had laws to the effect that guns couldn't be carried within their limits, except by local law enforcement, which didn't include federal marshals. The law was often ignored with regard to the locals, however, especially when the town was as quiet as this one, where guns were used more for shooting the kind of snake that slithered on the ground than the two-legged variety. But even fools knew that bartenders kept loaded shotguns behind their bars for these types of situations.

Eldon didn't spare Sam a glance. "I'd rather the marshal keep his."

The stranger leaned across the bar and got his face in Eldon's. "Then the sheriff can come here and get mine from me."

"The sheriff don't come in here except for church and on court days," the bartender replied. "She's a lady."

The stranger snorted. "I hear the only woman sheriff in these parts is Max Mayden's daughter, and she ain't no lady."

Eldon did look at Sam this time, just for a second, before his gaze flicked back to the stranger. "Perhaps you'd like to say that a little louder so's the marshal can hear it plainer, because he might decide to disagree. Seeing as how he's courting the sheriff."

One of the locals abruptly kicked back his chair, picked up his hat, and left, the batwing doors screeching behind him as he strode out. His footsteps faded away down the boardwalk. The two unknown men who'd been sitting quietly until now got up to leave, too. One of them accidentally bumped into Sam on his way out the door and muttered an apology.

Sam's gut instincts for trouble went haywire. The man at the bar had drawn too much attention to himself. If any of the three strangers were Sky People it would be the two who'd just left, and now Sam had a problem. He wanted to follow them and make sure they stayed away from Libby, but he could hardly walk away from the drama unfolding right here in front of him. The fool at the bar had come in here spoiling for a fight.

He didn't bother looking Sam's way. "I think I'll check Tilly and Bertha in with the sheriff after all," he said to the bartender. "I hear she's real pretty. And independent. Maybe see if she's interested in taking on a new suitor."

Sam saw red. The stranger had no right to disrespect any woman that way.

Especially not Libby.

He blocked the man's exit. "I believe you were informed that the sheriff's a lady," he said in a silky smooth voice. "Perhaps you didn't mean to sound quite so disrespectful."

The man swayed a little on his feet. Red rimmed his eyes, and Sam knew by the smell of his breath that he'd been drinking long before entering the saloon. Despite the apparent influence of alcohol, the man assessed Sam so carefully his sense of impending disaster flared again.

"My apologies, Marshal. Never knew it was disrespectful to call a woman pretty."

Sam risked a quick look in his eyes and caught the illusion of a fist headed straight for his face. He had to force himself not to duck. It wasn't real. The drunk blinked, not sure of what he'd just seen, and Sam stepped aside, convinced this one, at least, wasn't Sky. Libby wouldn't thank him for defending her honor, and if he started a fight, she'd arrest him as quick as anyone. Maybe faster.

And while he wanted to go check on the other two strangers and ease his mind, he decided it was best if he waited a few more minutes. If he stepped through those doors too close on the heels of this one, he was likely to take a bullet for his troubles.

Eldon had no such concerns. He walked around the bar, adjusting his bowtie, and went straight to the doors. He stood on his toes and peered over the bowed tops.

"Here comes Sheriff Mayden," he said with satisfaction. "And she don't look at all happy."

Libby normally let Eldon Caudel take care of saloon matters himself. The locals, for the most part, were harmless.

But when Boyd came into the jail and warned her that trouble was brewing, and Sam was involved, she decided it was time to assert her authority. She now had two marshals interfering in Coyote Bluff and Libby wasn't standing for it.

"I don't know if the marshal recognized him or not," Boyd said, "but that man's Garvin Haskell. No doubt. I saw his face on a WANTED poster at the telegraph office." Boyd's baby-smooth cheeks shone with hope. "Do I get the reward?"

Dismay filled Libby. She recognized that name, and she had a good idea what Garvin Haskell was doing in Coyote Bluff. Judge Roy had heard the rumors right. Would she never be able to leave her past and reputation behind her?

She strapped on her gun belt. "Yes, Boyd, if I capture him, the reward is yours."

"Dead or alive, right?"

She settled the belt over her hips and reached for the door. "That's what the poster says."

Haskell was coming down the front steps of the saloon just as Libby approached. From the size of the crowd beginning to gather, word of a possible gunfight had already spread.

The driver of a wagon rumbling down the main street toward them saw what was happening and reined his team in, knowing better than to proceed, because shots could—and usually did—go wild. He leapt from the box, unable to turn around because the road was too narrow. While Libby took note of his position, she couldn't afford the distraction of worrying.

"Well, well," Haskell said, a wide smile splitting his unshaven cheeks from one ear to the other as he stepped into the street to face Libby. His guns hung ridiculously low on his hips. "If it ain't Light-fingered Libby, herself."

She winced at the hated name. She hadn't earned it picking pockets, but for the ease with which she drew her guns.

Haskell had his hands positioned away from his sides and at the ready. When he flexed his fingers, Libby knew there was only one way this could end. She checked the streets one last time to make certain all spectators were well out of range. The wagon driver had gotten his team backed up and drawn as close against a building as he could manage.

She fixed her eyes on the outlaw. "Garvin Haskell, you're under arrest."

Sam's voice intruded, disrupting Libby's concentration for a crucial and disastrous second. "Put your hands up where I can see them."

He stood at the top of the steps in front of the saloon, his gun drawn and fastened on Haskell. The rest happened in a blur.

Haskell went for both of his guns. Later, it would occur to Libby that he'd anticipated Sam's presence and been prepared for it. Right now she, however, was not, and a tight ball of dread dropped like a cold stone in her stomach.

The distraction could have cost her Sam's life. Her own hadn't concerned her nearly as much.

Everything happened at once.

With a smooth, practiced movement, she threw her body to one side even as her pistol leapt into her hand. Her bad leg gave out on her and she went down on her knee—most likely saving her life.

She fired off two quick shots—one at Haskell's kidney, and one at his heart.

The shot Haskell aimed at Sam nailed the sign over the saloon, setting it swinging. The one meant for Libby hit her right arm, numbing it. Libby however, had drawn her weapon with her left. She struggled to her feet, her pistol now aimed at Haskell's head, ready to fire again if he so much as twitched.

He didn't move. Instead, he lay sprawled on his back in the dirt, his eyes wide open and staring at the sky.

"Libby!" Sam roared. His boots shook the wooden risers as he clattered down the stairs toward her. He rammed his gun back in its holster. "Are you hurt?"

Blood poured down her arm and dripped from her sleeve to water the dry, thirsty dirt. She stared at him in disbelief over the stupidity of the question, glad he was alive, but also so angry with him she could have shot him herself.

"Of course I'm hurt, Marshal Kyote," she said, as polite and professional as if speaking with a stranger, mindful of the onlookers. "I've been shot." She holstered her pistol with her good hand. The numbness was starting to fade and in its place a fierce, burning brushfire roared from her fingertips to her shoulder, and robbed her of her ability to concentrate on forming her words. "I thought I made it clear you weren't to interfere in town business?"

She could see in his eyes that he wanted to grab hold of her, to reassure himself that she was not seriously injured, and she was afraid if he did, she might fall to pieces.

To his credit and her everlasting gratitude, he didn't.

Instead, he shouted for the doctor.

Chapter Fourteen

Libby lost the argument with the doctor over the use of chloroform while he removed the bullet from her arm.

He was young, with a kind, plain face that gave him the appearance of a boy playing at being a real doctor, but he sounded as if he knew what he was about.

"I need you relaxed," he said, waving evil-looking forceps, "or the entry wound will contract and I'll have difficulty extracting the bullet. If I have to dig around the nerve for it, you could lose the use of your arm. As it is, you might lose the feeling in it."

Libby was reclining on the examining table. A tray of surgical tools stood near her head, the strong smell of antiseptic tickling her nose. She'd removed her fair share of bullets, and the cleanliness of the doctor's office boosted her confidence in him.

Still, she disliked the idea of being sedated.

Sam stood in a corner of the room, patiently listening,

but not interfering until now.

"If I were you I'd take the chloroform," he said to Libby. "A sheriff needs both hands."

She woke a few hours later with a dry mouth, a pounding headache and her arm heavily wrapped.

The doctor sat in a chair beside her, reading a paper. He looked up when she turned her head toward him.

"Wiggle your fingers for me," he said. Libby did so, and he gave a small, satisfied smile that made him look even more like a boy. "That's why I was top of my class." He set down the paper. "Marshal Kyote offered to escort you home when you're able to ride, since he lives so close to you."

"I'm able to ride now," Libby said. The words came out garbled, as if she had a mouth full of wool. *Mmmblrerdnew*.

"Let's give it another hour," the doctor said. "Besides, the marshal had some business to take care of and he hasn't returned yet."

Sam hadn't stayed with her. Libby had no right to feel as lost and disappointed by that news as she did.

He arrived at the doctor's office not too long after she woke.

"Sheriff Mayden," he greeted her, nodding in her direction before turning to question the doctor. "How'd the surgery go?"

"Without a hitch," the doctor replied. "That arm won't be much good to her for quite a while yet, but she should recover the use of it as long as she's careful. See that she's not left alone tonight. Chloroform can cause hallucinations and nightmares until it's out of her system."

"I'll see to it," Sam said.

Other than to check and make sure she was safely seated

in the saddle, he was unusually quiet on the long ride home. A few miles out of town, however, when it was well behind them, he stopped the horses and insisted she ride with him.

"You look like you're going to pass out any second, and I'm not taking any chances you'll fall off your horse."

He settled her into the saddle in front of him. Libby had to confess it was nice to be held in his arms even though it was plain he had more important things on his mind. She was the one who'd said they should spend time apart, so she tried not to let it sting. She'd been through gunfights before without anyone to help her. The old leg wound had been a lot worse than this. It wasn't as if her father had been a nurturing man.

But deep down, she was sick and tired of being strong on her own. More gunfighters would come, and while she was good with her left hand she wasn't likely to be as fast, anymore. She liked Coyote Bluff and she liked being sheriff, but maybe it was time to change her name and move on. The prospect depressed her.

When they reached Libby's place, the red sun had dropped to the horizon and she was beyond exhausted. She agreed to sit in her rocker on the verandah while Sam took care of her horse and the other animals in her barn.

"I have to ride over to my place and do my chores," Sam said to her when he was done. He scanned her face, his golden eyes serious and not teasing her the way they usually did. "I know you're tired and in pain, but you'll have to stay awake until I get back. Can you use your rifle one-handed if you have to?"

"With one eye closed," Libby said, trying to make him laugh, but her attempt at a joke was met with the thinnest of smiles.

She watched him ride away, uneasy. A lump formed in her throat. Not once had he tried to kiss her, or offer her any kind of consoling. She tipped her head back and stared at the deepening sky. She'd known she wasn't the sort of woman most men felt the need to coddle. But she'd thought Sam felt different toward her.

He'd said nothing to her about the new marshal either, which was also disquieting. It illustrated how very little she and Sam shared about themselves with each other. She knew no more about him than he did her.

The restless energy left over from the gunfight, as well as the nagging residuals of the chloroform, left her too wound up for sleep but not fully alert. The doctor's warning about possible hallucinations and nightmares increased her anxiety. In her head, over and over, she could hear her father's stern voice as well.

Never give up a hostage.

He used to tell her that once the hostage was freed, her life was worth nothing. She thought she should know why that advice applied to her current situation, but before she could put her finger on it, she realized she was no longer alone. She must have dozed off.

She grabbed for her rifle, her bandaged arm and aching head making her clumsy, and brought the barrel up to rest on her knees as she tried to identify the two riders in her yard. Twilight disguised them so that at first, Libby had no idea who they were. One was a mountain on horseback. The second, a slight woman with gingham skirts hiked up to her knees so she could straddle her pony. Her stirrups had been ridiculously shortened so that she'd need help in dismounting.

The mountain slid off his horse like a slow-moving avalanche.

"G'd ev'nin' Sheriff," he called to Libby, his voice gentle and quiet where one would expect gruffness and strength. He moved to the other horse and lifted the tiny figure from her saddle.

William and Mary Lou Bennett.

Libby relaxed her finger on the trigger. This was an unexpected visit. The hour was getting late and they were miles from home. She hoped William hadn't brought his wife out for her to arrest, because she wasn't up to the challenge tonight.

"Good evening," she said, and invited them each to take a seat on the verandah beside her. "I'd offer you something to eat or drink, but I haven't had a chance to prepare anything. I don't get much company."

"We heard about the gunfight. We came to bring something for you, not for you to wait on us," Mary Lou said.

The steps creaked beneath William's weight. He carried a large pot. "I'll set this in the kitchen. We already had it cooked so we brought it straight over."

"Thank you. It smells wonderful," Libby said, and meant it. Mary Lou's reputation for cooking was even more famous than her temperament.

William was back a minute later, settling his giant frame carefully onto a plain wooden bench.

Libby listened with half an ear as Mary Lou talked. She was used to her chatter, having spent many hours listening to it at the jail, although it felt odd to hear it in her own home. She wondered how long Sam would be, and hoped the Bennetts were gone before he returned. All she wanted right now was to crawl into bed and fall asleep in his arms, which just went to show how weak and dependent she'd become.

"What was it like growing up in an outlaw gang?" Mary Lou asked.

The question dragged Libby's attention back to her guests. In all the times she'd had Mary Lou at the jail, not once had the other woman expressed any interest in her.

"I didn't know anything else, so to me, it was normal," she said. "Most of the time it was dull." She'd been given an education, which was more than a lot of children living transient lives in the West could claim. Her father had surrounded himself with well-read, intelligent people who'd been happy to help teach her. Her father, too, had been highly educated. He'd once studied the law, an irony she found especially funny tonight.

William, too, was a well-educated man. It made his choice in women that much more perplexing.

"We heard the marshal escorted you home." Mary Lou looked at Libby's open front door as if she expected him to appear. Her face was alive with curiosity. "I don't see him anywhere."

"The doctor asked him to make sure I didn't fall off my horse. He has his own property to attend to," Libby said.

"It's for the best. I heard he's courting Bess Miller."

Libby couldn't figure out how everyone was hearing this rumor, which had little truth to it, and yet Bess and Cash managed to keep their romance a secret. She guessed people heard what they wanted.

"It's a shame, though," Mary Lou added. "Pretty woman

like you. If you'd like, I could give you advice on how to win the marshal back. Bess seems like a nice girl, but she'd never keep him in line. Not the way a man needs." She patted William's knee.

"Thank you." There wasn't much more Libby could say to such an offer.

Then her mind started to work on the reason behind the Bennetts' unexpected visit. They usually kept to themselves—other than the times Mary Lou spent with Libby in jail. She was starting to think that maybe the Bennetts were Sky People. Mary Lou certainly had the coldhearted part down. And while up until now all the ones Libby'd encountered had been male, she had no reason to believe they couldn't also be women.

But while she didn't know William well, she'd known him long enough. Unless someone had switched bodies with him, he wasn't one of the Sky People.

Maybe it was only Mary Lou.

Or maybe it was the gunshot and the chloroform talking.

"You could come home with us," Mary Lou was saying, "so you won't be alone tonight. You wouldn't want that gunshot to fester. Things like that can turn fatal real quick."

Libby's breathing picked up. Her fingers itched to grab the rifle she'd rested against her chair.

Hallucinations, she thought. Seeing and hearing things that weren't real. Reading too much into a simple, well-intentioned gesture because it came from an unexpected source.

"I appreciate the kind offer," she said, "but I'd rest easiest in my own bed."

The Bennetts stayed a while longer. When they finally

rode off, she took her rifle, went into the house, and closed the door.

If Sam thought too hard about it he'd never be able to leave Libby alone, not even for a second, so he mounted his horse and rode off without looking back.

He'd seen in her face, and known in his gut, that she wasn't as tough as she let on to the world—just as he knew she'd had no other choice in her life but to become that way. There was no doubting her ability to look after herself, though. Pride burned in his chest. He'd already seen how accurate she was with a rifle, but her skill with her pistols was something else again. She'd drawn across her body, left-handed, and taken down an armed man with two well-placed shots, and Sam knew for a fact that she wasn't left-handed. A few of the townspeople assumed she'd lost her touch because she'd needed that second shot, but Sam had understood why she'd aimed for a kidney first. It seemed she worried about Sky People more than gunfighters.

So did he.

While the doctor had tended to her, he'd tracked the two strangers out of town. They'd headed in a different direction from her small homestead, but he'd picked up their trail without too much trouble. He'd seen nothing to suggest they were anything other than what they seemed, which was two boys, down on their luck.

He buried Birch's body and bedded his animals down for the night.

The thin wedge of the moon's first quarter glowed

amongst the night stars as he stabled his horse in Libby's barn. He made lots of noise as he went for the front door. Libby would be groggy with the aftereffects of the anesthetic and the gunfight, and might very well be feeling trigger happy.

She sat waiting in the dark at the kitchen table, her pistol trained on him. Her hand trembled a little from the weight and she looked tired enough to topple onto her pretty face. When she saw who it was, she lowered her weapon to the table top.

Tension flooded the small cabin. It was plain from her expression that she anticipated some sort of confrontation with him. He'd had hours to think about this moment, however, and he didn't say any of the things that had bounced around in his head. He didn't scold her for scaring him, or criticize her for doing what, in the end, was her job. Nor did he ask her to quit, as he'd like. What difference would it make whether or not she was sheriff?

She'd always be Libby Mayden.

So he went with his heart.

"Could you tolerate me hovering around you, just for tonight?" he asked her instead. "Because I'm feeling the need."

The tension in her disappeared. Relief etched her lips. "If you wouldn't mind. I think I could use it," she confessed.

Sam had her wrapped in his arms in an instant, his chin resting on the top of her head, mindful of her injury. "The people in this town have an inordinate amount of interest in your life. I'm warning you of it so you won't be surprised by any conclusions they draw regarding my spending the night if someone should happen to ride out to check on you."

Libby sighed, her breath warm on his throat. "They've already been here. Mary Lou and William Bennett, of all people. They brought me dinner. There's some on the stove if you're hungry. And they've already drawn their conclusions. Pete's foolish legend has put notions in people's heads."

"It's not foolish at all. I am a Trickster. I'm also legendary."

"Of course you are." Her tone suggested she was rolling her eyes, and he had to smile.

"Forget about Pete," he said. "The Bennetts, too. And I'm not especially hungry. I want you to understand I did my best not to interfere in your job today. I'm not going to apologize for trying to keep you from getting shot," he added, not giving her a chance to argue the point, "because I would have reacted the same if any lawman was in a similar situation. I had no way of knowing for sure if that gunfighter came to town with the sole intention of calling you out. He could have been a Sky man. And yes, I admit I was fool enough to let him use me as a distraction. He knew I'd follow him outside once I figured out what was happening. But all that aside, I'm still going to remind you that you agreed not to interfere with my job, either. I need you to be honest with me about something because I believe it's important." He eased them apart and peered into her face in the darkness, wanting to catch her reaction. "What is it you know about Sky People that I don't? What have you been hiding from me?" He took a deep breath, softened his voice, and asked the question that bothered him most, with an answer he suspected he'd least like to hear.

"What happened that scared you so bad?"

She had no wish to dredge through her nightmares. Not even for him. Not when all she wanted was to be held in his arms.

"It's been a long day," she said. "Can't this wait until tomorrow?"

Immediately, Sam was all consideration. "Of course it can wait. We'll talk in the morning."

He helped her into her nightgown, then into bed. He undressed, turned down the wick in the lamp, and slipped in beside her, draping an arm over her waist.

Unfortunately, sleep wasn't going to come easily no matter how tired she was. She was too tightly wound, her thoughts chaotic. Her wound throbbed and burned. She tried not to fidget, to make him think she'd fallen immediately insensible, but he wasn't fooled. He was wide awake, too.

"What's wrong?" he asked.

"I've missed you," she confessed. "These last few weeks have been lonely without you." She'd meant to sound matter-of-fact. Instead, she sounded so…feminine.

"I missed you, too." He brushed her hair aside and kissed the curve of her neck, carefully avoiding the bandages strapping her shoulder. Her heart lurched in her chest. "I'm not going anywhere, Libby. It'll take more than you being skittish of marriage to get rid of me. But I don't want us to be sneaking around like this forever. You've got to learn to share things with me, and let me into your life."

He didn't know what he was asking of her. Her life in Coyote Bluff was built around secrets and lies. No one would want to be part of it. Not for long. And yet he'd had a long day too, and still, his thoughts were all for her. She had to admit, she liked the attention.

She laced her fingers through his. "I've shared plenty more with you than I have any other man. You're sharing my bed."

"Don't think I'm not appreciative. But there are other things you can share with me that would mean almost as much. For instance," his mouth moved to her ear, creating little ripples of heat that tickled her skin, "where is your favorite place in the whole world to be?"

The question drifted lazily in the darkness, wrapping comfort around her, making her doubly grateful for his presence. Squeezing his fingers, she gave it about two seconds of heartfelt consideration. "Right now, it's here with you."

He laughed under his breath. A rough palm moved to touch her cheek as he settled his weight on one hip so that he could look down at her. He propped his head on his hand. "That's a good answer. But pick somewhere else. Someplace special, even if it's a spot you've never seen before, but read about in a book and would someday like to visit. Or somewhere you have nice memories of, but haven't seen in a long time."

"You can do that?" The possibilities both intrigued and alarmed her. "Take something I describe and make an illusion out of it?"

"Sometimes, with certain people, I can take what you're thinking or daydreaming about and project it so that it looks real. It's easiest when you help out. Reality and imagination rarely match up though," he warned her, "so no matter what, it won't be an exact copy. Whatever's strongest in your mind is what you're likely to see."

She mulled over the dangers. She was afraid other

memories might work their way into the illusion. Not all of her secrets were hers to tell. But before she could ask any more questions, Sam tensed.

He lifted his head from the bed. "There's someone outside."

A knock sounded at the cabin door.

Chapter Fifteen

Sam couldn't imagine who'd be at the door at this hour of the night, and more importantly, what they might want. While they could be checking on Libby, the hour was too late for them to be wishing her continued good health.

His hand crept toward the night stand where she kept her gun.

"Don't make any noise," Libby whispered beside him. "Maybe whoever it is will go away."

"You're the sheriff. It might be important." As a lawman himself, Sam felt obliged to point that out.

"If it is, they'll have to ride into town and talk to Pete Gaster to get it sorted out. Until this arm mends I'm not much good to anyone."

Libby might be out of commission but Sam wasn't, and it went against all his instincts as a marshal to ignore a late-night knock on a door. For her peace of mind, however, and mindful of his promise not to interfere in her job, he remained silent. This was her town. She was its sheriff, and she knew it best.

The knocking turned to pounding. Whoever it was at the door, they weren't going to go away.

"You in there, Libby?" a man's voice rang out.

That sure sounded like her deputy.

Libby recognized the voice, too. She sat up, alarm etched on her face. Her alarm, Sam knew, was over the possibility he might be discovered in her bed, but for his part, he wasn't concerned about that in the least. She knew how to stop it from being a problem. All she had to do was marry him.

He locked his hands behind his head and waited to see how this would play out. She'd shown less panic over a gunfight.

"Give me a minute, Pete," Libby called back. Then, "Quick," she commanded Sam, giving him a shove. "Get under the bed."

Sam snagged the back of her nightgown before she could swing her feet to the floor, no longer finding the situation entertaining. Too many things could go wrong.

"Hold on just a minute. What if that's not really Pete at the door?" he asked.

Libby paused. "Who else would it be?"

It didn't matter. He wasn't hiding in safety under the bed while she opened the door to potential danger. "Has he ever come to your door this late at night before?"

Libby made a face. "Lots of times. I don't know if you've noticed, but he's not very good at his job."

Yes, Sam had noticed. Someone was going to have to go to the door, and if it was Pete on the other side, he knew she wouldn't let it be him.

He pressed her pistol into her good hand and draped a blanket over her shoulders. "I'll keep the rifle trained on him from the bedroom," he said. "Don't get between us."

Libby stood to one side of the front door as she lifted the wooden bar, then swung the door wide so the visitor was in Sam's line of vision. It certainly looked like the deputy who was standing on her verandah with his hat in his hands. If not, it was a danged good imitation.

"What's the matter, Pete?" Libby asked. "Is there a problem?"

"Thought I'd check up on you and make sure you're comfortable. The doc says you're going to be laid up for a while." Pete cast a long look into Libby's cabin through the open door, but Sam was confident it was too dark for him to see much of anything.

"I'm fine. But thank you for inquiring," she added as a hasty afterthought.

She sounded surprised by his concern, and a smidgeon of compassion weaseled its way into Sam's heart. She'd been raised by a band of outlaws, which was no fostering environment for a young woman. Not much wonder she found gunfights easier to deal with than courting.

Pete continued to hover in the doorway as if he expected Libby to invite him in, in spite of the late hour. "I'm looking for Marshal Kyote," he finally said.

Sam snapped to attention. Why would Libby's deputy be looking for him?

She leaned against the door frame, casually blocking Pete from entering. "Did you try his place?"

"Yep. He weren't there."

"Is there something you need me to do for you, then?"

she asked, her tone sharper this time.

Sam worried a bit for Pete's safety. Libby didn't get angry, she got impatient—and when she was impatient, there was a real danger her gun might go off.

Pete, it seemed, had a careless disregard for his life. "Thought you might know where he is, seeing as how he escorted you home this afternoon."

"He brought me home, and then he left."

That was true enough. Libby merely neglected to mention that Sam had come back.

"Well, he ain't at his place." Pete shot another quick look over her shoulder.

Either curiosity finally got the better of Libby, or she thought it might look odd if she didn't express more interest in what had the deputy out looking for Sam in the middle of the night.

"Is there an emergency that requires his attention?" she asked.

That was what Sam wanted to know. He lowered the rifle and propped it against the wall, confident the deputy was who he claimed, and posed no danger to Libby other than maybe to elevate her blood pressure.

"Some cows with his brand on them was spotted over in the Rosenbergs' pasture land."

Sam relaxed. There was no emergency. This was Pete Gaster being nosy—and not trying very hard to hide the fact. He waited to see if Pete would bring up that legend. If he did, he was a dead man. At least the moon wasn't full.

"It's late. Marshal Kyote is probably in bed. I'm sure some of the Rosenbergs' cattle are on his land, and mine too, for that matter. We'll get them all sorted out at roundup time." She yawned. "Thank you for your concern." She started to inch the door closed.

Pete stuck his foot over the threshold to keep it from shutting in his face. "If he comes back to collect his horse from your barn, would you mind letting him know I was looking for him?"

"I'll be sure to tell him if I see him. Good night, Pete," she said.

Sam was impressed. She'd made her response without any pause or inflection that might give away her true thoughts. As always, she remained exceedingly polite. She closed the door and dropped the bar in the brackets, then waited with her ear pressed to the panel. After a few seconds, Sam heard the sound of the deputy's boots thudding down the front steps, then hoof beats as he rode away.

Once Libby appeared convinced Pete was gone, she tugged the blanket more tightly around her shoulders and padded back to the bedroom on her bare feet. Sam wondered if he was about to shoulder the blame for whatever conclusions Pete had drawn regarding the horse in the barn. He eased over to let Libby into the bed.

She stretched out on her back and stared at the ceiling. A tiny frown crinkled her forehead. "For the life of me, I can't understand why he's so interested in everything I do."

Sam threw caution to the wind. "While I agree Pete was being nosy, he was checking up on you to make sure you're safe. If you were a bit more open with the local people, they'd be less interested in your personal life and not as apt to interfere."

She turned her head to look at him, as if trying to read his face in the darkness. "How much do you plan to tell people in Coyote Bluff about yourself?"

This was going to be one of those conversations he'd soon wish he had never started. "That's different," he said. "I'll be away most of the time because of my work. I won't be as much a part of the community. They won't get to know me as well as they seem to want to know you."

"Hold on a second." Libby sounded a little too reasonable for Sam's comfort. "You asked me to marry you even though you don't plan on being around much?"

"I'm a marshal." He figured he still was, since his new partner was dead and Washington had no way of knowing if he'd delivered his message. There was also the matter of how a Sky man had managed to get inside the Special Division. He'd known too much about Sam for him to have manufactured it. "My work requires me to travel."

"I met the new marshal. He said you were suspended."

So Birch had stopped at the jail to see her before coming to find Sam. He didn't like that. "He decided not to stay once he heard my side of the story. Seems Sky People scare him. Besides, it's not a suspension. It's sick leave. My ability to create illusions is still somewhat new."

Rather than becoming upset by the news, she seemed relieved. And pleased. "That's perfect."

Sam wasn't sure which way this conversation was now headed. He chose to remain optimistic. "Does that mean you'll marry me?"

"Your work leaves you in no position to marry anyone. Our original arrangement suits both our needs. If you continue to keep to yourself, as soon as you're gone back to Washington everyone will forget about a possible connection between us. That means whenever you're in town, you can come and go here as often as you please."

He counted to ten. "Before I come over, should I send you a telegram to warn you? In case you're exercising that decision of yours to be non-exclusive?"

There was a heartbeat of silence.

"You're angry," she said.

"Damn straight, I'm angry." And disappointed. Unlike Libby, Sam couldn't turn his emotions on and off.

There was a second, longer stretch of silence.

"You'll never be content with any arrangement between us unless you set the terms, will you?" she asked, although it was more of an acceptance of something she couldn't change than a question.

He almost wished she were a yelling and screaming, throwing things kind of woman, but that wasn't her way, and it made it difficult to read her mood. He checked to make sure her gun was on the nightstand and not in her hand. "That's not what I said."

She prodded his chest with one finger, a sure sign she wasn't happy. "Admit it, Sam. You like the excitement of the hunt, and you like to win. That's why you're a marshal. Getting me to marry you has become a challenge to you."

"You're wrong." But an uncomfortable feeling suggested she might be dead right, and that she could read him easier than he did her. "I could say those same things about you."

She didn't get defensive or thrown off balance the way he had. Instead, she agreed with him. "Yes—except I'm being practical and you aren't. Why can't you accept that marriage isn't for every woman? Or that every woman isn't meant for marriage?"

He scrubbed a hand down his face. He wasn't going to

get anywhere by fighting with her. Libby was as stubborn as he was. She wasn't wrong about him liking the excitement and the challenge of pursuing her, but she wasn't right, either. He wanted to marry her because he was in love with her, but it was too soon to tell her so. Not when she wasn't being honest with him—not about her involvement with the Sky People, and not about her feelings for him.

Disappointment gnawed at his heart like a dog chewing on a bone. She couldn't be honest about her feelings for him because she didn't know what they were. Not if she couldn't even carry on a proper argument with him.

So, for the time being, he let the subject of marriage drop. He'd work on her involvement with Sky People instead.

"I promised you another illusion."

She stifled a yawn with her fingers, and her eyelids drooped. "Could I have it tomorrow?"

"Whenever you'd like."

The hour was late now, and she shouldn't have any more difficulty falling asleep. Afraid he might injure her arm by accident, rather than holding her as he would have preferred, he placed a small amount of space between them so that they faced each other in the bed but didn't touch. It was going to be a long night for him, to have her so near and yet be unable to reach for her. His desire for her had grown deep enough roots by now that she filled his thoughts no matter how hard he tried to clear them.

"Sam?"

Her voice, drowsy and more sensual than she could possibly intend given the hour and the circumstances, made him smile and ache with desire at the same time. "Yes?"

She slid a hand under his head and leaned closer to kiss

him. She tasted sweet and smelled warm, like sunshine, and he tried not to think about how much he wanted her because this wasn't the time.

"You'll never need to send any telegrams to warn me that you'll be coming home to spend the nights with me," she said. "I'm not interested in marriage, but I don't want to be adventurous with anyone but you."

Chapter Sixteen

"Are you ready for this?" Sam asked.

They were seated beside Libby's kitchen table, facing each other, their chairs pulled close together so that their knees were touching.

Libby wore a man's white shirt over her heavy bandages, a pair of shabby buckskin breeches, and plain-buckled shoes. Sam decided she could make wearing a feedbag seem gorgeous to him. If she were in pain this morning, she wasn't letting on. Her lovely face, with its strikingly slanted, wide blue eyes and high cheekbones, had taken on a hue of serious determination.

She looked as if he were leading her to a lynching rather than offering to share an illusion. She'd been frightened by what had happened to her—and it took a lot to scare Libby Mayden.

"Yes," she said in response to his spoken question. "I'm ready."

Her eyes on his face radiated a trust he hoped he deserved. He took her good hand in his, not because it was necessary for what he was about to do, but because he liked to touch her as often as possible. Her fingers were cold as ice. The sooner they did this, the better.

He concentrated, focusing on his ability to project an illusion. The kitchen, and Libby's cabin, all disappeared, leaving the two of them surrounded by desert. Sam experienced a burning sensation in his throat and mouth, suddenly desperate for a drink of water. Wind blew skirls of sand and debris that prickled his face, but Libby's memory of the sensation was faint and eroded by time. Her emotions, however, were not. He felt those, too. This was a new addition to his abilities, one that was far more disturbing.

They were on horseback. Beside them, a tall, thin man swayed in his saddle, his Stetson pulled low on his forehead, and a red and white striped bandanna drawn up so that only his eyes remained visible. There was something not right about the man, Sam knew at once. It was more than a feeling Libby had that he picked up on. The man's pupils swallowed the light of the glaring sun rather than shrink from it.

And his hands...

The fingers on the reins were too long, and hooked like claws at the tips. They were more human than the ones on the Sky People Sam had buried, but close enough to theirs to make him think that this one wasn't able to maintain his human form anymore. That he wasn't well.

The horses plodded along for several more minutes. Libby's anxiety level stayed steady until they reached a jagged crack in the sandstone cliffs. The crack led into a canyon.

The Sky man urged her forward. Libby refused to move.

This is as far as I go, she said. *You can find your own way from here. Pay me the rest of my money and I'm gone.*

The money's in the canyon.

Then I'll make do with what I've already got and you're on your own.

The Sky man must have realized that Libby wasn't going to budge. He made a move for his pistol, but Libby, prepared for it, drew first. Her shot caught him in the chest in what should have been a direct hit on his heart. The Sky man's bullet caught her in the thigh and grazed her horse. The animal reared back, screaming in pain, and tossed her to the ground.

Outside of the illusion, where they sat in the kitchen, Sam could hear her ragged inhales of air. He tightened his fingers around hers, glad he'd thought to take her hand. She squeezed back and her breathing steadied.

The Sky man lifted her to her feet by the back of her jacket and forced her to walk to the canyon, her injured leg dragging as blood from the wound seeped through her trousers. Sam knew by her emotions that the leg wasn't troubling her nearly as much as what waited on the other side of that narrow rock opening.

They passed into the canyon. It took a few seconds for her to gather together her memories of what was inside, as if she found it difficult to make any sense of them. Her thoughts swirled at first before settling into an image of an enormous mechanical ship, crumpled and broken to several large pieces that were buried nose-down in the desert floor. Sam tried to get a better look at it. Round, and gleaming golden in the sun, it looked like two inverted brass dinner plates had been mashed together and soldered into place.

The Sky man dropped any remaining pretense of humanity. When Libby remembered him now, he appeared identical to the dead ones Sam had seen. Then her thoughts were running too rapidly now for him to capture. Everything was becoming a blur. He snatched fleeting images of rows and rows of panels inside one of the pieces of the wreckage, with flashing colored lights and odd-shaped switches, and two chairs to the left of where Libby now stood.

"Nothing can hurt you here," he said to her, hoping to lend reassurance. "Can you concentrate harder and give me a better look at the whole room?"

Her thick fear choked him with tight fists, and if he could take it from her he would, but he needed as much information as possible because he wouldn't do this to her again. The problem was that the information he was getting this time wasn't going to be entirely accurate. She'd already had her memories of the ship corrupted by the one they had seen in the gorge.

Overall, however, he was impressed with her level of recall, whether or not it was accurate. One image in particular recurred over and over in her thoughts, as if she couldn't tear them away from it. It was of a large silver box still attached to the top of a long, broken bench, or maybe a table, partially covered in sand. Whatever the box was, it held some significance for Libby. The emotions she attached to it were complex, and difficult for Sam to peel apart and extract.

The Sky man gestured for her to work it free.

Then all hell broke loose.

The Sky man, too, bled from the wound she'd inflicted on him, although his blood was blue. Libby's elbow rammed into the hole in his chest where she'd shot him. He let out a grunt of pain and loosened his grip on her enough for her to break free. She clawed at the back of her short leather jacket for another gun she'd kept hidden and blasted two more bullets into the Sky man, aiming for internal organs that weren't where they should be. He dropped at the second shot, which struck him in his side—right where Sam knew its heart was contained.

She stood over the Sky man's body, staring at him until her panic and anger subsided and logic returned. Rather than run, as she should, Libby bent down and rifled through his pockets. She yanked out a heavy-looking coin purse before turning her attention to the box on the table.

She pried the box loose from the casings that held it attached to the bench. After another quick look around, she limped away from the wreckage.

"That's enough," she said from where she sat facing Sam, in her kitchen. She sounded ill.

He dropped the illusion at once. Libby, although pale, was composed.

"That's all I know," she said. "When my father was killed, I needed the money so I accepted the job in his place. I knew how to deal with untrustworthy men, but this one was something I'd never come across before. I knew things were wrong when the Sky man started asking me odd questions, mostly having to do with the differences between men and women, but until he started to physically change, I guess my common sense wouldn't allow me to believe he was anything other than what I could see him as." She inched back in her chair and away from Sam so that they weren't sitting so close as she gazed out the window. "That's a mistake I'll never make again."

"What was the box you took from the wreckage?" he asked.

"I don't know." She fidgeted with the sleeve over her bandaged arm, which told Sam she was uncomfortable discussing it with him. "It was heavier than it looked, so I buried it in the desert rather than carry it with me. I didn't need anything useless weighing my horse down."

Rubbing his forehead, he leaned back in his chair. The fear Libby had felt during the illusion crawled through him. It must have been ten times worse for her.

He tightened a fist. Something about that box was important. "Do you think you could draw me a map to where you buried it?"

Libby lied to Sam and said no.

She'd taken that box because the Blue man had wanted it. She'd been injured and scared, and it had weighed her down, so in the end, she'd hidden it in the desert. But the fact that it had been so important he was planning to kill her to keep it a secret from his own people meant it could have no good purpose for hers.

This was her hostage. No one could ever find out that she knew where it was.

Sam's sun-bleached hair had flipped forward. It needed a trim. She'd offer to cut it for him when she could use her arm again. She was out of practice, but she'd been cutting men's hair for years. Shaving them, too. Men on the wrong side of the law tended to be nervous about letting strangers carrying sharp instruments get too close to their throats.

The sun streamed through the kitchen window, turning Sam's skin the same shade of gold as the flecks in his eyes. He was shirtless and barefoot, his chair drawn close to hers, and heat pooled in her belly. Her shoulder and arm throbbed and burned, but she didn't care. He made her forget about gunshot wounds, gunslingers, and Sky People. When they were alone in her house, she liked nothing better than giving him her whole attention, and getting his in return. She didn't want him thinking too hard about that cylinder, or recalling that her skills had guided her across that desert a time or two already.

She slid from her chair to his lap, easing her good arm around his shoulders. The blond scruff on his jaw tickled the underside of her chin as he wrapped his arms around her.

"Can I have another illusion?" she asked.

His lean face expressed his doubt and concern. "Are you sure you want to try it again?"

"This one's different," she assured him. "You asked me last night if there was somewhere I'd like to visit. It's not a place I've read of, although I've seen pictures in books. It's somewhere my mother used to tell me about when I was a little girl. Her father took her to Italy the year before she came out in society. She loved the canals of Venice the best." Libby smiled, although she felt a little sad over the memory of her mother's happiness whenever she spoke of that trip. "She met my father the following year and ran away with him. She wasn't at all prepared for life in the West. She was dead before I turned six."

"I'm sorry," Sam said.

"Don't be." She pressed a light kiss to his lips. "No one forced her to marry my father or cross the Atlantic with him.

She made a hasty decision and lived to regret it."

He frowned. "I see."

That frown told Libby he was reading too much into what she was telling him. "I'm not my mother."

"You're not your father, either," he pointed out. "But they both helped make you who you are."

"Your parents must have influenced you too, then."

She waited for him to say something about them. He knew a lot about hers, or her father, at least. But most of what he knew was a matter of public record. Everyone thought Max was reckless, and he was, but he was also a good judge of character.

And an opportunist. Libby loved him, but she wasn't blind to his faults.

"I suppose they did," Sam said.

His silence with regard to his own family didn't seem fair to Libby. He was the one who kept talking about marriage. She'd think he would want her to know what to expect. "What are they like?"

"Not nearly as colorful as yours. My mother comes from Atlanta and my father's a Yankee banker in Boston, so we've had our fair share of conflict, too. I was too young to get involved in the war, but two of my uncles fought for the North while one fought for the South." He made a face at her. "I had front row seats for the battles on the home front. Dinners were interesting at times."

"That didn't put you off marriage?"

"Not a bit." His voice softened. So did his eyes. "All sorts of things separate families, Libby. But mine pulled through it." He slipped his hand under the hem of her shirt and rubbed her back with the heel of his palm, from the base of her spine to the aching spot between her shoulders, carefully avoiding her wound. "My father picks his battles. He knows how to make my mother happy."

Sam's methods were working on Libby, too. She shifted so that she straddled his thighs. Beneath her, she could feel his rising level of interest.

"Do you want that illusion or not?" he asked, shifting her weight with both hands, but he was smiling.

"Eventually," she said. "First, you could practice figuring out what makes me happy."

"I can do both."

Sam stood, hiking Libby into his arms, and carried her back to bed. He made love to her in a gently rocking gondola on the waters of the Grand Canal, with the sun glittering off the white stone facade of the Rialto Bridge.

They spent the rest of the morning at his place in order for him to finish some fencing on a new corral. Later, in the afternoon when it became too hot to work, Sam planned to go to town and send a few telegrams.

She'd promised to stay close to the house, and her rifle, and try to rest while he worked. It wasn't long before she became restless and bored. Since Sam had told her to make herself at home, she wandered into the parlor and took a book off a shelf. It was a biography. She recalled that her father had once kept a journal and hoped to publish his memoirs someday. His notes, however, were long gone.

She replaced the book and walked through the remainder of the house. A portrait of a young family hung on a wall in Sam's bedroom. When she turned it around to peek at the back she found his name, and those of what must be his parents and two younger brothers, written on it in pencil, along with a date and location. *1855, Boston, Mass.*

She returned it to its original position and examined the portrait with a critical eye. In it, Sam looked to be about five years old. A close inspection revealed a tiny tear on the knee of his linen suit trousers, and mischief lurked in the glint of his eyes. Libby suspected his mother's hands had been full while raising him, and wondered what she thought of his chosen career.

Or what she'd think of his choice in a bride. Libby's family might have been lords and ladies in the old country, but she herself was born and raised in the West—disowned, the same as her disreputable, infamous father.

Her family life had been nothing like Sam's.

Libby went back to her exploring. The whole house was spotless. He had better taste than she did, and fancier things, which didn't surprise her. He could also cook—all of which confirmed for her that Sam didn't need a wife any more than she needed a husband. The current arrangement between them was by far the best for them both.

One of the empty upstairs bedrooms had a window with a good view of the corral where Sam was fencing. Libby watched from the window. She knew in intimate detail how his body felt against hers, but she rarely got the chance to admire it.

He had his shirt off, showing tanned skin to the top of his low-slung trousers. Muscles on his arms and across his shoulders worked as he swung the post maul, pounding the posts into the holes he'd dug with an auger. It was hard, time-consuming work, but if anything, he seemed to enjoy it. Every once in a while he'd stop, stand the post maul on the ground, and bend to grab a canteen of water.

As he tipped his blond head back to take a long pull from the canteen, Libby thought she saw a flash of light off in the desert. She shifted her gaze to the spot, wondering if perhaps she'd been mistaken.

No. There it was—the reflection of sunlight off glass. Someone was watching Sam, either through a rifle scope, or some sort of telescope. The glare off field glasses would create a different patch of light.

Libby turned from the window and ran for the stairs. The fact that they hadn't shot at Sam yet suggested they were more interested in watching his activities, or maybe waiting for something, but she wasn't staying here to find out.

She didn't bother taking her rifle. Trying to shoot it one-handed from a standing position would be next to impossible. She'd have to rest the butt under her arm, not against her shoulder, and the kickback would make her aim unpredictable. She'd make do with a pistol, and that meant she'd need to get close to her target.

She couldn't go out the front door or through the kitchen without being seen, so she headed for a window at the back of the house. Climbing out with one arm was impossible. Libby sat on the ledge, swung her legs over, and jumped. The drop wasn't far and she landed on her feet, cat-like, in a crouch.

It took her a long while to work her way into position, but when she did, she discovered two men, not one—although only one had a rifle. A large wooden box sat beside them, but from this distance she couldn't tell for certain what it might be. One of the men blocked her view.

She took cover behind a clump of rock and mesquite, not daring to approach any closer. She was too far away to have an accurate shot but she figured she could at least scare them off. She lifted her pistol, bracing her elbow on her knee.

Her bullet fell short, but kicked up dirt near the man with the rifle. He rolled away, then swung the rifle in her direction. Rather than return fire, however, he snapped a command at his partner.

The second man reached for the box. When he moved, Libby got a better look at it. It had a plunger on top.

She went cold all over. Now she knew what it was.

"Sam!" she shouted, just as a blast went off that knocked her flat.

Chapter Seventeen

Sam heard a gunshot.

He grabbed for his gun as he threw himself to the ground. His immediate concern was for Libby, but he'd spotted her watching him from an upstairs window just a little bit ago. She was safe in the house.

Seconds later, an enormous explosion rocked the earth, so close that he felt the hot air as shock waves washed over him, raining dirt and debris. He flung his arms over his head for protection, dropping the gun. A chunk of wood struck him on the back. His legs went numb.

When the dust finally settled, he took stock of the damage. His ears were ringing, leaving him partially deaf, but he knew that was temporary. His back hurt, and was most likely bruised, but other than that, everything worked. He could move his legs. He was fine.

Which was more than he could say for his house. A large crater, strewn with broken beams and crumpled panels of plastered wood and siding, occupied the place where it had sat less than two minutes prior. He scrambled to his feet with complete disregard for his safety, his brain seizing on one single, all-consuming thought.

Libby.

He ran for the rubble, knowing it was already too late but not caring. Frantic, with no plan other than to find her, he began tossing the smaller pieces of wreckage aside. A fragment of the china he'd bought for entertaining her crumbled beneath a carelessly placed boot heel.

Gradually, however, his hearing and common sense both returned. A sound came at him from a distance, as if carried through water, and it took a few seconds to place it.

Libby was shouting his name.

He looked up, afraid to believe it was more than his hopeful imagination, and saw her running toward him from the desert. The sling strapping her arm to her chest left her with an awkward, lopsided gait. He'd never seen anything more wonderful. The numbness in his chest eased its grip as he stumbled to meet her, sweeping her into his arms and holding her tight, scarcely able to grasp that she was alive.

"Sky People," she panted. "They were watching you through a rifle scope. I saw the reflection and went out to investigate. We've got to hurry. They could be back any minute."

Why blow up his house in the middle of the day? Why hadn't they simply shot him when they had the chance?

It was as if they wanted to draw the whole town's attention.

"This doesn't make any sense." He scanned their surroundings more carefully this time.

A buzzard circled lazily overhead, but he saw no signs

of Sky People or anyone else. Nothing moved. Whoever had blown up his house was long gone. To be safe, he carefully constructed an illusion around them that left anyone who might be watching with nothing but rubble to see. He and Libby were hidden.

"They might have been waiting for me to go in the house, trying to get us both together," he finally said. "That's my best guess."

She looked doubtful. "If so, they could have killed us last night at my place."

"There was a high level of interest in your place last night," he pointed out. "My house was empty, and made it easy for them to rig it to explode. Luckily for us we make a good team," he added, holding her close. "We're hard to kill."

Although this time, he conceded as he stood in the midst of what remained of his house, they'd gotten lucky. It was a good thing Libby was attentive.

She looked around at the destruction. "What are we supposed to do now?"

Gambling with his life was one thing. Endangering Libby's was another. His heart was still pounding over what had almost happened to her. It might be time for them both to disappear.

"We're getting out of Coyote Bluff," he said. "That's what we're doing."

"And go where?"

"Someplace no one's ever heard of, where no one will find either one of us."

She got that stubborn look in her eyes he was becoming all too familiar with. She intended to argue. He braced himself for it.

"Why do you think I came to Coyote Bluff in the first place?" she asked. "The Territories are getting more and more settled every day. There's nowhere left to hide."

"We'll change our names."

"No." Her mouth set. Her blue eyes darkened. "I'm not running. And I'm not changing my name. It's all I have left."

"Left of what?" Sam demanded. "Your reputation got you shot. You almost got blown up just now. I'm afraid for your life."

"I never asked you to worry about me. I'm not your responsibility."

Where he'd raised his voice, she'd lowered hers. Libby, with her gunfighter instincts, never got truly angry. She kept a clear head. But for Sam, this had become a full blown argument. His patience snapped. And he had no trouble with displays of emotion.

"Of course you're my responsibility," he said, his voice harsh, although more from frustration and fear for her safety than actual anger. "I love you."

Those three words hung between them, as heavy as the dust in the hot, stagnant air. This certainly wasn't how he'd wanted to say them to her for the first time. He was as surprised as she seemed to be—not that he loved her, because he'd known that already, but by the depth of his feelings. She was far more fearless than he was, and she made him afraid. He never worried too much about danger to himself, but if anything ever happened to her, he wasn't sure life would be worth living anymore.

Her gaze broke from his first, her lashes dropping to hide what she was thinking. "It's been my observation that it doesn't take men long to recover from love. As soon as someone or something better comes along, it's forgotten. I'm sure you'll get over it, too."

Sky People, gunfighters, and his problems at the Special Division were all forgotten. So was his frustration with her. This was the most fascinating conversation they'd held so far because it explained so much about her.

"Are you calling me fickle?" he asked, wanting to be clear.

"Not at all." She leaned in close and kissed him on the cheek. "I believe you're sincere. I'm simply pointing out that I've seen men fall in and out of love hundreds of times over the years. There's a distinct pattern to it. Trust me. As soon as you move on you'll recover."

"Maybe I will. Maybe I won't. But how long will it take for you get over me?" Sam asked. "When do you suppose you'll be ready to move on to somebody new?"

She said nothing, as if his question startled her, which meant she'd given no thought at all to her getting over him. He found that encouraging. He tugged her toward him. She'd had a bad few days, and an unusual life overall, and he wanted so much to change those things for her.

But standing in the rubble of an explosion that could have killed them both might not be the best time to try and change her opinions. Instead, he thought he'd give her a few things to think on. In most situations she was unflappable. But he figured he now knew what scared her, and he wanted her as terrified as he was so she'd understand how he felt.

"I believe I've been remiss." He slid one of his hands from her hip, over her waist, and to the small of her back. He took a half step closer so that they were touching from the tops of their thighs to their chests. She was slender and feminine, soft in the right places, and he doubted he'd ever get over her. Not in this lifetime. "I can't recall if I've ever told you how beautiful you are, or how much I desire you. There is no one better. Not for me. I spend each night at your place with you because I want to be near you. I love to sit on your front steps and hold you while we talk and watch the stars. When I'm with you, my life feels complete. I'll always come back to you."

He kissed her until she was breathless and clinging to him with her one good arm. She could move the fingers of her right hand, he noted, relieved. The doctor had told him the truth when he'd said she'd regain the use of her arm. She'd hooked her thumb in the waist of his trousers.

A smile trembled in her eyes. "You might not be fickle, but you sure are a sweet talker."

She didn't tell him she loved him, too. He was disappointed, but far from discouraged. She liked to think things through, but he remained confident of the conclusion she'd eventually reach.

"We'll spend tonight in the desert, under the stars," he said. "No one will find us."

That was a temporary solution, however. He had to come up with something longer term. The only person at the Division he could safely telegraph for help was Louis. Whatever he wanted of Sam, it was safe to assume it wasn't him dead.

The same couldn't be said of the Division's director. A Sky man wearing a marshal badge had tried to kill Sam. The message Sam sent to Louis would have to be carefully worded.

"First, we're going to town." He took her hand and started for the barn, hoping the horses weren't overly spooked by the explosion. "I need to send a message to a friend."

He left Libby at the jail, which was empty as usual, and headed for the telegraph office. He was still limping a little, but had managed to shake off most of the dust.

By Coyote Bluff standards, the main street was bustling. Three older men sat on a bench in front of the mercantile, out of the sun. Two women in bonnets strolled along the boardwalk, carrying baskets over their arms.

Pete Gaster lounged against the post outside of the telegraph office, smoking a crumpled cigarette. "Howdy, Marshal. Did you get my message?"

Sam had to think for a minute. "About the cattle?"

Pete's eyes sparkled with triumph. "Then that was your horse in Libby's barn."

"Of course it was my horse. I'm spreading my livestock around. I've got my cattle grazing on the Rosenberg property, and my horse stabled at Libby's. Saves me a fortune on feed."

"Now you're just foolin' with me," Pete said. "The ground shook out your way a little bit ago. Happen to know anything about that?"

"I was busy all morning, looking for those cattle. Could have been an earthquake. Excuse me. I've got to send a telegram."

"Wait one second, Marshal. I'd like to have a word with you." Pete looked uncomfortable. He dropped the butt of his cigarette on the ground and stubbed it out with the toe of his boot. "Libby's an awful good woman. She's un-or-thee-dox, I admit, and might take some persuadin', but a man could do a lot worse. I'd hate to see anyone treat her dishonorable."

Her deputy was worried about her. That was so... perplexing. Sam's opinion of him shot up a notch.

"No dishonorable intentions here," he replied. "But Sheriff Mayden's a woman who makes up her own mind about the way things are going to be."

Sam left Pete to puzzle that out.

Pastor Endicott was coming out of the telegraph office as he was going in.

"Good day, Marshal," Endicott said. He held the door open, but blocked the entrance so Sam couldn't pass through. "How's Sheriff Mayden feeling this morning?"

"About as well as can be expected."

Endicott got that same worried look to his eyes that Pete had been wearing. He let the door close so that he and Sam were outside. On either side of them, the boardwalk was empty. "May I speak with you for a moment?"

"Is it about Sheriff Mayden?"

"I thought I might give you some advice."

"No offense, Pastor," Sam said, "but I've been getting a lot of unsolicited suggestions for courting the sheriff, and I have to say, none of them have been especially useful. How about if I tell you my intentions are honorable and we leave it at that?"

"It's not your intentions toward her that concern me," Endicott said, "although that's good to hear. Rather, it's more her lack of experience with convention." He hesitated as if searching for the right words. "The sheriff isn't exactly the kind of woman most men want to marry."

"Careful, Pastor, or this time, I may be the one calling you out on your disrespectfulness," Sam said.

"You could." Endicott shrugged off the threat. "But you

comprehend what I mean. I'm not being disrespectful. Most everyone in Coyote Bluff wants what's best for the sheriff. She needs a man who doesn't mind that she's got a bigger reputation than his. And who isn't worried that someday, he might find himself facing another Garvin Haskell come looking for her."

From the moment he'd met her, Sam had wondered over Libby's situation in Coyote Bluff. She was a single, beautiful woman without any suitors in a town filled with bachelors. He was starting to piece a few things together.

"I thought you claimed she got her job because Pete can't read."

"She got her job because Judge Roy Rowe is backing her, and that means her reputation is legitimate. It doesn't mean the town—or Rowe—wants everyone to know that it is. Look what happens once they find out." Endicott rubbed his forehead with his thumb beneath the band of his hat. "We end up with Pete Gaster protecting the town while she recovers. All I can say is, praise the Lord for Judge Rowe. He keeps the worst outlaws away."

Outlaws, yes. But there were other, worse things loose in the world.

Sam narrowed his eyes. "Why this sudden interest in me courting the sheriff? Why is the town talking about me courting a certain young lady of good reputation? And what about a rumor I heard regarding Cash Robson and that same certain young lady?"

"I'm fairly confident that last rumor is true." Endicott grinned. "What might have been somewhat exaggerated was his outrage at being called out over it in church. He's not the most exemplary of men, but he's not a bad sort, either. And he likes to fight. Although he's not very good at it."

"Robson had the sheriff convinced the young lady needed protection from him. Is the entire town in on a conspiracy to get me and the sheriff together? And if so, who thought it up?"

"To be truthful, I'm not really sure. It just sort of happened," Endicott admitted. "But back to my original offer of advice with regard to Sheriff Mayden. It's not so much about how to court her as it is a general concern for your health. You might want to make an honest woman of her before Judge Rowe finds out you have any intentions toward her at all — even honorable ones."

"I'm not sure I understand Judge Rowe's particular interest in Libby," Sam said. He had to confess, that had him confused. "She's a grown woman. If he plans on courting her himself, why hasn't he spoken up before now?"

"He's not courting the sheriff." Again, the pastor appeared to be choosing his words with particular care. "I first met Rowe about five years ago, at a time when he was anxious to make a fresh start. We shared an interest in baseball and politics. Over time, he opened up. He had a few worries to get off his chest, and needed a private, educated ear to help talk them through. He's a fascinating man, but when he puts his mind to something, he's a dog with a bone. He can be dangerous. Let's just say he's come to think of the sheriff as his own daughter."

A few more pieces fell into place. Sam had wondered how many secrets Libby was keeping from him. She'd been forthcoming about so many other things with regard to her past that Endicott's careful wording — and warning — made Sam suspect this particular secret might not be hers to tell.

Since the first attack against him had happened before he'd met her, it was doubtful that she was the reason anyone wanted him dead. And today's attack might well have killed her instead. If his suspicions were correct Rowe, more than anyone, would want to prevent that from happening again.

The sun was at its hottest point in the day. Other than the two of them, the boardwalk remained empty.

"I have a telegram that needs to be sent. Then," Sam said slowly, "I think I might be in need of a private, educated ear at the moment, myself. Maybe you and I should have a little talk."

Louis sat at his desk in his laboratory, smoothing the paper in front of him with his fingertips as he pondered its message.

THE SKY IS FALLING STOP YOUR HEAD IS IN THE CLOUDS STOP.

Whitley had taken action. That the telegram had been sent indicated that so far, Sam had survived it. Next time, he might not.

The experiment Louis had been working on was in its final stages, but the air quality in his laboratory remained poor and his head was aching. A stroll around the neighborhood was in order. A few streets over was a church. Its rector was a man with whom he had a better than passing acquaintance. They went back a number of years. They also had a mutual friend.

One who would be very interested in what was happening in Coyote Bluff at the moment.

Chapter Eighteen

I love you.

No one had ever said those words to her before.

Libby stared out at the street through the narrow window of the jailhouse, willing Sam to appear, safe and sound. She'd had lots of experience with waiting. She'd once lived a life on the run with her father and his men, never certain from one day to the next if they'd come back from some venture alive, and had accepted it as normal because she'd known nothing else.

These days, she liked being settled. But her life would never be what anyone else might call normal. Sam had complicated it even further with his declaration of love, and by asking her if she could so easily forget him, because the answer was no.

She had no idea what to do about it. She'd been raised to understand that loyalty and survival went hand in hand.

Her loyalties were divided.

He wasn't gone more than a half hour.

"From the talk at the telegraph office, so far, people think that was an earthquake they heard, but it won't take long for them to figure out the truth," he reported as he came through the door. We need to be gone before then."

"I'm not leaving Coyote Bluff," she said. "If you go, you're going without me."

"The heck I will. I—" Sam began, then stopped, his attention caught by a movement behind him. Greta Rosenberg stood in the doorway. None of the children were with her. Libby assumed that meant they were napping in the back of the Rosenberg wagon.

"Am I interrupting?" Greta asked, shifting her gaze from Libby to Sam. She placed both hands at the small of her back as if to ease a great strain on it.

"Not at all," Libby said. "Come in."

With steps slow and careful because of her advanced pregnancy, Greta took the chair Sam offered her.

"What can I do for you?" Libby asked.

"There have been strangers around our barns the past few nights," Greta said.

Libby's attention had drifted to her pending argument with Sam. Now, it swerved back to the conversation she was currently supposed to be engaging in. "I beg your pardon? Could you repeat that, please?"

"I told you about those shots I heard in the gorge. Now we've seen strangers around our barns, too. Then today, the ground shook. Ira's talking about moving." Greta clasped her hands over her round belly, the lacing and unlacing of her fingers an indicator of her level of anxiety. "I don't want to run for the rest of our lives. Not with children to care for."

The gorge made a good hiding place. While a horse could only be ridden in from the mouth, it had many little crooks and bends to camp in, and plenty of deer paths up and down its banks for escape routes and ambushes if a man was nimble-footed enough. Libby had watched over that gorge most of the time Sam was in Washington, but stopped checking it after he came back. Guilt settled into her stomach. She'd been more interested in spending her nights with him.

But not everything that happened in and around Coyote Bluff could be blamed on the Sky People. Greta's concern over bounty hunters was well-founded. Or someone could be out for revenge. The Mayden gang had made enemies on both sides of the law. There was also the possibility of those two young cowboys, who hadn't lasted long at the Double U ranch, causing trouble. They appeared to be shy as far as work ethic went. Sam claimed to have seen strangers at the saloon, too. And someone had taken that shot at the stagecoach.

"Was anything stolen, or did any damage occur?" Libby asked.

Pete Gaster walked in as she was asking the question. The deputy removed his hat when he saw Greta.

"Afternoon, Missus Rosenberg." He nodded to Sam, looked at Libby, then back to Sam. "Couldn't help but overhear. A couple people is complaining about strangers nosing around their property at night, and the saloon's been seeing more traffic than a wh…" He cut off the word *whorehouse* when he realized two women were listening. "A lot more than usual," he amended. "Some's apprehensive of that earthquake too, Marshal Kyote. Said it felt more like a dynamite blast. You know what I think." He turned his hat around in his hands. "I think the local spirits is restless and Coyote Trickster's gettin' anxious. A full moon's coming soon."

"I think you need to spend more time learning the local language before you go trying to figure out what motivates the local spirits," Sam replied. "I'm not discounting them, mind you. But full moons roll around every month. Maybe Coyote Trickster thinks people should mind their own business."

"I think someone's looking for something," Greta interrupted. "Although I can't imagine what they think they'll find in our barn. And I have no idea what the ground shaking might mean."

"Who else has been complaining about strangers on their property?" Sam asked.

Pete ticked them off on his fingers. "We've got the Rosenbergs, Harley Temple, and the Bennetts."

Libby had no trouble connecting the dots. Sam's place used to belong to Billie Hernandez. And the saloon was run by Eldon Caudel. All of them were former Mayden gang members. What if Sam wasn't the target at all? What if someone was searching the properties, looking for something that an explosion wouldn't damage because it had survived a shipwreck unharmed?

Each of those men knew the location of the wrecked Sky ship. No one but Sam had any idea that she knew it, too.

"I'll ride out and take a look in that gorge," Sam was saying to Greta. "If someone's made a hideout for themselves, it won't take long to find them."

Libby didn't want him going out there alone. If she

propped the butt of her rifle properly, her aim with her left hand was still better than most. She could help. Besides, this was her problem, not his.

"I'm the sheriff in Coyote Bluff," she said, tapping the badge she'd pinned to her shirt, "and the Rosenberg property is inside county lines." Mindful of Greta and Pete, she didn't add that they'd blown up a house in her county, too. She threw his own argument right back at him. "I'm not going to apologize for trying to keep you from getting shot. I'd do the same for any lawman in a similar situation."

Sam cast a grin at her that caused her heart to do a queer little dance. "I'm glad you were listening. But this is no longer about the law between you and me. You've been shot once on my watch and I'm not letting it happen again."

She followed him to the door of the jail and put a hand on his sleeve, uncaring that Pete and Greta, and anyone on the street, might be watching. He turned back to her with a question in the lift of his brows, and she could think of a million things she wanted to say to him, but found no words to express them.

As always, Sam seemed to understand what she couldn't spit out. He drew her into his arms, pressing his lean body full against hers. She slid her good arm around his neck and held onto him, their faces scant inches apart. He leaned over to kiss her, scraping his whisker-rough chin along the line of her jaw to tease her.

"I'm coming back, Libby." His voice spread over her skin like warm honey on toast. He kissed her again, harder and longer this time, until she was weak-kneed with wanting him. "Don't think for a minute that you'll be rid of me this easily."

He eased them apart, then clattered down the steps of the jail. She watched him mount his horse at the hitching post. He waved to her from the saddle with a wide, reassuring grin on his face, and although she lifted her hand in response, she couldn't find it in her to smile, too.

He rode off in a cloud of dust, saddlebags flapping, leaving her unsettled. Worried.

And annoyed.

Judging by the number of faces pressed to the window of the general store across the street, half the town had witnessed Sam kiss her goodbye before riding off. Her cheeks burned. So much for the rumors of his pending engagement to Bess Miller.

She made up her mind. He didn't get to decide to leave her behind. Whether he liked it or not, they were in this together.

She stepped back inside the jailhouse and reached for her gun belt. She fumbled with the buckle, the fingers of her injured arm still numb at the tips and her shoulder throbbing with pain, making it awkward.

"Where are you going?" Pete asked.

"Since you've got things covered here in town, I'm riding out to take a look, too."

"You can't do that," Greta said, aghast. "You're injured. Marshal Kyote expects you to stay here. What if there's danger?"

Libby finally managed to strap on her gun belt. She reached for her hat on its hook near the door. "I'm the sheriff in Coyote Bluff, not Marshal Kyote. I get paid to handle dangerous matters. Besides, we don't know for certain what's going on. We could be jumping to all the wrong conclusions."

The other woman's face grew even more anxious. She pressed a hand to her breast. "I'll ask Ira to go with you. We've got a right to protect what's ours."

"If whatever's out there ain't dangerous," Pete added, "then why did Marshal Kyote send a krip-tick telegram to Washington asking for help? Missus Rosenberg is right," he added. "This is our town. We got a right to defend it. I say we put together a proper posse."

Matters were getting more and more out of hand. Libby didn't want the whole town involved. The fewer people who know about Sky People the better.

"Why don't I head out now to check on Marshal Kyote, and in the meantime you can round up Pastor Endicott, Eldon Caudel, and Harley Temple in case we need to deputize them?" she suggested to Pete. "Once Marshal Kyote and I find out what's going on, we'll meet you back here and talk about the need for a posse."

Pete slapped his hat on his head with more enthusiasm and energy than Libby had ever seen from him, before.

"If they's thievin' outlaws," he said, a glint in his eye, "they'll learn better than to mess around with the people of Coyote Bluff."

Sam's conversation with Endicott had been enlightening, more for what wasn't said than what was.

Libby had a strong sense of loyalty. Nothing new there. Her father had loved her more than anything. Well, most fathers did. But it was the comment regarding how loyal Mayden's men had been to him — and therefore, to his daughter—that had made Sam see the light. Wanted men spread to backwater places Like Coyote Bluff so they could disappear.

Sheriff Libby Mayden was harboring fugitives, just as Birch had intimated.

It stung a little that she hadn't come right out and told him so. With Max Mayden dead, his gang disbanded, and its former members no longer of more than a passing interest to the federal government, what did she think he would do if he knew?

He wiped his damp brow with his sleeve. The heat rising off the baked rocks at the top of the gorge swallowed any breathable air, and what little remained scorched the insides of his lungs. If he looked behind him, shimmering waves distorted the desert landscape.

When he peered into the gorge, however, he had an excellent view of a camp. Only one man stood guard in it. Sam tried to determine what he was doing. It looked as if he was waiting for something. Or someone.

Sam rested on his elbows in the scorching sand while he contemplated his current situation.

He'd been experimented on and sent to Coyote Bluff to recover, and told to prepare for a special assignment, but given no more information than that. Coyote Bluff had Sky People snooping around it, either trying to scare him away or kill him. Possibly both. It had members of a retired outlaw gang in its population—men who'd once lived near the same area of New Mexico where the Sky People had crashed. It had a judge with plenty of high-powered connections in Washington—and an inordinate interest in the local sheriff. Which all brought him back to Libby, who'd had her own brush with the Sky People in the past—only he'd swear on a bible that she'd told no one about it but him. He couldn't quite figure out how the pieces all fit together, but somehow, they did.

Right now, there was a good chance he had one of the Sky People cornered alone in the gorge. He had to be sure of it, though. He could climb into the gorge under cover of an illusion and catch him off guard. Then, once he was certain the stranger was Sky, maybe he'd start asking questions. He felt no need to be delicate in how he posed those questions, either. Not after he'd been shot at and had his house blown to pieces. Libby'd been threatened, too.

Habit had him checking over his shoulder. A small cloud of dust rose off the desert floor, growing fast as it drew closer. He rolled into the dubious cover of some nearby sage, wondering if the other Sky men were returning already.

It wasn't Sky People, however. That was Libby approaching. Resignation settled in. So this was what their future together was going to be like. He liked independence in a woman, but sometimes she took it too far.

Hell, who was he fooling? He wouldn't have her any other way.

He tracked her progress. She left her horse about a half mile back and set off on foot, carrying her rifle in her good hand, her gait somewhat awkward because of her arm strapped to her chest. He sat back to wait for her. Since she was already here, she might as well make herself useful. She could cover him while he climbed into the gorge.

When she drew near he waved an arm to get her attention. She headed in his direction, her slim, long legs covering the short distance in no time. It was a good thing Sam wasn't angry with her because he could never have stayed that way. She was too pretty for words.

A canteen of water hung around her neck. She tucked it under her injured arm to unscrew the cap, took a long draw, then offered the canteen to him. Settling her hat back on her head, she squeezed her eyes to slits against the glare of the sun.

He might not be angry, but the same couldn't be said about her. And Libby, all fired up, was a sight to behold.

"I have a few things to say to you, Sam Kyote, and you're going to listen." She propped her rifle on the ground between her knees and settled her good hand on her hip. "Don't ask me to marry you, then leave me behind the first chance you get. Either we're a team or we're nothing. Do you want me or not?"

"Oh, I want you, all right." For better or for worse, because she needn't think she could leave him behind, either. But first things first. They had some Sky People to bring back to earth. "And since you're here you can make yourself useful. I need you to watch my back. I'm going down to get a closer look at what's in that camp while there's only one of them there."

"Are you *insane*? You'll be out in plain sight."

"I know how to hide myself. We don't know who that is down there, Libby. Not for sure. My gut says it's a Sky man hunkered down in that gorge. But I could be wrong. And I'm a lawman too, remember? He could as easily be one of those innocent newcomers you said we shouldn't randomly kill."

That gave her pause. She went to her knees and poked her head cautiously over the lip of the gorge. "It's still not a good idea. The handholds are too tricky. The brush won't have deep roots. The soil's so dry those rocks are going to work themselves loose if you put any weight on them. You'll start a landslide and he'll know something's wrong."

Sam rubbed the back of his neck under his bandana. "That's why I need you to cover me."

She laid her rifle on the ground beside her. The long barrel gleamed. "He won't get a chance to shoot you because if you fall, I'll shoot you myself."

"Then I reckon that gives me two good reasons to make the climb a success. You concentrate on the Sky man. Do me a favor and shoot him before you shoot me."

"Fine." Now that her temper had been somewhat expended, she looked at him with more warmth in her eyes. "But if I have to kill you, I'm finding another man straight away to replace you."

Sam chuckled softly as he bent to give her a kiss. Once this was done, they were having a long talk about marriage. No way was he having another man jump his claim. He planned to defend what was his. "I'm irreplaceable, darlin'."

Lying on his stomach he eased his lower body over the edge of the gorge, his fingers clenched tight around deep-rooted scrub. His back was sore from where he'd been struck by debris when the house exploded. The rest of him ached. But he could do this.

"Sam?"

He lifted his gaze to find her expression even more anxious. She seemed to want to say something important but was having a great deal of difficulty finding the words, which he was coming to learn wasn't unusual for her. He loved her, and believed she returned his feelings, but she was terrible at expressing herself. Sooner or later she'd figure out how to tell him she loved him. Until then, he wasn't putting the words in her mouth.

"Yes?" he prompted her, daring to hope.

She hesitated. "Be careful. I don't want to have to replace you."

That was good enough for him, at least for the moment. "I'll be as careful as you'd be," he promised.

He pieced together an illusion that made it seem as if the cliff face was untouched. Then, he let himself drop.

The toes of his boots fumbled in the loose dirt for anything that might support him. When he glanced down, the floor of the gorge spun beneath him in slow semi-circles, first left, then right. It was a long drop to the bottom, and the wall was steeper than he'd thought, but it took a sharp angle part way down. That meant he'd most likely end up crippled if he fell, not dead.

He hated to admit it, but Libby might have been right. This wasn't a good idea. Not at all.

He'd managed almost three quarters of the descent before a bush he grabbed at pulled free. One arm spun wildly in empty space, then for a few seconds, he was airborne. He'd reached the point where the wall angled out, however, so he didn't have far to fall.

He landed hard on his back, already sore and bruised from the explosion, then tumbled the rest of the way to the bottom in a tangle of stones, loose dirt, and dislodged prickly shrub to sprawl in the rubble of the landslide Libby had predicted. His forehead connected with a rock solidly embedded in the ground. The world went gray, spinning into a colorless void. He couldn't hold the illusion together. It fragmented, peeling apart, exposing the real world—and

Sam—hidden beneath it.

He raised his aching head. He tried to get to his feet, but the world refused to cooperate.

Any time now, Libby. Go ahead and shoot.

Past his wavering vision, he saw the Sky man grab for his gun. The movement no doubt saved the Sky man's life. Instead of hitting its mark, Libby's bullet rang against the gorge wall and ricocheted off a rock, burying into the ground a scant three inches above where Sam lay spread-eagled in the midst of disaster.

The Sky man returned fire against Libby at the top of the gorge.

Sam's head pounded with a fierce, piercing pain that lanced straight to the backs of both eyes. His stomach lurched when he moved.

Ignoring the pain in his head and his protesting stomach, he lunged to his feet. She'd missed her shot, which meant she couldn't defend herself, either. He'd known she wasn't ready for this. Not so soon after her gunfight. He should have made her head back to town straight away. If any more Sky People were lurking about—and there had to be others—she'd be all alone. He had to get her away from here.

The only way to drive her away was to give her no reason to stay. Gritting his teeth he reconstructed the illusion, this time casting it across the entire floor of the gorge.

Chapter Nineteen

The rifle had been harder to steady when it kicked back than she'd anticipated because her bad shoulder made her shaky, but that was no excuse. Left-handed or not, she shouldn't have missed such an easy shot. Sam had trusted her with his life and she'd let him down.

Worse than that, she suddenly saw with crystal clarity how blind and foolish she'd been. Up until now she'd worried about how her loyalties belonged to her father and the men he protected. She'd been so wrong. It wasn't a question of loyalty, but that she'd gotten her priorities confused. Her father, his men, Coyote Bluff…None of them needed her as much as she needed Sam. He would always come first. A few words spoken by a pastor made no difference at all. If marriage meant that much to him though, then they'd get married. If he wanted to leave Coyote Bluff forever, then she'd go.

She hadn't told him she loved him. To do so, she had to

keep him alive.

The problem, however, was that the camp at the bottom of the gorge had disappeared. So had Sam and the Sky man.

She kicked at a rock in angry frustration. Climbing into the gorge with one useless arm was impossible. Even if she could, she'd be too easy a target. She studied the sky. It was going to take forever to work her way around to where the head of the gorge narrowed and flattened. She'd need to walk a half mile back to get her horse first. The thought of the time it would take filled her with panic.

But she saw no other option than that. She couldn't stand by and do nothing.

She set out, praying for sunset so the air could cool off. By the time she reached her horse, the sun had dipped low and her injured arm throbbed with pain at every step. As she started to lift her foot into the stirrup to mount, praying she could make it into the saddle one-handed, she felt a faint rumbling of the earth that came from the direction of town, as if a stampede of horses approached. She looked across the desert. Coyote Bluff was little more than a blur on the horizon in the fading light. A shadow grew, soon taking shape.

It wasn't a stampede. It was Pete and his posse. A fast count told her there had to be at least thirty more people, armed with everything from rifles to pitchforks. She spotted Pastor Endicott riding alongside Harley Temple and Eldon Caudel. While at least three men were now present who knew how to kill Sky People, the problem was that they couldn't shoot them in front of the townspeople. If the public found out about Sky People, or where they came from, then Coyote Bluff would no longer be a peaceful hideout for the retired Mayden gang.

The whole world would arrive on its doorstep.

Pete reined in, looking quite pleased with himself. Libby drew him aside so she could speak with him in private. "I thought I told you three special deputies and we'd talk about the need for a posse later."

He spit a wad of chewing tobacco into the dirt. "Shoot, Libby. A pastor, a saloon keeper, and a one-legged man ain't gonna be no good against outlaws."

If Pete only knew.

Libby couldn't very well argue the point without giving too much away. Instead, she tried to visualize a plan that would help Sam but keep the townsmen—as well as the Sky People—from getting killed.

A pink bonnet and long swathe of blond hair in the crowd caught her eye. "Is that *Mary Lou Bennett*?"

"You expected me to say no to her when she volunteered?" Pete asked. "She was in town buyin' a new frying pan. Seems her old one disappeared and she was all riled up about it. Thought it might be a good idea to let her work out all that aggression afore she headed home."

"Tell me you didn't give her a weapon." The possibility was appalling. There was no telling who she might shoot and then try to pass it off as an accident.

"Nah, she's got her frying pan. Everyone knows enough to stay out of her reach."

Libby thought fast. "From what we could see there's some sort of camp at the bottom of the gorge. It could be outlaws, wanting to set up some sort of home base or hideout. We only saw one stranger acting suspicious, but Sam thinks there are others. Keep ten men with you, Mary Lou, too, and hide along the sides of the gorge entrance. I'll take the others with me. If anyone you don't recognize approaches, stop them. But don't kill them," she added hastily. "We don't know for certain anyone's done anything wrong. Whoever they are, we'll bring them in for questioning."

Pete was less than thrilled with her plan. "Why can't you take Mary Lou?" he complained. "It's because she's a little bit of a woman, ain't it? You don't think she can hold her own in a fight and needs to be paired with a man."

Libby longed to point out that Mary Lou put the fear of God into most of the men in Coyote Bluff, but time was running out. All she could think of was Sam, and how she needed for her head to be clear. She wasn't missing any more shots.

"Yes," she said. "That's exactly the reason I don't want her with me."

She wheeled her horse around and the two of them got down to work, dividing everyone into two groups. She sent Pastor Endicott and Eldon Caudel with Pete, keeping Harley Temple with her. Then she led her group into the gorge on horseback while Pete and his people left their mounts hobbled in a sparse stand of yucca nearby and took up the rearguard on foot.

The place where the camp had been was about a mile deeper into the gorge. By the time Libby and her men reached it, twilight had fallen and the land was a wash of ripe purples and blues. Stars twinkled to life, one by one, but the moon hadn't yet crested the ridge.

There was no trace of the camp.

It had to be here, buried somewhere beneath one of Sam's illusions. That meant he was alive. She bit her lip, her heart in her throat.

What was she supposed to do now?

With the pain in his head, and prickles of light interfering with his vision, Sam had a hard time focusing his concentration to hold this larger illusion together. The fall hadn't helped his bruised back any, either.

The effort, however, was worth it. The Sky man could no longer see him. He'd be unable to see himself, either. It gave Sam the advantage.

The Sky man's gaze scanned the area. "We've been wondering how you manage to do this. It's very impressive."

Sam wasn't about to enlighten him. Let him figure it out on his own. He gauged the distance between them and took a step forward. The Sky man's head swiveled in his direction. So did his gun. Sam froze. The Sky man fired a shot in his direction that went well wide of its mark. He might not be able to see Sam, but there appeared to be nothing wrong with his hearing.

Sam picked up a rock and skimmed it low to the ground so that it kicked up dirt a good distance away. The Sky man spun toward the noise. Sam dove at him, punching him in the kidney where he was most vulnerable, then got his heel behind the other man's knee and jerked. Rather than falling, the Sky man blindly grabbed Sam by the front of his shirt and head-butted him in the exact same spot on his forehead he'd struck on a rock when he fell. Sam wrenched free of his grasp but tripped, hitting the ground, and cracked the back of his head, too. He gagged on a fresh wave of nausea. The world spun like a top. The illusion wavered. He fought to keep it in place.

The Sky man groped around blindly, unable to find him. When he came up empty-handed, he stopped to listen. Sam lay very still, trying to keep from throwing up, passing out, or breathing too loud. Anything that might give away his location before he could recover his balance. Seconds went by. Neither of them moved.

And then the Sky man began searching for him, walking in a widening circle. Sam bided his time. When the Sky man was standing next to him, he shot a straight-armed fist upward. It caught the Sky man in the groin. With a grunt, the Sky man doubled over and fell to his knees. Sam lashed out with a boot, striking the Sky man's kidney again. He curled into a ball, then went limp.

Sam, however, wasn't about to have the same possum trick he'd just pulled played on him. He kicked the Sky man once more for good measure. The Sky man stayed motionless.

He was out cold.

Sam began searching the camp for something to tie him up with. He found some rope that had been used to tie packs to the horses. Once he had the Sky man trussed with his hands bound together and tied behind his back, then lashed to his feet, Sam gagged him. He crouched on his heels at his side, looking down at him.

"It's my turn to ask questions. You can nod yes or no."

A sound rumbled through the gorge like the approach of a steam locomotive, distracting him. Horses were coming. He didn't know who it might be. Night had descended, steeping the gorge in deep shadows. He sat and waited.

Libby rode into sight at the head of what appeared to be half the town. He stepped into her path. Her horse reared back, startled by his sudden appearance from out of the darkness. He grabbed for the bridle, dodging the mare's flailing hooves. A group of riders drew up behind her, seeming uncertain as to what they should do.

"Where the heck did all these people come from?" he asked Libby. "I thought you said a few men had been deputized?"

"Pete raised a posse."

"So I see." Red speckles swam behind his eyelids again. He had a hell of a headache, both from the fall and holding an illusion together too long. "What's all the shouting about?"

It sounded as if people were being murdered at the mouth of the gorge. Libby frowned, tipping her head and trying to make some sort of sense out of the noise. "I'm guessing they caught themselves some prisoners."

She directed two men to stay behind and keep a watch on the camp and the trussed up Sky man while the rest of them checked out the ruckus at the mouth of the gorge. Sam swung into the saddle behind her and buried his face in her hair, thankful she was safe.

When they reached the members of the posse who were on foot, they found them gathered around two prone figures lying in the dirt in the dark. A woman stood over them, brandishing a cast iron frying pan.

"Is that *Mary Lou Bennett*?" Sam said to Libby. The red spots grew worse, to the point he didn't dare close his eyes too long for fear he'd pass out or throw up.

"I'm afraid so. It appears Pete was right. She needed to work off some hostility," Libby replied. A note of worry slipped into her voice. "I hope those are Sky People she's bludgeoned. They look like men."

"The one I caught is Sky for certain. We can sort out what these two are later."

The townspeople turned out to be as good a posse as any, and more helpful than some. They rounded up all three prisoners, and then marched them back to town as if it were something they did every day.

Libby left Pete in charge of the jail.

Harley Temple stayed behind to help him. "Even a one-legged man can shoot an escaped prisoner," he said.

It was the early hours of the morning by the time Sam and Libby rode through the quiet desert sunrise to her place. Sam rested his chin on her shoulder and closed his eyes, one arm around her waist while he held the reins loose in his hand. The mare was tired too, and he wasn't too concerned she'd head for anywhere but home. She'd had her tantrum for the night. The only thing that interested her now was her barn and a bucket of oats.

He kissed the side of Libby's neck. She tasted like salt, soap, and sweetness. *This*, he thought drowsily, *is how a woman should taste*. He kissed her once more for good measure.

"If you were to propose to me again," she said, wriggling deeper into the saddle and the crook of his arm, "my answer might be different this time."

Sam peeled one eye open. Bright fingers of orange and gold reached over the horizon and groped at the desert floor.

"Let me think on it," he said.

Carson Whitley stepped from the front door of the Capitol Hill townhouse where he rented rooms.

He turned left and headed past the rows of townhouses barricading the empty, unlit street, planning to take a shortcut through the grounds of nearby Christ Church.

At the street corner, he picked up an unwelcome companion. Judge Roy Rowe had been waiting for him in the shadows. Carson had to wonder how closely his movements were being monitored that Rowe knew where he'd be at this hour.

And for what purpose Rowe was monitoring him.

"Walk with me," Rowe said, moving into step beside him and taking his arm.

Carson swiveled his head, but there was no one nearby to witness his abduction. He considered shouting for help, but that would accomplish nothing but embarrassment. He could hardly tell the police he believed Judge Roy Rowe, a known friend of the president, wished him harm. Besides, Rowe wouldn't dare. He wasn't the only one who had powerful connections.

"What's this all about?" Carson demanded, hiding his fear behind his impatience.

"I thought I'd made it clear that if anything happened to Libby Mayden, you'd be held accountable. And yet I've heard disturbing reports with regard to her safety, and from several different sources. Someone saw fit to blow up the marshal's house a few days ago. They didn't, however, check to see if anyone might be inside. Luckily for you, the sheriff escaped."

"She isn't my concern," Carson replied. "Maybe the question you should be asking is what she was doing in his house in the first place."

Rowe's fingers tightened on his arm and Carson knew he'd hit a nerve. His curiosity was piqued. Why would Rowe care what Max Mayden's daughter did with her evenings?

The two men continued to walk as if out for a companionable, early morning stroll. Rowe guided Carson down the next street. Christ Church wasn't too far away. Carson debated breaking free and making a run for the rectory. He could bang on the door. The rector wouldn't ask questions and wouldn't tell tales, and Rowe wouldn't dare shoot him in the back on church property.

"You should spend more time making allies and less on acquiring enemies," Rowe said to him. "Paying attention to small details would be of considerable help. For instance, why do you suppose I'd care what happens to Max Mayden's daughter?"

Carson despised men who thought they were more clever than everyone else. "You're interested in finding out how much she knows about Sky People. How much he might have told her about that box you're searching for." The church grounds were within sight now.

"True enough." Rowe seemed in no hurry. He kept their pace steady. "But let me tell you a little more about Max Mayden. You never knew him, did you?"

"Everyone in the Territories knew him," Carson said.

"Fair enough. But if you knew him personally, if you'd met him, you'd know he was a good judge of character. He surrounded himself with men who were loyal. Most were well educated, with good connections, but they'd fallen on hard times. He treated them well. They were always the first to be paid. In return, he trusted them with his life."

"That didn't do him much good." Carson calculated the distance to the front door of the rectory.

"I think it did." Rowe sounded amused. It was chilling. "He also had a deep and abiding love for his daughter. He knew she could take care of herself, he saw to that, but he wasn't one for leaving anything about her to chance. He miscalculated a little, however. He didn't realize she'd get herself involved with a marshal."

"How could he?" One hundred paces. "Mayden's dead."

"Which is why a man with a lot of enemies should spend as much time, if not more, making allies. They can tie up those loose ends for him he couldn't predict."

Rowe wasn't walking past the church yard. Instead, he steered Carson into the path that led through the grounds to the rectory—right where Carson wanted to go. Safety was not far away.

The front door of the church opened. Carson relaxed. He'd been to many Sunday morning services here. The rector knew him, at least by sight. He wouldn't have to run for the rectory. He wouldn't forget how Rowe had ambushed him this morning, either. By doing so, he'd signed his own death warrant.

"Good morning, Reverend Saunders," Rowe called out as the rector stepped outside, turning to close the tall wooden door behind him.

The rector looked up. He lifted a hand in acknowledgment, then appeared to be scanning the church grounds. "Around back, to the cemetery," he said to Rowe. "We need to be quick, though. I have a wedding scheduled in a few hours and I don't want to introduce anything unpleasant into their day. Young people should start their lives together in happiness."

The black cord wrapped around two pieces of wood clutched in the rector's hands caught and held Carson's attention. It was a garrote. While on one level he couldn't comprehend the rector's part in this, it only took a few seconds for him to figure out what was happening.

When he did, all the blood rushed from his face, leaving him dizzy.

"You're Max Mayden," he said to Rowe. His chest felt as if it had been crushed by a load of bricks. A stabbing pain shot down his left arm. He tried to jerk free of Rowe's grasp, but Rowe didn't let go.

The rector came down the steps and seized Carson's other arm. Between them, they wrestled him around to the back of the church. Before Carson could think to scream, Rowe had him on the ground, on his back, with his knees on Carson's arms while he sat on his chest. The rector wound the garrote around his neck.

Carson bucked, trying to throw Rowe off him, kicking with his legs. The garrote tightened until he couldn't breathe.

"I went to a lot of trouble to make sure my daughter wouldn't be troubled by men like you," Rowe said. "She should be happy, too."

Chapter Twenty

CLOUDS HAVE CLEARED. FIVE RAYS OF SUNSHINE ON WAY.

The telegram had come from Louis over six days ago, although it was possible that someone else had sent it in his name. Sam would find out for certain once those five marshals arrived. He expected them to ride into town any day now.

In the meantime, convincing Libby to agree to allow him to assume responsibility and guard the three jailed Sky People hadn't been as difficult as he'd anticipated. She'd even conceded he might be more suited to the task, at least for the time being.

What she hadn't done yet was tell him why she was suddenly so willing to marry him. If they were going to plan a life together, she needed to refine her communication skills. It couldn't possibly be too hard for her to say three little words. He meant to hear her say that she loved him.

Preferably after calling his name during a highly intimate moment, but he wasn't going to be choosy.

Until the marshals came to collect the Sky People, however, he was stuck right here at the jail. It didn't seem the same to him without Mary Lou Bennett in residence, but Libby said she was going to have to overlook the woman's transgressions until after the current prisoners had been transferred.

The three Sky men who sat behind bars sported sullen expressions on their faces. They looked as human as he did. Even he couldn't testify that they weren't, and they weren't admitting to anything. It was the coldness in their eyes that gave them away, however. They had nothing inside them. No human emotion. He couldn't create any illusions from them. He'd tried.

Harley Temple limped into the jail, disrupting Sam's thoughts. He stooped his shaggy black head as he brushed through the door. The man was enormous. When he'd had the use of both legs, he must have been terrifying.

"Good afternoon, Marshal," he said. "Judge Rowe wants to see you over at the Evening Lily. I'm to sit with the prisoners for a spell."

Except for Eldon Caudel and a lone man at a table, the saloon was empty when he entered. Sam paused at the door to study the stranger.

So this was Judge Roy Rowe. He looked much like any of the middle-aged men who'd spent most of their lives in the West. He was hard-bodied and lean, with skin toughened to leather by the sun and the wind. He wore a black suit and hat. Sam looked in his eyes.

Cold certainty ran through him. He recognized the

shape. That particular shade of blue. While Libby's eyes were clear and direct, however, Roy Rowe's were as hard as the rest of him. Not much wonder grown men shriveled in fear.

And now he knew why Libby hadn't wanted to tell him all of her secrets.

Rowe saluted him with a shot glass of whiskey filled to the brim. "Why don't you pull up a chair and join me for a drink, Marshal Kyote?"

"I'm on duty."

"Is that a fact?" Rowe tossed back his drink and set the empty glass on the table in front of him. He fixed Sam with a thoughtful stare. "I heard you're suspended."

Sam couldn't argue with that. He shrugged. "Then I guess we can make mine a double."

Eldon brought them their drinks. Sam didn't touch his. Instead, he waited.

Rowe cast him a faint smile that deepened the creases around his mouth. "How would you like to have that suspension lifted?"

"It's probably best if you don't do me any more favors, Judge," Sam said. "I haven't recovered from the blood transfusion." A surge of fresh anger coursed through him. "You set Whitley on me, too. You used me as bait. Worse than that, you used Libby."

The smile widened. "You both can take care of yourselves. And neither of you have any more worries on that account. The crime rate in Washington is disturbingly high. It seems Carson Whitley met with an unfortunate accident. As of this morning, the Special Division has a new director." He withdrew a piece of paper from his breast pocket and waved it at Sam. "That would be me."

Sam didn't think he could know about Roy Rowe's past and work for him, too. Max Mayden the outlaw might be dead, but Roy Rowe the judge shared his lack of morals.

"I'll be handing in my badge," he said.

"I thought that might be your reaction. You're still angry about a harmless blood transfusion."

He was. It didn't help to have Rowe act as if it were nothing. But it was Rowe's negligence with his own daughter's life that really stuck in Sam's craw. "If you try and tell me I'm government property because of something done to me without my permission, I'll shoot you right now."

"You aren't government property. You are, however, a government employee. A rather special one." The smile disappeared as Rowe leaned closer, dropping his forearm to the table. "And don't think for a second you'd have won a woman like Libby if you didn't have that something special to set you apart."

Sam would be damned if he'd admit to any doubts about his worthiness of her. He refused to be intimidated, either. "Is that what this is about? You want me to leave her alone?"

"Hell, no. Rumor has it you're sleeping with her. If you know what's good for you, you're damn well going to marry her. No, I'm interested in recovering something I believe she may have taken off that Sky ship in the Chihuahuan Desert. If she did she won't give it up. Not even to me."

If she wouldn't give it to Rowe then Sam wouldn't, either. "Let's say she did take something. Exactly what might it be?"

"A tool box, one that was built to withstand a crash landing. It contains a type of replicator. The replicator designs and builds those tiny bits of technology in the Sky People's blood that helps their bodies adapt to a new world. It's the same technology Louis injected in you. But that's just the beginning of the things that one little silver box can do." Rowe's expression grew more intense. "It can build machines so small they can't be seen under a microscope, or an entire, defensible colony if the Sky People were to land on a potentially hostile world."

A little silver box.

Libby had ridden into the desert with someone so anxious to have it and keep it secret that he'd planned to kill her. "Maybe it's better off lost."

"Maybe it is. But the Sky People will never give up looking for it. That replicator means survival to them. If they get their hands on it, they can build things with it you and I can't even begin to imagine. They can change the future of this entire world. Why do you think they were working with someone like Carson Whitley? What did he want more than anything else?"

Power.

"And what do you suppose they've been searching for in Coyote Bluff? Who would be the only people other than themselves who'd know anything about that shipwreck and what might be on it?"

"Why should I trust anything you say?" Sam asked. "Carson Whitley isn't the only ambitious man in the world. Maybe you have Sky People working with you, too."

Rowe didn't appear to be offended. "I may be a lot of things, Marshal Kyote, but the most important one for you to consider is that I'm loyal to those I believe in. Look around you. Coyote Bluff exists because so many of Mayden's men remain loyal to me. I earned that. I look out for them, too. But nobody is truly trustworthy in all situations. As long as that replicator is missing, the people here — Libby included — won't be left in peace. It's better off found. That shipwreck has been claimed as United States government property. I believe in the government as an institution. I also believe in our President. He's a good man. But the only person I truly trust to oversee the study of that shipwreck and the replicator is me. So the real question you should be asking yourself is not why you should trust me, but who would you trust to have watching over something like that?"

The answer, of course, was the same as Rowe's. No one but himself.

No. That wasn't true. There was one other person he'd trust.

"We need good men to stand against the Sky People, Marshal," Rowe continued. "I'm hoping you'll be one of them. As long as you trust yourself, then I'm willing to trust you."

"Before I can make up my mind on that," Sam said, "I have one more question. How did you get the blood sample Louis injected me with?"

"It was given to me."

"I find that hard to believe. Why would one of the Sky People up and give you a sample of their blood?"

Rowe played with the shot glass in front of him. He took his time answering, as if formulating the best response. Sam hoped it was good. This was going to decide matters for him.

"When you work with the law as long as I have, no matter which side of it you're on, you learn a few things about men," Rowe finally said. "One is that none are the same. Another is that they all make mistakes. The same rings true for the Sky People. Living in exile is a harsh enough punishment. Everyone deserves a second chance. Some take it right away. Others need time to readjust their line of thinking. Then, of course, there are always those who need to be shot."

Of all the stories Sam had heard about both Maxwell Mayden and Judge Roy Rowe, one fact remained consistent throughout. They were tough men, but fair. While a few things were going to be hard to forgive, Sam reckoned that was one thing he could live with.

"I'll need a few weeks before I report back to duty. I have personal matters to settle here first," he said. He stood. Then, he turned back to Judge Rowe. "I'll be marrying Libby, sir. If she'll have me, that is. But let's get one thing straight. It's because I want her. Not because you threatened me."

"I'm glad we understand each other." The judge tipped back in his chair. While his eyes weren't as cold as the Sky People's, they held little warmth. "If you'd only agreed to marry her because you were threatened, then you'd be dead."

Eight days after the three Sky People were captured, five US Federal marshals arrived in Coyote Bluff on the afternoon stagecoach.

Tonight was the first chance Libby'd had to be alone with Sam, and instead of spending the evening in bed together as she'd planned, he'd insisted they ride out to his property. She shifted her weight in her saddle, doing her best to hold her reins in one hand while keeping it close to her holstered gun.

Old habits died hard.

Their horses had no difficulty picking their way through the familiar desert scrub by the light of the full moon. The smells of horseflesh, creosote and sage lay thick in the air. The night sky blazed a rich, midnight blue, heavily peppered with stars so bright and clear that Libby thought if she extended her arm far enough, she could reach out and touch them. She could think of no place on earth, or even beyond, where she'd rather be than right here, at Sam's side, at this moment.

He hadn't proposed to her again. After eight days and nights, Libby had finally gotten over the disappointment. She'd been the one all along who'd resisted marriage and she could hardly blame him for changing his mind about wanting it, since she'd changed hers, too.

He was with her right now, and that was what mattered.

They'd had little time to talk about anything at all. The Sky People held in the jail required constant attending, and Sam's marshal friends had only just arrived on the afternoon stage coach to relieve him and escort them back to Washington. Libby wondered if Sam planned to go along, or if he'd hang around a while longer.

Worry had her sitting too stiff in the saddle, and her horse shifted uneasily beneath her in response to her mood. Maybe she'd been right, and it was the thrill of the chase that Sam enjoyed most. Now that she was willing, he might not want her as much.

Either way, she'd decided she owed Sam more information. If he did still want to marry her, he should know what he was getting himself into before he made any commitment.

"There might be one or two things about my past you

should be aware of," she said, breaking the silence. "I might have held something back, but it's not really about me."

"If it has to do with your father," Sam said, "then I know all I need to. You can keep his secrets, Libby. I'm not going to ask you to betray him or anyone else. It's probably best if you don't."

She wondered how he'd found out. Perhaps that was what had made him change his mind about wanting to marry her. If so, she couldn't blame him for that, either. Her father was good to the people in his inner circle. Other than that, he was a dangerous man.

Sam reined in his horse at the top of the knoll overlooking the gaping black hole where his house used to be.

"I'm sorry," Libby said to him as he surveyed the damage.

"It can be rebuilt." He shifted in his saddle to face her. "Before we can start in on planning our new house though, you and I are going to have to talk about that box you hid. The government has claimed the Sky People's wrecked ship as salvage. It's now government property. That means everything that was on it is, too. Can that box be found?"

He already knew she'd once had the box. If she'd trust anyone with its hiding place, it was him. "I suppose anything's possible, although I can't imagine how. It's deep in the desert in New Mexico Territory. I threw it into a pit in a limestone cave. I didn't hear it hit bottom."

"Then we're going with the answer is no. Maybe that's for the best, too."

She thought of what else Sam had just said. Hope had her heart beating faster. "We're building a new house together?"

"I like the idea of starting out with something that's ours, and not yours or mine. What do you think?"

She wasn't sure what to say. Was he asking her to marry him, or for them to live together?

She'd take what he offered, but she wanted to know which it was. "Are you talking marriage, or are you asking me to set up light housekeeping with you?"

Sam slid from his horse, then reached up to help her dismount. He'd left his hat at home and his fair hair flopped over his eyes. He flicked it aside with a toss of his head, keeping his hands at her waist, his gaze probing her face in the darkness.

"Why are you so interested in marriage all of a sudden?" he asked. "What made you change your mind?"

Because she couldn't imagine her life without him. "I've gotten used to you being underfoot."

His lips jerked up at the corners, but his voice stayed serious. "There are going to be days and weeks, and maybe even months at a stretch, where you'll be all by yourself."

"I don't mind my own company. I'm used to that, too." Libby rested a palm on his chest and eased a bit closer. "But since I met you, I realized I've never gotten used to having no one I can call mine."

"I'm definitely yours. You don't need to marry me for that to be true." Sam's hands tightened on her waist. "I'm a little curious as to what difference you think marriage will make to our current relationship."

Libby hadn't anticipated the subject to become this complicated. "I don't suppose it will make any difference. You already know I won't make a good wife. I like being the sheriff and won't give it up. You'll do your job, I'll do mine, and when you're able to be in Coyote Bluff, we can be here together." She curled her fingers into a fist against his chest. "You don't have to marry me. I thought it was what you wanted."

"I do want it. But I never asked you to be anything other than who you are right now, so why all of a sudden are you ready to say yes? Why wouldn't you say yes before?"

"Coyote Bluff isn't always as peaceful as it seems. You're a federal marshal, while my father was one of the most infamous outlaws in the West. I have a past, too. That's going to be difficult for you to explain. You could have any woman you want," Libby added, a little tired of having to point out her shortcomings when they were already well documented, and plain for the whole world to see. "I'm not a great beauty and I'm far from domestic."

The flecks of gold in his eyes caught the light of the moon. "Let me make sure I understand your meaning," he said. "To summarize, you think me marrying you would be the worst mistake of my life?"

A lot of the magic died out of the evening.

"It's not like you're perfect either," she said.

"If I can have any woman I want, I'd say that makes me the next best thing." Sam drew her closer and kissed the tip of her nose. "And it seems I'm not interested in any other woman. I knew the second you wrestled Mary Lou Bennett into the dirt that you were the one for me. That's partly why I asked you to marry me. Your shooting arm is another good reason. The doctor swears you'll recover it." His lips caught the corner of her mouth in another light kiss. "Your shortcomings are all in your head, Libby Mayden. You are, without a doubt, the most beautiful woman I've ever laid eyes on. But the real reason I asked you to marry me is because I love you. My family will love you, too. You're perfect, all right. At least, you're perfect for me." He pressed his mouth full onto hers, and for a few moments, Libby forgot how to breathe. When she was thoroughly kissed, he lifted his head. "Now, tell me the real reason you want to marry me. Try saying the first thing that comes into your head. Don't think on it too much."

The stars spun in the wide, velvety sky, from one side of the earth to the other, leaving her dizzy.

"*BecauseIloveyoutoo*."

Libby blew it out in such a rush that it sounded like a single word.

Sam's arms tightened. "Was that such a hard thing to say?"

"No," she replied, so surprised by the discovery that when Sam laughed at her, she had to smile, too. "I love you," she said again, with more confidence this time.

His smooth voice went rough. "Then yes, Libby Mayden, I accept your proposal."

"I wasn't the one who proposed," she protested.

"When I repeat this story to our grandchildren—and there will be grandchildren—they'll be hearing my version of this courtship, not yours."

Libby had only just reconciled herself to marriage. Her feelings for Sam were both new and overwhelming, and she wanted to savor them, so she pushed away thoughts of grandchildren, or any kind of children, for her to examine at another time. The possibility of them no longer frightened her, though. Libby thought she might like having little people around for her to love. Her friend Greta seemed content.

"As long as we're married when you tell it to them," she said, and leaned against him to nestle her cheek into the curve of his throat. Contentment filled her.

Somewhere out in the desert, a pack of coyotes took up a serenade to the moon. Under the circumstances, Libby thought it quite fitting.

"Oh," she said, suddenly thinking of something. "Pete's going to be so disappointed that the moon never walked. He puts a lot of faith in his legends."

"After everything that's happened, we can't have him disappointed. Besides, that legend's true. This Kyote's caught his Mayden and he's not letting her go." Sam turned her around so that her shoulders were pressed to his chest and tilted her chin upward with the tip of one finger.

Before Libby's laughing eyes, the full, pale moon sprouted two arms and two legs, and Sam made it dance a little jig before letting it strut like a satisfied rooster across the star-speckled night sky.

The End

Acknowledgments

As usual, the team at Entangled is awesome. Many thanks to Vanessa Mitchell and Heidi Stryker for all their hard work and attention to detail, and to Syd Gill for the beautiful cover.

About the Author

Paula Altenburg lives in rural Nova Scotia, Canada, with her husband and two sons. Once a manager in the aerospace industry, she now enjoys working from home and writing fulltime. Paula writes fantasy and paranormal romance, as well as short contemporary romance.

Also by Paula Altenburg…

THE DEMON'S DAUGHTER

BLACK WIDOW DEMON

THE DEMON LORD

THE DEMON CREED

DESIRE BY DESIGN

HER SECRET, HIS SURPRISE

Made in the USA
Charleston, SC
11 November 2015